THE DREAM THIEF

Violet Fenn

First published by Harker House Publishing 2024

Copyright © 2024 by Violet Fenn

All rights reserved. No part of this book may be reproduced in any form or by any electronic or mechanical means, including information storage and retrieval systems, without written permission from the author, except for the use of brief quotations in a book review. It is illegal to copy this book, post it to a website, or distribute it by any other means without permission.

This novel is entirely a work of fiction and the names, characters and incidents portrayed in it are the work of the author's imagination. Any resemblance to actual persons, living or dead, events or localities is entirely coincidental.

Violet Fenn asserts the moral right to be identified as the author of this work.

Cover design by GetCovers.

"Just because you're paranoid doesn't mean they're not after you."

Joseph Heller

Well, That's The Doormat Ruined

There's nothing quite like the sound of a corpse landing on your doorstep to distract you from a *True Blood* binge-fest. I'd started from the beginning, because Aunt Kitty had never seen it. Kitty's only just getting to grips with the idea of colour television, let alone twenty-four hours a day streaming on demand. We'd just got to the bit where Sookie finds her dead grandmother in the kitchen when I heard a buzzing noise coming from my bedroom. Concerned that the electrics might finally be giving up and about to set the building on fire, I got up to check. When I stuck my head around the door everything seemed normal, but I could still hear the buzzing. It took me a few seconds to register that the noise was coming from the crown hanging from my dressing table mirror. It had been given to me by an erstwhile fling who'd turned out to be a famous ancient king. Could happen to anyone, right? Anyway, he'd dumped St Edward's Crown on my doorstep. Yes, the original and most important one, the one that was supposedly melted down by Thomas Cromwell but clearly hadn't been on account of how it was now in my flat. Bastard didn't even bother to run through the terms and conditions beforehand. You'd know the fling in question as William the Conqueror, but I like to call him 'that devious bellend Liam O'Connor'. Because a) that's the name he goes under these days; and b) he really is the most devious of all the bellends. And I know a *lot* of bellends.

Just as I was stepping very carefully forward to check what was up with my temperamental piece of royal memorabilia, there was a loud crashing noise outside, followed by something thudding heavily against the back door. I shot out of the bedroom so fast that the cat exploded into a ball of angry grey fur and bounced off Kitty's lap onto the windowsill, before leaping on top of the television and yowling under his breath. Luckily for Kitty she's a ghost, so doesn't have to worry about the sharpness of Grimm's claws. I might be immortal with super-quick healing powers, but those scratches still hurt like a bastard. The cat and the phantom watched from a safe distance as I wrenched open the kitchen door. To my absolute horror, Katja—the small female vampire who sits on the rooftop to guard me every night—was slumped outside. A wooden stake that Buffy would have been proud of was sticking out of her chest and she was rapidly disintegrating into a sticky mess on the doorstep. One side of her face was already melting into the 'G' of "GO AWAY" that was printed on the doormat alongside a cartoon drawing of a cat flicking the V's. I'd really liked that mat. Izzy had bought it for me for Christmas. Stepping over Katja's gruesome remains I bounced up onto the roof. Movement in the distance made me turn in the direction of Toxteth. Two figures were just about visible, disappearing across the roofs. The first was running on two legs, but even from here, I could see that the second was on four. With any luck, Katja's attacker would trip over a handy chimney stack and the gigantic cat that was chasing them would get a well-deserved snack. Sighing, I clambered back down off the roof, stepped gingerly over what was left of my bloodsucking bodyguard and asked Kitty to go fetch our friendly neighbourhood vampire chief.

"Oh dear," said Aiden, surveying the sorry scene outside my kitchen door. "Oh dear, oh dear, oh dear." It had started raining, and what was left of Katja was rapidly being washed down the steps of the fire escape that everyone uses as the main access to my flat. There was already a replacement guardian up on the roof—a middle-aged man who looked thoroughly unhappy at being given his deceased colleague's job and was currently hunched miserably against the chimney. When he'd first arrived I suggested I might be better off alone than lumbered with someone who clearly didn't want to be there. Aiden had just sniffed and said the new sentry should feel honoured to be asked, then refused to discuss it further.

"Why have you got Colin Robinson sitting on your roof?" Izzy nodded up to where the new vamp had turned his back to us and was sitting with his face resting against the chimney bricks. Izzy had turned up just after Aiden, apparently alerted to the gruesome drama by what she likes to call her 'spidey senses'. I think it's far more likely that Kitty keeps her informed of anything that happens to me, because she knows damn fine Izzy's the only person I ever listen to. Iz might be a mere mortal, but she's known me since we were both eight years old. If she tells me not to do something, there's usually a good reason. Okay, so that reason is often, 'because you'll make an absolute fool of yourself yet again, for fuck's sake'. Still, everyone needs an Izzy in their life. She'd arrived still in her purple pyjamas and fluffy slippers, having clearly decided it wasn't worth the effort of getting dressed for the two minute walk over to my place. "You won't be able to wander around in public dressed like that when you're living at Albert Dock," I'd said when I saw her heading up the fire escape, stepping carefully around the lumps of greasy ash that were splattered down the steps. Izzy had lived in her flat on Button Street for well over a decade and had no plans to move, until Eadric Silverton—technically my landlord, and also my go-to source of undead information—had offered her a penthouse apartment overlooking the river down on Albert Dock. To be fair, he'd offered it to me first. It was, apparently, 'far more suitable' than the flat in which I was currently standing. But the Harrington Street flat was, to me at least, the perfect home. It was high above the street, with my beloved cafe at ground level underneath it. Grimm only had to hop out of the kitchen window and he had free run of the city's rooftops—or at least, the ones this side of Lord Street. He tends not to go much further, because—according to Kitty, who seems worryingly adept at translating his expressions—other cats keep stopping him to ask for advice on matters of a feline nature. Grimm is head of the local cat population in the same way I'm the top of the undead pile, and he knows it.

Aah, yeah. Did I forget to mention I'm Queen of the Dead? Not that I asked for the job. And I definitely didn't actually want it. But spooky society unilaterally decided that my arrival into the netherworld —which I like to call the nether*weird*, just because it pisses Eadric off— courtesy of an unexpected back flip off the top of the fire escape out of my kitchen heralded the dawn of a new undead age. Or something. Which is why the most famous king in British history dropped that crown on my doorstep, and is also why his even older rival has decided I'm destined to be the other half of his planned neo-Viking rule. I've told both of them to piss off and go play in the traffic, obviously, but that hasn't stopped either of them trying to push the issue. And Eadric —who I'm technically usurping by my mere existence, because he's been local leader for centuries—is annoyingly pleased about the current situation. If I manage to unite the kingdom, he gets to be free of a centuries-old curse that ties him to the living world. Eadric would very much like to swap local politics for an eternity in the arms of his erstwhile fairy-wife (a long and complicated story even by my standards), and I would very much like Eadric to get the fuck over himself and stay put so I don't have to deal with everything on my own. Mind you, most Queens don't have a pair of gigantic metal birds watching their back all the time, so that's one up for me. Yeah, I'm looking at you, Queen Vic. Looming up there on your bloody big monument in Derby Square. You might have been Empress of All Oppressed States, but did you have a Liver Bird at your shoulder whilst doing so? Thought not. Mostly because they'd have literally knocked you off your royal perch and told you to give it all back, like the thieving brat you were.

Anyway. When I'd survived the whole time-slip farrago a few months earlier and finally accepted my royal undead fate, Bella had been the first person I'd gone to for advice. Okay, so a giant metal bird isn't technically a person. And she certainly can't give much in the way of verbal suggestions. But she's very good at making her feelings known. After I'd turned down the move to Albert Dock, Eadric had offered me space in the Liver Building itself as an alternative, and had been very surprised when I'd turned that down as well. "I assumed you'd want to be closer to Bella," he'd said. "Not all the way up on Harrington Street in that poky little flat." I'd pointed out that he'd been just fine with me living in the poky little flat back when I'd been renting it from him as a normal human, to which he said he hadn't even been aware of my existence at that point. I'd given him a short sharp lecture on the perils of remote landlords. And also about how dangerous it was to ignore the humans, because even the most intelligent of humans are very stupid en masse and guillotines could still make a comeback. Anyway, Flora's is only a ten minute walk from the river, even at human speed. And if I do it in the early hours when no one's around to see me, I can get down there in a minute or so, leaving nothing but a slight breeze behind me.

If there's anything really disappointing about the undead life, it's that in order to fit in, you have to learn to behave like a human again. You know that scene in the final *Twilight* movie, where Bella's being given instructions on how to 'act human' and ends up looking like an absolute lunatic? That's a pretty good illustration of what it's like being a revenant in the early days of your afterlife. It's way too easy to forget that people are definitely going to notice if you decide that skipping over the rooftops is a quicker route up to the Bombed Out Church, rather than just walking up Bold Street like the rest of the population. And it wasn't as if I'd even been your standard newborn revenant. I'd since learned that most newcomers are bewildered enough to let the Liver Building overlords ship them off to the remotest location they can think of, until everyone who knew them is dead and they've learned how to act reasonably normal. Bloody-minded to the core, I'd refused to be shipped anywhere, much less give up my daily human life. Nikolaus Silverton—publicly Eadric's brother, in reality no connection except also being dead (and far too famous to keep his original name)—liked to suggest I wouldn't know normal if it jumped up and slapped me in the face. But then Nik's an over-opinionated gobshite who ought to stick to bad poetry and inappropriate romantic crushes.

Anyway, that's my story. I woke up dead one day and discovered that Liverpool is, in fact, overrun with spooky weirdos. Who even knew the bloke with the funky bookshop up on Renshaw Street had actually been dead this past eight hundred years? Not me. Or that the stories about the ghost dancing around the graves up in Anfield Cemetery are not only true, but the ghost in question is called Alan and is currently dating the vampire who lives in the flat below mine? And now I'm the north-west's answer to Queen of the Damned, only without Aaliyah's figure. Or dress sense. Like I say, it's been a strange year. And now someone—or something—had tried to get into my flat and was prepared to kill in order to do so. Thank gods for the were-cats and their unexpected loyalty to me. Oh yeah, so it turns out were-cats are a thing. Apologies in advance if any of this is coming as a shock. The cats' loyalty was quite possibly fuelled by their fear of being disembowelled by Grimm if anything happened to disturb his constant supply of gourmet kitty food, but I take the small wins where I can. I still relied on the Silvertons for advice, though. And they've been doing their best to educate me in the ways of the afterlife, but I'm a terrible student and they're a pair of boring old men who can't use one word when three very lengthy ones will do.

"You'd better let Eadric know," said Izzy from the kitchen, as though she was reading my mind. She held a cup of tea in both hands and was watching proceedings from a safe distance. "Someone was clearly trying to break in." Kitty suddenly appeared next to her. "Fuck*sake*, Kitty!" hissed Izzy, "Can you not just *walk* into the bloody room, like a normal person?"

"Sorry," said my late lamented great-aunt. "I forget how to walk when I'm stressed. You do need to call Eadric, Lil," she said to me. "He'd want to know."

"No need," said a politely clipped voice from further down the fire escape, "he already knows." Nikolaus was making his way up towards us, tip-toeing carefully around the mess on the steps. Rachel, the vampire from the flat downstairs, popped her head out of her door to see what was going on. Then she immediately retreated and slammed it shut again. Which was a reasonable response to finding one of your friends rapidly disintegrating on your fire escape, I thought. "Oh my god," said Nik, "this is *disgusting*."

"That," I snapped, "is Katja. And she is not disgusting." Nik looked unconvinced. "Someone killed her."

"I can see that," he said. "One must assume they were looking for you, no? She presumably got in the way, the poor child. Espresso please, Isobel."

"What did your last servant die of?" Izzy grumbled, but she was already turning to do it. She says Nik's a spoiled brat who needs to learn the ways of the twenty-first century, but she secretly adores him. Everyone loves Nik. He's so utterly ridiculous that it somehow ends up being endearing, rather than annoying. Most of the time, anyway.

"Exhaustion, probably," said Nik. "Never could get the staff. I'm sorry about this, Aiden," he went on, turning to the worried-looking vampire standing next to him on the platform that forms the balcony area outside my flat. "This wouldn't have happened had Lilith taken our advice and moved to more secure premises."

"Don't you *dare* blame me for this," I snapped. "I am entitled to live wherever I choose without worrying about it putting either me or my friends in danger, same as anyone else."

"But you're not the same as everyone else," said Nik calmly, "are you? And your insistence on living in this..." he looked around as though for inspiration, "...*hovel,* is only adding to everyone's stress levels."

"I'm not moving," I said doggedly.

"Yes," said Nik, "you keep saying that. Perhaps we should ask Bertie if he'd like to flap over and sit on the roof for a while? That might put people off."

"Don't be ridiculous," I snapped.

"I'm learning from the best," he said. "And it's no more ridiculous an idea than you still living on this dingy little back street."

"It's a ridiculous idea because he'd be way too heavy for the roof," I said. "Not because I wouldn't want him living here. Bella would get jealous though. Maybe if I strengthened the roof, they could take it in turns." I looked up to where my reluctant vampire guard was sitting on the apex tiles with dawn breaking in the distance behind him. Contrary to common belief, sunlight doesn't kill vampires—that was a trope invented by the film director F. W. Murnau for *Nosferatu*. Murnau added it in the hope it might give weight to his claim he'd created a new vampire story, rather than just ripping off *Dracula*. His claim failed—mostly because he really had ripped off *Dracula*—and his film company went bankrupt soon after the movie came out. But the idea of sunlight being fatal to vampires had stuck ever since. It's a wonder Bram Stoker isn't being used as an ethical energy source, given all the spinning he must be doing in that grave of his.

A polite cough brought me back to the current situation. "This wasn't anyone's fault" said Aiden politely, when he felt he had our attention back. "Katja was at her happiest when she was guarding Lilith. She'd have wanted it this way."

"Well, *I* don't want it this way," I said. "I didn't choose to be the bloody queen and I don't need a vampire guard on my roof."

"As a matter of fact, you clearly do," said Izzy, appearing in the doorway, "because if Katja and the cats hadn't intervened, it could well have been you lying on this doormat. Here you go, Monsieur Ponce." She handed Nik a tiny espresso cup filled to the brim. "Try not to spill it on the corpse, aye."

"Don't you start," I said. "I didn't ask to be undead, and I certainly didn't have 'take over the immortal realms' down on my list when we spoke to that careers advisor at school."

"No one asks to be born in the first place," said Izzy in an annoyingly reasonable tone, "yet here we are. Suck it up, Your Highness, there's vampires at stake. Stake! Ahahaha—sorry," she'd seen Aiden's expression, "couldn't help myself." She perched herself on the kitchen counter and produced a small pouch from her dressing gown pocket, before settling to the serious business of rolling herself a cigarette. Izzy knows I don't like her smoking in the flat but she generally only does it when she's really stressed, so I left her to it.

"Please could I request some water, Lilith?" said Aiden. "I think the best option is to just wash the steps and be done with."

"Seriously?" I squinted at him. "You want to wash Katja down onto the car park and leave her there?"

"She'd be happier with that than with people arguing whilst standing on her remains," said Aiden politely. "And she'd have liked the idea of always being here with you, I think." Stunned into silence—which is a very rare occurrence in my life—I headed into the kitchen and filled the washing up bowl with water. "Thank you," said Aiden as I passed it to him. "Go peacefully into that good night, my child," he said, before sloshing the water down the steps and turning back to me. "One more bowl will do it, I think."

When the stairs were as clean as he could get them, Aiden left with a promise to return the next night, 'just to make sure everything is as it should be.' Fighting the urge to point out that 'as it should be' was a moveable feast in my world, I settled for thanking him politely and apologising again for Katja's untimely demise. "These things happen," he'd shrugged, before disappearing into the darkness. I was just heading back into the flat where Izzy, Nik and Kitty had settled in to watch the devious shenanigans of Vampire Bill without me, when there was a clattering noise from a nearby roof. Colin the guard-vampire made a hissing noise and stood up, his sweater and beige slacks as incongruous as was possible to imagine against the brightening skyline.

"It's fine," I reassured him. "It's just Finn. He won't hurt you." Colin looked unconvinced as the massive cat slunk across the roof of the building opposite, before dropping down with the soft thud of heavy paws onto the rough ground in front of Basil, my ancient but beloved Beetle. As he loped across to the stairs I realised he was limping. "What happened?" I asked, as he appeared around the last turn of the fire escape and padded slowly up towards me. He made a grunting noise, his ears scrunched down against the slope of his big cat head and his eyes squinting in pain. "Christ," I said, "was it you who chased Katja's attacker?" He nodded heavily. "You'd better get inside and let me have a look at you."

"What happened?" asked Izzy, coming out of the living room to meet us. "Bloody hell, Finn," she said when she saw him, "what have you done to yourself?"

"He was chasing off whoever killed Katja," I said. "Can you grab some towels from the bathroom? We need to get him onto the kitchen table so I can have a proper look."

"Remember when we used to moan about how boring our lives were?" said Izzy. I nodded. "Just occasionally," she said, "I really miss being bored."

THE DREAM THIEF

～

"Will you just stay bloody still? I can't help you if you keep fidgeting like that." Finn tilted his head to give me a sad look, but did at least stop wriggling. He settled for making forlorn meeping noises instead. "You know that sounds ridiculous from a cat your size?" I said. In response, he flopped dramatically down onto the table and let out a heavy sigh. Kitty and Izzy were watching with interest, while Grimm sat on the worktop next to the sink pretending he couldn't care less. Occasional snorting noises coming from the living room suggested Nik wasn't entirely impressed with the Deep South vampires. "You've sprained something," I told Finn, "but nothing's broken. There's a few cuts and bruises, but it looks more like you fell through a bush than anything more serious." He gave me a sideways look that suggested yes, something undignified might well have happened during his high-speed chase. "You need your dew claws trimming again though. Might as well do it now, as you're here. Stop being so bloody dramatic," I said, as he flinched away from me. "It's just like cutting your nails, for gods' sake." I'd only known Finn a few weeks, but I was already aware of his tendency to grow out long dew claws that curled round and dug into his paw pads. "Don't move." The giant cat stayed obediently where he was while I rooted round in the cutlery drawer for the nail clippers I'd put in there for just this sort of job. I'd had to tell the customer assistant in Superdrug that they were for my nanna who had tough toenails. She'd been very sympathetic and suggested some foot cream to soften things up, but I was pretty sure that wouldn't work on cats. I squinted and angled the clippers carefully before snipping off the offending claw with a loud snap. Finn gave a dramatic squeal, leaped off the table and disappeared into the living room. "Don't you *dare* get on my bed!" I yelled after him. "I've just put clean sheets on it. I'm sick of having bloody cat hair on everything." Finn slunk back into the room and bounced up onto the sink, settling down next to his smaller sibling with a petulant look on his face. "Don't you ever miss the days when it was just me and you?" I asked Grimm. He gave what I chose to interpret as a noncommittal shrug. Grimm is actually very big as far as cats go—more your Norwegian Forest variety than an average British moggy. But even he was tiny in comparison to the enormous black beast sitting next to him. Finn had draped himself along the entire length of the kitchen counter and his tail *still* hung down over the end of the worktop and swished gently against the floor tiles. "You," I said, pointing to Finn, "are way too heavy to be on my worktops. Shoo!" I gave him a shove and he reluctantly dropped down onto the floor. "I'll make you up a bed on the sofa. Hopefully you'll turn back into your human form when the adrenalin wears off a bit, then you can have some paracetamol. I really need to get some animal medication in." This was to Izzy, who was standing next to me. "If I'd realised just how much big cat care there was going to be in my life, I might have done that veterinary nurse course I was talking about back in sixth form."

"You wouldn't have lasted a week," said Izzy. "One old pooch coming in for a one-way trip to Rainbow Bridge and you'd have been out the door and breaking your heart in the car park."

"True." I'd always been a soft touch when it came to animals. "A first aid course would come in handy, though. Reckon Jenny would run one for us?" Jenny was a member of our local knitting club. She was also designated first aider at the local police station, where she worked as a special constable.

"I think she might wonder why you need advice for animals rather than humans," said Izzy.

"Nah," I said, "she's known us long enough to just accept the weirdness, I reckon."

"You okay if I go home now?" said Izzy. "Only it's my turn to open up today and it's almost morning already." She was right—low-level traffic noise was becoming audible from down on North John Street. And so another day dawned in the mysterious metropolis.

"I'm fine," I said. "Nobody's going to try anything else tonight. This morning," I corrected myself. "They know I'll be on alert now, anyway. Go back to bed and come in at lunchtime—I can cope on my own for one morning."

It was an indication of just how tired Izzy was that she gave it some thought. Under normal circumstances she'd say no immediately, on account of how I am, apparently, a 'liability' in the café. "Isn't it your morning to see Eadric?" she asked. I'd taken to spending one morning a week over at the Liver Building, going through paperwork with Eadric and learning about who wanted to kill who (it usually involved vampires) and why (motives range from 'he looked at me funny down in the tunnels and now I'm going to rip his fangs out' to 'his sire killed my granny's sister's babysitter before the war and now it's down to me to avenge the family name'). I'd been surprised by just how much admin is caused by having vampires on your patch. Revenants live as (and with) humans most of the time, were-cats generally sort themselves out, and ghosts are often annoying but mostly harmless. Vampires, though—vampires are a pain in everyone's undead ass.

Far from being the glossily sexy visions of darkness you see in the movies, they're mostly just grubby and annoying. *Really* annoying. Eadric once said he'd never been able to figure out quite why vampires were such a letdown in the flesh. Especially as the occasional one—and Aiden was an excellent example of this—turned out to be as carnivorously Byronic a bloodsucker as any goth could ever hope to meet on a dark and stormy night. I'd pointed out that the vast majority of the vampires we knew were unfortunate relics of the Victorian era, when being poor literally meant fighting over whatever meat you could get off a rat and being swept down an alleyway for a bit of how's your father with a dark and interesting stranger was probably seen as a welcome distraction. And then a new baby vamp staggered back out of the alley with a thirst for both vengeance and human blood, and their neighbours' lives suddenly got a whole lot more interesting. Not many of Aiden's immortal community had been to finishing school before joining the ranks of the undead. "Anyway," I'd told Eadric, "at least they're learning to pass as humans these days. Even the fangs just get passed off as an affectation." It's no accident that the younger ones often pretend to be art students. And some are finally learning how to make themselves look more presentable. Only the previous week, Katja had excitedly shown me her new hairdo—a bold and choppy pixie cut that really suited her. Which was lucky, because vampire hair doesn't grow—if it had gone wrong, she'd have had to wear hats for all eternity. But Katja's eternity had been cut short by someone who had apparently been after me instead.

"Yeah," I said, pulling myself back to the conversation, "but it can wait 'til later. I'll make coffee whilst pondering bloody revenge on whoever it was that killed Katja."

"Why would anyone want to kill Katja in the first place?" said Izzy.

"Someone who wants something badly enough to kill whoever gets in the way," I said. "Simple as that."

"Which rules out Liam and Ivo," said Izzy.

I stopped what I was doing and looked at her. "What makes you say that?" As it happened, the pair of them had been top of my mental list of People Who Would Kill To Get What They Want.

"Because," said Izzy in the sort of tone kindergarten teachers use for kids who've been told three times already why they shouldn't eat the crayons, "they're both ridiculously besotted with you and wouldn't harm a hair on your frankly ridiculous head." I automatically put a hand up to my head and remembered I'd twisted my mop of red curly hair into a weird kind of pineapple arrangement in order to keep it out of my eyes.

"I wouldn't bet on it," I said, pulling the scrunchy out and shaking my hair until it stood up around my head like a particularly carroty halo. "Doesn't matter how much either of them are led by the contents of their trousers. They'd sacrifice their own grandmothers if it meant getting what they want."

"What you're forgetting," said Izzy patiently, "is what both of them actually want is you."

"Humph." I wasn't convinced. I had, undeniably, once spent a very energetic night with Liam. But that was before I knew his true identity, let alone just what an egotistical ratbastard he could be. And I'd certainly never been fully up close and personal with Ivo, however much he seemed to think we were destined to be together forever, like some sort of cheesy love song from the eighties. If I'd known, back when I was still alive, that one day I'd be genuinely annoyed because two of the most eligible bachelors in history were constantly trying to remind me of their existence, I'd have wondered whether Future Me somehow lost her mind along with her pulse. Then I'd have peed my pants in excitement at the thought of future adventures. But these days romantic adventure invariably takes second place to trying to stop the entire undead world killing each other permanently. And anyway I lost the ability to pee when I died, so my pants are safe. Sometimes I missed being able to shut myself in the bathroom for a bit of peace and quiet. "Anyway," I said to Izzy, "I'll worry about that another time. Go get some sleep. I'll hold the fort until you come back."

"Thanks Lil," she said, already heading out through the door. "You're the best." She blew me a kiss and pitter-pattered off down the steps, her silky dressing gown flowing behind her like a cloak. A Royal Mail delivery man was walking up Harrington Street and he did a classic double take when he saw her. Izzy gave him a cheery wave and headed off home, leaving him looking faintly stunned. Some things never changed. I was turning to go back inside the flat when something caught my eye. A lock of grey-white hair lay on the top level of the fire escape, just outside the kitchen door. It was on the side nearest the drop, which was presumably how it had missed being washed away by Aiden and his dishwater. I bent to pick it up and dropped it into the palm of my hand for a closer look. I initially thought it might have somehow come from my grandmother, when she'd arrived unannounced back in January and turned everyone's life upside down. But Gran was a ghost—and the one thing I knew about ghosts was that everything about them is an illusion. It doesn't matter how real they look and feel—and some of them are as solid as you or I, capable of passing undetected even at a recording of *Most Haunted*—it's all a trick. They can change their appearance as well. When I'd first got to know Billy, the ghost who used to 'live' in the empty shop doorway opposite Flora's, he'd been as scruffy as any rough sleeper I'd ever seen. But then Kitty had trained him in the ways of regeneration, and suddenly he'd been the sharpest ghost on the block. I forced myself away from the sore subject of Billy and back to the matter in hand. Literally. The hair curled in my palm, a small twist of greasy-looking strands that didn't seem quite natural. Holding it up to the light, I realised that was because it wasn't. A quick sniff confirmed what I thought—the curl was made of horsehair. And it was old and smelly horsehair, at that. I only knew one person who wore an old-fashioned wig, and I hadn't seen him since he'd walked through seventeenth-century Toxteth with me a few months earlier. It must have been him outside the flat, but I didn't think he was capable of murdering Katja in cold blood. Not even when the blood in question has long since

Well, That's The Doormat Ruined

congealed. I tucked the little curl into my pocket and headed back into the flat. Above me, I thought I heard the faint sound of a vampire grumbling to himself about being forced to do overtime.

∼

Finn was asleep on the sofa, still in his cat form. Nik was sitting in my armchair with Kitty cross legged next to him, both of them still engrossed in the television. I went into my bedroom and opened the wardrobe door. As I pulled a pile of old blankets out of the bottom of it, a bright glow flashed in my peripheral vision. I stood up so fast that I cracked my head against the wardrobe door. Its small hinges were no match for the strength of my inhuman skull and the top one sheared off from the wooden frame, leaving the door hanging. "Fuck*sake*," I muttered, closing the wardrobe doors and locking them so they'd stay shut for now. It was just one more thing to add to the ever-growing list of 'Things Lil's Broken By Accident Cos She Doesn't Know Her Own Strength'. Already on the list was the cold tap in the back kitchen downstairs in Flora's (I'd turned it off too fast a few days earlier and must have broken the washer, because it had been dripping constantly ever since) and a stone lintel on the top level of the Liver Building (I'd climbed up it at speed one night just for the hell of it, and broke a piece off with my foot—impressive even by my standards, because I'd been wearing Converse at the time). The glow was coming from the crown. It did this occasionally, usually when it was pissed off about something. The problem was that I could only figure out what it was trying to tell me by putting it on. And that was an unnerving experience both for me, and for anyone else unfortunate enough to be in the vicinity at the same time. That crown holds an awful lot of memories—many of them deeply unpleasant—and it likes to make them my problem. The amount of power stored in the fragile circlet of thin and ancient gold is enough to send anyone mad, let alone someone who'd only been dead just over a year and still wasn't entirely sure what they were doing a lot of the time.

The first anniversary of my death had been a month earlier. Much to Izzy's disgust, I'd refused to have a party for it. "Are you fucking *mental*?" had been my actual response, when she'd first suggested it.

"What would I put on the invites? *'Come along to Lil's deathiversary, yeah sorry we forgot to tell you she's actually dead, please don't tell the newspapers'?*"

"Don't be ridiculous," Izzy had replied. "We'd just invite people who already know about it."

"We're pushing our luck as it is," I'd said. "Too many people know already, that's our problem. Anyway," I went on, before she had a chance to speak, "since when was my *death* worth celebrating? Anyone would think you were pleased about it, for christ's sake."

"You can't deny that life's more interesting these days," Izzy had shrugged. "All the ghosts and vampires and zombies running around."

"I am not a bloody zombie."

"Yeah, yeah," she grinned, "whatever. You could wear your crown and everything." I'd given her my patented Hard Bear Stare before stalking off and refusing to discuss it again. And now I was standing in my bedroom staring at said crown and wondering what was upsetting it.

"I'm not putting you on," I told it. "You're dangerous." There was a faint shimmer to the glow for a second. "I'm not being rude," I said, "I'm being sensible. Anyway I need to go make a bed for a giant cat. We can discuss this later." I picked up the blankets and walked out of the room. Behind me, the crown flared.

Queens Gotta Queen

I was just tucking Finn in on the sofa when there was a loud "Cooooeeeee!" from the kitchen door, announcing the arrival of Gaultier Mapp, my very favourite undead friend. "Good morning, Your Majesty," he said, walking into the room and sweeping downwards in an unnecessarily ostentatious curtsey. "I carry news from the outlands, for royal ears alone." The fact he was wearing what appeared to be several metres of gold satin fabric that he'd tied round his waist in a makeshift sarong made his entrance even more dramatic. Gaultier Mapp is very tall, very dark, and *very* handsome, which is how he gets away with his somewhat esoteric wardrobe choices. He is also approximately eight hundred years old and cheekier than a pallet of peaches.

"You heard the man," I said to Kitty and Nik, who'd clearly settled in for the entire series. "Off you go." Behind me, the television was paused with Bill and Sookie in the bathtub. *If only vampires were that interesting*, I thought. "Aladdin here clearly has gossip," the twinkle in Mapp's dark brown eyes confirmed this, "and it's about time I started hearing bad news ahead of everyone else in this ridiculous city. Go on," I flapped my arms, "shoo!"

"Are you actually 'shooing'" Nik did air quotes for emphasis, "me, Lilith?"

"Yes," I replied firmly, "I am. You were all happy enough to lecture me about how I had to take charge. You don't get to whine about it now. Out you go. Let me conduct my royal business in peace."

"Charming," said aunt Kitty. "He was my friend first, you know." Kitty and Mapp had had a fling back in the sixties, which I only found out about after I'd died and discovered my long-dead great aunt was haunting my flat. There were a lot of things to discover back then. Not least the fact that although I was technically dead as the proverbial doornail, my brain had somehow failed to get the memo and I was doomed to spend all eternity roaming the land as a supernatural creature of the night. In reality, I'm actually an often-grumpy thirtysomething who mostly just roams the bit of the city centre that sits between the Cavern Club and the Liverpool One shopping centre, but you get my drift.

"I'm not trying to steal your friends, for heaven's sake," I said, flapping at her again for emphasis. "But right now he is my lowly subject, come to inform his monarch of the machinations troubling her super-spooky lands. Now bugger off." Kitty gave me one last narrow-eyed look then disappeared, winking out like a lightbulb. Nik raised his eyebrows but got to his feet, anyway.

"This is going to take some getting used to," he observed, as he fussed over his jacket, which now had a decorative coating of cat hair.

"It's a modern world we're living in," I said, passing him a lint roller from the coffee table. When you share your living space with a full-time moggy and a part-time were-cat, you learn to buy lint rollers in bulk. "Well, maybe not actually living. Existing in. Feminism has come a long way since your day, Nik. Better get used to it."

"I have nothing against feminism," said Nik. "Nor feminists. Some of my best friends over the centuries have been strong women. They're often more fun than the men. What I meant was that I'm struggling with the concept of our entire territory being run from a grubby little flat on a backstreet."

"Charming," I said. "Anyway, I've got a decorating budget." A ridiculously enormous decorating budget, as it happened. Eadric had been so rich for so long he'd clearly lost any perspective on what constituted 'reasonable' for pretty much anything to do with money. The first time he'd dropped some petty cash into my bank account—just to see me through my first trip to London on revenant business—it had landed so heavily into my basic current account that the bank had called me up to check I wasn't being used as an unwitting money launderer. Let's just say I was currently getting over my dislike of being patronised by writing very long wish lists of the sort of wallpaper you see on Instagram accounts run by interior designers who think 'migraine' is a valid design choice.

"Does it cover the cost of bulldozing the entire place and starting from scratch?"

"Nikolaus Silverton," I said, "you are a terminal snob. We're not in the nineteenth century anymore, you know. Now go!" I gave him a shove. "Tell Eadric I'll come see him later. We'll need to have a chat about this."

"He's already on the case," said Nik. "I left him attempting to find the current whereabouts of both Laithlind and the Bastard."

"I don't think either of them would be so direct," I said, thinking about the curl of horsehair tucked away in my pocket.

"She's right, you know," said Mapp. "I suspect they'd both prefer to seduce Lilith here into submission, not attack her out of nowhere."

"Well, one of them's already tried that," I said, "and it hasn't done him any good so far." I shrugged. "Just getting it out there before either of you are tempted to make unfunny remarks about the state of my love life."

"As if we'd mock your personal life, my darling," said Mapp, a distinct twinkle in his eye. "Although I do think it could be a bit more adventurous, no?"

"He's right, you know," said Nik. "You're letting the side down, Lilith. We're creatures of the night—"

"We go out in daylight all the time," I interrupted. "Mapp here runs a bloody shop, for fuck's sake!"

"As I was saying," Nik went on, "we are immortal creatures, doomed to an eternity of lustful indulgence." He gave me a sharp look. "About time you started cracking on with it, I reckon. Chop chop!"

GO AWAY.

Both men looked at me in genuine surprise. *Ha*, I thought, *you weren't expecting me to have practised, were you?* It was true that The

Voice ('of Doom', Izzy likes to add) had unnerved me as much as anyone else when it had first made its presence known. But I didn't have much control over it, back then. I'd get annoyed at something, finally lose my temper and then suddenly I was intoning my words as though I should be carrying a scythe and riding a horse with a name that rhymes with Winky. Mine wasn't the voice of the End Times, though—even I wasn't that cool, dead or not. It reminded me more of that feeling you get when you've got music playing loud enough for the bass to be rattling your chest. It's making you feel sick and you want to turn it off, but you know you're going to listen to the end of the track first. The voice was also way more commanding and, well, *meaner* than I would ever be. It would pop up out of the blue and have me informing people they were my underlings and needed to get used to it quickly or I'd be hoofing them into another dimension, that sort of thing.

After frightening both myself and other people with it for longer than was comfortable, I took myself off to a quiet spot on the waterfront one evening and practised. To begin with, I couldn't even get it to work. I knew it was there, somewhere, but it kept slipping away from me like the memories of a dream that fade to nothing even as you're just opening your eyes. Or like when you're a kid learning to ride a bike, and something inside you knows you can do it, if only you can build up enough courage to just push yourself off and pedal as hard and fast as you can. Fear of failure makes you nervous and you don't pedal hard enough and then fall, making failure a self-fulfilling prophecy. I'd thought a lot about that idea of failure, whilst sitting with my back against the wall and waiting for an unwitting test subject to walk past. About whether I could even do what was being asked of me. Whether this beautiful, ridiculous city had bet on the completely wrong horse to lead its charge into the future. And then I'd had a surge of furious clarity and I knew there was nothing for it but to pedal forward with all my strength. Unfortunately the only thing around for me to take this newfound mental strength out on had been an unsuspecting seagull which must have wondered what the hell was happening when I murmured *UP* under my breath and it veered off course and soared upwards to land on Bella's beak. Since then I'd persuaded Izzy to be my guinea pig a few times, and it was a mark of her affection that she'd done it. Okay so she pulled faces and made theatrical retching noises, but even she admitted that the Voice was far more bearable when it wasn't being boomed at her with the acoustic range of the Philharmonic when there's a full orchestra in residence. She wasn't impressed by me using my newly controlled talent to make her curtsey, mind—she was halfway to the floor when she suddenly snapped upright and shouted at me for abuse of power. Then she'd asked if I could teach her how to do it herself. Apparently she fancied the idea of making her boyfriend Damon bend to her every whim. I'd pointed out he did that already, pretty much—she'd huffed and informed me she'd smack me in the face with a dishcloth if I ever tried to pull that trick on her again.

The sound of the kitchen door closing brought me out of my mental meanderings and I just caught sight of Nik's confused face as he headed down the fire escape.

"Impressive," said Mapp, "if somewhat manipulative."

"Says the man who makes a career out of manipulating the pants off people."

"Can't even deny it, girl," he grinned. "Gonna put the kettle on? I'm parched."

"Coffee?" I said. "I've got a new machine."

"Ooh," said Mapp, following me through and settling in at the kitchen table, "don't mind if I do. Mine's a double espresso, ta."

"That bad?" I turned to poke buttons on the fancy coffee machine that was way too complicated for my liking and wished—not for the first time—that I'd never agreed to this stupid bloody refurb. Eadric gifted me the entire building out of guilt, after discovering that my untimely death had been precipitated by the actions of his then-wife. She's his *late* wife now, on account of how I lopped her head off with a machete, but he doesn't hold it against me. What he does resent is my refusal to move into the fancy-schmancy Albert Dock apartment, because he genuinely can't understand why anyone would want to stay living on Harrington Street when classier alternatives are available. Anyway, like I said, Izzy's far more susceptible to the temptations of a twenty-four-hour concierge service and balcony views of industrial shipping as far as the eye can see. Which was why she was currently in the midst of packing up a decade's worth of clutter, ready for her move.

Unfortunately, Eadric then decided it still wasn't acceptable for me to be living in what he deemed to be 'absolute squalor' and sent a crack team of decorators round to do something about it. So far, they'd stripped the walls and emptied the place of what I like to call 'character', but Izzy calls 'a fucking mess worthy of an extended episode of *Hoarders*'. They were now waiting on me to decide on colours, whilst Eadric had indulged his new love of online shopping by replacing all my ancient electrics with fancy new stuff.

That one was entirely on me—I'd been astonished by the discovery that some people still didn't know the deep joys of the materialistic side of the internet and had given him a crash course in the delights of overnight delivery. Not needing anything for his own living quarters—which take up most of the front tower of the Liver Building and are furnished as lavishly as you might expect—he'd amused himself by shopping for me instead. Within days, the nearby John Lewis store had politely dumped many thousands of pounds-worth of gadgetry on my doorstep. Izzy also did well out of his tendency to forget what he'd already ordered, mind. She too now had a very shiny coffee machine, as well as the most expensive kitchen bin either of us had ever seen. Which was why I was currently sitting in a dilapidated flat with nothing more than lining paper on the walls, surrounded by lots of fancy new machines that I didn't know how to use. "Fucksake," I stabbed the machine with my finger again, "why won't it just do as it's *told*?"

"Because you're asking it to pre-heat the milk steamer," said Mapp, "instead of dispensing coffee." He pushed me gently out of the way and pressed a button I hadn't even noticed. The display magically cleared itself and sat waiting for further instruction. He tapped another button, and the machine miraculously began pumping out piping hot coffee. "Have you read the instruction manual?"

"What a silly question," I said, flopping down onto the chair. "You know very well I haven't." Mapp arched an elegant eyebrow, but said nothing. "Why can't I just keep things how they were?" I whined, as he put the first tiny espresso cup in front of me and found a larger one for himself.

He waited until he was sitting opposite me at the table before replying. "Because things are different now," he said.

I sighed. Things *were* different—really, hugely bloody different. In the year since I fell to my death, I'd had to kill people and fight for my (after) life on more occasions than I felt was either acceptable or necessary. And that was before the surprise discovery that I was also, apparently, the Second Coming Of Undead Kind. That's how I liked to interpret it, anyway. Other people would tell you I just happened to be in the wrong place at the wrong time and the Fates were bored and looking for trouble. Whatever the reason—or lack thereof—my loveable yet distant landlord had made it very clear that, whilst he was fully prepared to hang around until I knew what I was doing, it was high time I stepped up to my new responsibilities.

"Heard from Laithlind?" asked Mapp. He gazed innocently at me over his raised coffee cup as I scowled. Ivo Laithlind was even more devious than Liam O'Connor, although possibly fractionally less of a bellend. The jury's still out on that one. Ivo's even older than Liam, but looks about forty and is every bit the urbane, well-dressed gentleman about town. He's also a duplicitous toad who'd fathered a child with Eadric's wife (yes, the wife I killed; I told you this shit is complicated) when she was still human. That child had, in turn, attempted to kill me the previous summer, before I'd chased her down to the river where I watched her get chomped by feral mermaids.

Then, only a few months ago, Liverpool had developed a nasty case of time slips and I'd fallen—literally—into the middle of the Second World War. To top it off, when I finally got back to the future, I discovered the entire mess had been orchestrated centuries earlier by Ivo sodding Laithlind and his foolishly misguided belief that I was fated to be his partner in crime. Partner in something, anyway. For someone who's never had much luck in their love life, I'd spent a surprising amount of time since my death fending off the attentions of ancient and powerful rulers. Ivo once admitted to still being friends with Emperor Constantine and honestly, if the Byzantine leader had walked through the door of the cafe and asked for a flat white to go, it wouldn't be the weirdest thing that had happened since I died.

"Why do you ask?" I said. Two could play at that game. As it happened, I hadn't heard from Ivo since the time slip insanity. He'd once told me I was dangerous, which was hilarious. I'd taken it as an insult but had since decided to see it as a compliment. *Let them quake in fear*, I thought to myself. *Witness the might of the mardy cafe-owner.*

Talking to yourself again? asked the city that lives in my head. When it first started popping uninvited into my skull I'd assumed it was the ghost of Liverpool itself, but rapidly discovered it was actually made up of everyone who'd ever been born, raised or lived in the city. The spirit of the City—note the capitalisation—is far older, and far more powerful. And often downright rude as well. But luckily it chooses not to inhabit my head too often. Its smaller sibling, however, is a different matter. Popping in and out seemingly at random, it never lets the basic human desire for personal privacy get in the way of its need to gossip.

We do not gossip, it said indignantly. ***We discuss important matters with the reverence that is due to them.***

You reckon? I snipped silently back at it. Mapp looked unperturbed. All my friends were now long used waiting for me to finish conversations in my head before I can continue those I'm having out loud. *You're the ones who woke me up the other night to tell me about the couple having it away on the steps of the World Museum.*

You don't sleep, it said. ***So you can't be woken up.***

That's not the point. I was resting, and you disturbed me. What were you expecting me to do, go tell them to stop?

As it happens, yes.

Who am I to interfere in the course of true romance?

It didn't look very romantic to us, it persisted. ***And you're always saying people should treat the city with the respect it deserves.***

I meant on a sodding political level, I snarked back, *not people shagging on the concrete.* A polite cough brought me back to the matter in hand. Mapp was looking at me with that sympathetic expression he saves for those less fortunate in the intellectual capacity department.

"Anything important?" he asked. "Only I'm supposed to be meeting Heggie soon. We're going to play crazy golf down at that new place in Baltic Triangle." Heggie is what I can only describe as Mapp's 'companion'. A doughy man in his twenties, Hegs is strange enough that I assumed for ages he was just some kind of paranormal creature I hadn't yet heard of. So it had been a surprise to discover he was actually fully human, and very much still alive. Even after more than a year of friendship with the pair of them I still had no idea what their relationship really was, but decided long ago it was none of my business. The two men—one dumpy and still breathing, the other the epitome of long-dead glamour—openly adored each other. That was enough for me.

"Won't your skirt get in the way?" I said, nodding at the puddle of shiny satin pooled around Mapp's ankles.

"I'll hook it up," he said with a grin. "Got m'boots on underneath." He waggled a shapely leg in the air to show that he was, indeed, wearing black patent ankle boots. They had a crepe sole that was at least four inches thick and were fastened with glittery gold laces.

"Christ," I said. "Careful you don't squash any small animals with those."

"I am fully respectful of life in all its different forms and glory," he said. "Only yesterday I removed a trapped pigeon from the storeroom in the shop." Mapp's shop is a Liverpool legend in itself, situated in one of the few buildings on Renshaw Street to have survived the German bombing campaign of WWII. In theory he buys and sells books and antiques, but in reality it's more a curiosity shop containing everything from expensive Victorian mourning jewellery to a heap of plastic tableware from the seventies that he bought for a pittance at auction because they apparently made him nostalgic.

"Uh huh," I said. "Have you got round to cleaning the pigeon shit off the roof yet?"

Mapp narrowed his eyes. "You know I can't climb up there," he said. The roof of the upper floor of Mapp's shop is mostly taken up with an enormous glass skylight, which would let in a lot of light if it wasn't permanently coated with a layer of pigeon guano. "It's not safe for someone as delicate as myself."

"You're about as delicate as a rhino charging around the china section of Marks and Spencer."

"That's as maybe," he sniffed, "but I don't like heights." He ignored my rolling eyes. "I'll get a man in," he said eventually.

"I just bet you will," I said. "Anyway," I went on before he could respond, "you'd better spill the tea before the Scooby gang reappears. Finn's going to want a snack soon." Finn's eating habits were a source of almost constant bemusement to me. Even in his human form he favoured the sort of food cats like—salmon and prawns were his favourite, but he'd never turn down a chicken nugget. I once suggested it would be cheaper to just buy him a bulk pack of Whiskas, and he took it so personally that he hid down the side of the sofa for an entire evening. I ended up going out to buy him a KFC boneless banquet as a peace offering. I'd been thinking more about simplifying life than balancing my budget, anyway. My personal finances are just fine and dandy—they can't really not be, when you don't need to eat, don't pay rent and don't feel the cold. I kept the heating on for the cats, but that was about it. Eadric kept wanting to talk about sorting out a proper income for me courtesy of the company coffers, but I was putting it off. He thought I was being prideful. Truth was, I was terrified that having money would change me. When you're born working class and then spend your entire adult life in a city so left-wing it's practically on another continent, that shit sticks with you. Shiny gadgets were enough for now.

"Something's rotten in the state of Chester," said Mapp. "You're probably going to have to intervene." I frowned. Chester isn't far from Liverpool, and it's absolutely within our territory. I'd also been hearing rumours about it not quite fitting in with the rest of us ever since I'd died and woken up in the Scouse edition of *Buffy*. When I asked Eadric about it, he always said it was complicated and he'd explain when I had a day free to go through the paperwork. Admin being my least favourite occupation, I'd carefully never found the time. And it hadn't mattered anyway, because nothing ever happened in Chester. Until now, clearly.

"Why did you have to come and tell me about it?" I asked. "Wouldn't Eadric be a better choice?"

"Well now," grinned Mapp, "you'd think that, wouldn't you? But you forget, ma'am," he doffed an invisible cap, "that you are now, to all intents and purposes, our beloved monarch. Queens gotta queen, Lil. Time to make your grand entrance, innit?" Depending on who you talked to, as well as being head of the north-west territory I was also possibly queen of the entire country. The whole bloody lot of it, from

Land's End to John O'Groats. In theory this also included Ireland, but I'd made it very clear I would not be messing with them. "The Irish have been arsed around enough," I said to Eadric, when we'd met in his office high over the Mersey to discuss the most amicable takeover in history. "I'd rather they just looked after themselves." I felt the same about Scotland, but hadn't dropped that one on him as yet.

"It's not that simple," Eadric had said. "If the rest of the country is under your protection but Ireland isn't, it will be the primary target for those who'd like to extend their own territories by stealing some of ours."

"Oh, this is all just stupid," I'd said, displaying the full extent of my political opinion. "Okay, so I'll worry about our bit first. The rest can wait."

"I'm not so sure about that," Eadric had fretted, getting up from his desk to gaze out of the window across to the sunny delights of the Wirral. "I don't think William wants to wait."

"He doesn't have much choice," I said. "I'm not going to work with him, and he can't do it without me, so he's shafted. And he knows it." Liam's unexpected gift of the crown—which he'd literally just left on my doorstep one day, for all the world like a teenage boy casually dropping off the world's most expensive Valentine's gift—had turned out to be a solid gold Trojan horse. It absolutely belonged to me, there was no doubting that. Sometimes I was tempted enough to stroke it, and it talked to me. Not out loud, and not even in words. The crown wasn't anything like the city in my head, wittering on at me whenever it had gossip, or sometimes just because it was bored and wanted company. The crown was *alive*. Just the act of touching it with the very tips of my fingers allowed it to transmit its memories and power, showing me endless reels of the awful things that had happened to it—and because of it—over the centuries. No wonder I avoided putting it on my head. The biggest surprise had been the discovery of just how much the crown struggled with the concept of monarchy. I'd found this bizarre to begin with. After all, wasn't a crown—*the* crown, no less—the epitome of what it meant to be, well, *royal*? The crown in question clearly disagreed. I'd once spent several hours lying next to it on by bed, my fingertips the only connection. I'd been only vaguely aware of the night fading and daylight rising through my bedroom window as the crown spun my mind through the centuries of turmoil that had somehow collected within the fragile precious metal. I'd only broken the trance when I heard noises from far below me, suggesting Izzy had arrived to open Flora's for the day. I'd hung it carefully back up on the mirror before striding down to the Liver Building to inform Eadric I'd decided to face the inevitable and maybe he'd like to start giving me lessons in ruling. I'd asked him to carry on with the paperwork side of things for now, mind. I'm pragmatic, not stupid.

"Go on, then," I sighed, giving in to the inevitable. "Hit me with it."

"Aah well," said Mapp, "that's the problem, innit? There is no 'it' to speak of."

"Then why have you come to tell me about this nonexistent it?"

Mapp looked thoughtful for a moment, as if he genuinely didn't know the answer to that. "Well," he said finally, "something's wrong. In Chester, I mean. More wrong than usual, anyway." He frowned. "Has Eadric really never told you about it?"

"No," I said, carefully failing to mention that this was entirely my fault, "he hasn't. So how's about you jiggle that pretty little head of yours and spit it out?" There was a long silence. I was just about to say something about needing to go check on Finn—not even a lie, because that boy could get into trouble in an empty room—when Mapp finally spoke.

"Chester's weird," he said. "Like, *really* weird. You know?" I shrugged to imply that no, I did not know. "It's as though..." he trailed off, before rallying, "it's as though it doesn't fit in with the rest of us. Got a chip on its shoulder. That sort of thing."

"My dad used to say Granny Ivy was evenly balanced, cos she had a chip on *both* shoulders," I said helpfully.

Mapp looked horrified. "For god's sake, Lil," he said, "don't be bringing your grandmother into this! Things are difficult enough as it is, without that..." he paused, trying to think of the appropriate word, "without that *woman* getting involved."

"Don't you start," I frowned. "I know Kitty doesn't like her, but Ivy helped me, didn't she? When..." Now it was my turn to run out of words. Ivy was indeed my grandmother, but she was also Kitty's sister.

The two sisters hadn't got on while they were alive, and they definitely weren't going to let something as minor as being dead change that. Personally, I thought Ivy had mellowed a bit, but Kitty was so clearly traumatised from a childhood with the most scathing sister on the planet that she wouldn't hear a word in Ivy's defence. Not even when my grandmother helped me travel back in time to fix a hole in the space-time continuum that was unravelling and threatening to take all of us with it. And yes, it was as complicated and hair-raising as it sounds. Anyway, it had been Ivy who'd pushed me in the right direction, and she'd disappeared off immediately afterwards, saying she was going to visit family on the Wirral. I hadn't even known we *had* family on the Wirral, let alone the sort that wouldn't mind the ghostly apparition of one of their ancestors turning up without warning. But Kitty was threatening to perform an exorcism on her own sibling by that point and although I genuinely love my gran and wouldn't want anyone to hurt her, she really is hard work. So she went away, and no one was overly sad about it. I did occasionally wonder about the mystery relative, though.

"Yes," said Mapp, rescuing me from my own thoughts, "she did. And we're all very grateful for that. But if we could get back to the matter at hand?"

"Chester," I said. "Weird."

"Weirder than usual," he said. "And let me tell you, Lilith O'Reilly, I know weird when I see it."

"Years of practise," I said drily. "Anyway, so Chester's playing up and you want me to do something about it. Yes?"

"Yup," said Mapp.

"Then you're going to have to come up with some better information than *'ooh it's all a bit weird, no idea why, you'd better go look'*," I said. "I like this normal daily life and I'm not going to go gallivanting across the country without very good reason." I sighed heavily. So much for normality. It had been nearly four months since the incident with the carousel horse and the unexpected bombing raids and the ancient castle that had appeared out of nowhere, and—well. I'd been enjoying the peace, it was as simple as that. I'd even had coffee with Sean a couple of times. Sean Hannerty is exactly who you think he is—famous crime writer, very personable, your mum probably loved him on *QI*. He's also a regular in Flora's, and we once went on a date that ended in me having to suck his memory right out of his head after an unexpected bout of mermaid carnage. Think that's bad? By some absolute miracle, he eventually asked me out on a second date—and promptly got shot by someone who was out to kill me. To my utter astonishment, none of this has dampened his ardour in the slightest. He broaches the idea of another attempt at romance every couple of weeks, and—after the inevitable mental fight with my own libido—I turn him down each time. However undeniably fanciable Sean might be—and he really is, all floppy hair and puppy-dog smiles—I'd quite like to not be responsible for him becoming the *late* Sean Hannerty.

    I'd also enjoyed just hanging out in Flora's over the past few weeks. Admittedly, I mostly sat in the staff kitchen reading through the piles of paperwork that Eadric insisted were part of the whole 'taking over the kingdom' thing. But I could see through to the cafe itself, and Izzy would often come to stand in the doorway for a chat between customers. It helped that the bookwork hadn't been nearly as dull as I'd expected. I'd assumed it would involve endless reams of accounts and legalities, and there was a bit of that—mostly contracts and leases for properties across the north-west. But a large part of it was a stash of ancient notebooks that Eadric had produced from a small, unassuming cupboard in the corner of his office. I'd taken one look at the cracked, yellowing paper and the ancient fading ink and asked him why the books weren't in a museum, which was when he'd informed me they were his own diaries. "A record of events, if you like," he'd said, a faint smile crinkling the edges of his beautiful face. And Eadric really is beautiful, if you like that sort of thing. I mean, obviously I do indeed like that sort of thing—it's hard *not* to be attracted to someone who looks like he stepped off the set of a film shoot that probably involved lots of dramatic fighting and some hefty bouts of romance. But he's also reserved and quite formal, and I like my men rougher round the edges. And my women as well, come to that.

    Anyway, I'd got into the habit of taking a couple of books at a time down to the back room of Flora's. I'd been reading diligently every day but had still only got as far as the turn of the twelfth century. This country had been *busy*. Werewolves stalking Yorkshire, an uprising in Cheltenham—Eadric's theory at the time was that it had probably been started by a bishop with a grudge—and selkies coming ashore to wreak havoc amongst the menfolk of south Wales. I'd asked if he thought the selkies might actually be Asrai—the 'mermaids' who live in the Mersey. He'd said no. "That would be like comparing catfish to seals," he'd said, but refused to tell me which ones he thought were the fish.

"You still with me, Lil?" asked Mapp. When I'd first met him, Mapp had insisted on calling me Lili, because he said it sounded more elegant. These days he went with Lil, same as everyone else. I sometimes wondered whether it was just because it was easier to say, or whether he'd decided I wasn't actually elegant enough to deserve the extra effort.

"Yeah," I said. "Lots going on in my head."

"I bet there is," said Mapp. "You spoken to the big cheese recently?" He meant the City itself—the real, deep-down soul of the entire place.

"No," I said truthfully. "It hasn't popped up since the Billy stuff was sorted out." The City had helped me fix the time slips that had popped up back at the beginning of the year. Unfortunately, said fix had involved us losing Billy, our favourite ghostly rough-sleeper, who'd inhabited a doorway opposite Flora's. But he'd gone off to spend eternity with the love of his life, so we couldn't be too upset about it.

"Still missing him?" asked Mapp kindly.

"Always," I said. "Anyway," I sat up briskly in my chair, "what are we going to do about Chester?"

"I'm sorry, Your Majesty," said Mapp with a grin, "but I reckon that's up to you."

Won't Somebody Think Of The Goldfish?

Mapp left in a flurry of satin and air-kisses and promises to bring Heggie over for a catch-up soonest. After checking Finn was still asleep on the sofa, I headed downstairs to Flora's. Turning the key in the control box for the shutters, I gazed around me as I waited for them to creak their way open. It was always quiet on Harrington Street at this time in the morning—it's not really a shortcut to anywhere unless you're very local. Late spring sunshine was already warming the stone and reflecting off the mostly empty windows of the Cavern Walks shopping centre. I've always loved Liverpool the most first thing in the morning, when it's shaking itself awake and preparing for yet another day as the coolest city on the planet. Not that it even needs to try—who needs London when you can have a *proper* port city, with seaside and industry crammed in cheek by jowl, and cruise ship passengers jostling with locals, who get annoyed by the traffic, but are secretly proud of their beloved town and would defend it to the death. Leaning back against the old bricks, I breathed the city deep into my cold, dead lungs.

It's impossible to explain why breathing as a revenant is so different from breathing as a human. It's an unnecessary act, for one thing—our metabolisms are so slow that we absorb enough oxygen purely by existing in the world. And humans don't risk hurting anyone around them when they breathe. Which is lucky, or humanity would have died out pretty bloody quickly. But whereas humans just, well, *breathe*, we take in everything. Oxygen, nitrogen, argon (even as a human you're pulling in a tiny amount of argon every time you take a breath, so there's your random useful fact for the day, you're welcome), scents (both good and bad) and sometimes entire human souls. Yeah, that one had come as a shock to me as well. Turns out we're so good at absorbing energy that we also absorb *literal* life force. So, the general rule is 'don't breathe at all, but if you do, make sure it's away from humans'. Trouble is, humans are *delicious*. I'd never really been into heavy drugs when I was alive, so had little to measure against, but I was pretty sure none of them could come close to the sensation you get from absorbing human energy. The initial high is a bit like when you're three gins into an evening out and everything's fun and funny and you're filled to the brim with a glowing warmth that makes everything right in the world. So obviously you decide that what you clearly need is several more gins to make things even better, but by the time you're onto the sixth glass you're getting angry and tearful, and boy, are you going to pay for it in the morning. If humans could invent a way of staying at that 'early evening drunk' level, the world would be a much better place. Anyway, I digress. It's a habit of mine. So, a light little breath of *eau de human* gives you that three-gin-feeling. Which means you breathe a tiny bit deeper next time, because it feels nice, and those dopamine receptors don't let something as minor as death stop them pinging off in your brain. And so you take a deep breath and your legs feel weak and you might orgasm on the spot if no one was looking, but you settle for feeling your dead heart explode with light and energy and power, and the gods-given right to do whatever you want because you are Death, destroyer of worlds... Which is when the shouting starts and you look down at the unconscious people scattered on the floor all around you and decide maybe it's time to get the fuck away from the scene of the crime before anyone starts questioning why you're the only one unaffected and then it's a short enforced trip to the hospital for standard blood and urine tests and suddenly you're in a high security science laboratory with no guarantee you're going to survive past the technicians' first coffee break of the day.

You do a lot of breathing yourself, said the city, *for someone who doesn't need to breathe.*

What's that supposed to mean? I frowned.

Just saying.

Well I'd rather you didn't. The shutters had finished their clanking journey back up into the top of the window frame, so I unlocked the front door and let myself into Flora's. I loved the atmosphere in here, even when it was empty. There was a warmth that somehow seemed to emanate from the bricks themselves, and a welcoming brightness that wasn't just down to Izzy's interior design talents. I could smell the remnants of yesterday's cakes, the last of which were boxed up next to the till, ready for one of us to go dish them out to the local rough sleepers. We'd done the same for Billy when he was here, and hadn't wanted to drop the tradition after he left us. It wasn't quite the same, though. God, there was a plastic sandwich box filled with yum-yums—those sticky pastry twists that are a bit like fresh doughnuts but with even more sugar and icing. I really missed yum-yums, I decided, lifting the lid so the sweet aroma wafted up at me. Not as much as I missed baklava, but close. I missed cakes in general, really. You don't realise just what a joy it is to push a sticky cake into your mouth—eyes bulging with your attempts to chew it instead of choking—until you can't do it anymore.

You're doing it now.

Doing what? I stomped around behind the counter and began setting up the coffee machine.

Breathing.

Am not.

Well you're not **now**, said the city, *because I brought it to your attention and then you stopped.*

It's just cake, for god's sake!

Cake today, said the city, *humans tomorrow. That's how it goes.*

Well that's not how it's going for me, thank you.

You're very confident in your own self-control.

And you're very confident in your ability to be a patronising asshat. I was holding the box in which we store coffee for the machine, and pulled the lid off with such force that a small spray of beans bounced out of it and onto the floor. *Look what you've made me do now!* But before the city could think of a suitably snarky clap back, the first customer of the day came through the door and I kept myself distracted until Izzy came in to take over. And I absolutely, definitely did not do any breathing. Cross my heart and hope to die.

~

"How's things down at the petting zoo?" Nik Silverton swung his legs over the side of the antique chair he was wedged into and grinned at me over the top of a battered copy of *Lace* by Shirley Conran. "Found yourself any sentient squirrels yet?"

"All squirrels are sentient," I said. "And cleverer than most humans I know." I nodded at the book in his hands. "Have you got to the goldfish yet?"

Nik frowned. "No," he said, "I don't think so. Why?"

"Oh, you'll know when you get there." I walked past him to where Eadric sat at his desk and heard the distinct sound of pages flipping frantically behind me. "A'right?" I dropped into the chair opposite my landlord and leader. "How goes it in the world of spooky shenanigans? Got any more books about wolves roaming the streets of Birmingham in the sixteenth century?"

Eadric smiled despite himself. "Those weren't wolves," he said, "as you know very well. The vampires had killed all the wolves off by then. And yes, I have more books. But I suspect that's not the real reason for your visit."

"Do I have to have a reason?" I did my best to look affronted. "Am I not a permanently welcome and integral part of your delightfully weird network? One of the fam, as it were?"

"Of course," said Eadric. "You will always be one of the fam, Lilith." I could practically hear his teeth gritting at the enforced use of slang. Mind you, this is the bloke who regularly 'hangs' with Ifan—our favourite local busker—so I didn't think the terminology would be that alien to him. "But what is it you're really here for?"

"Is it that obvious?" I griped "I was hoping to look friendly and chatty and 'ooh, just popped in for a cuppa' before starting the quiz session."

"Yes," said Eadric, "it's that obvious. What's up?"

"Chester," I sighed. "Chester's what's up." Eadric raised a querying eyebrow. "Mapp says things aren't right there," I explained, "and I'll need to go sort it out."

"And do *you* think you need to go sort things out?"

"Yeah," I said slowly, "I do. Cos if it's kicking off enough for gossip to have reached Mapp's delightfully fragrant ears, it's already gone too far. And I'm curious. About Chester," I added, in case Eadric hadn't fully understood.

"I offered to go through the history with you," he said, raising a mildly reproachful eyebrow. "It was always going to be an issue again, eventually."

"Again?" I asked. "How long is it since the last time things kicked off there? And more to the point," I heard Nik making spluttering noises behind me, but chose to ignore him, "what's the problem in the first place? Why is Chester such a big deal?"

"Oh, my *lord*!" shrieked Nik, getting up from his chair and stalking over to where Eadric and I sat. "This," he flapped the book in the air, "is absolute *filth*. That poor fish!" Eadric blinked in confusion.

"Told you," I said with a grin. "No one forgets the goldfish." Nik made a show of doing goggle-eyes at me. "Don't read it then," I said. "Maybe you've finally found your personal limit."

"Don't be ridiculous," said Nik, already turning away. "It's a goldfish, not a shark." With that, he walked off toward his private rooms. I noticed he was careful to close the door properly behind him.

"Care to explain?" asked Eadric. "Or am I better off not knowing?" I looked at his ancient, handsome face, the features barely weathered by time and an air of quiet reservation in his expression.

"Best just leave it," I said finally. "It'll only make you cross about the mistreatment of small creatures. Now, tell me about Chester."

~

Won't Somebody Think Of The Goldfish?

You can't grow up in the upper-left bit of England without knowing about Chester's history as a Roman city. It's the prime destination for school day trips and tourists alike, all wandering around sections of old brick walls with expressions of polite interest masking the desire to head off onto the main shopping streets instead. Founded sometime around 70 A.D. as a base for the Legio XX Valeria Victrix, it was initially named Deva Victrix, after both its residents and the goddess of River Dee, within whose curves it lay. By the time Rome abandoned Britain to an uncertain future in the fifth century, Deva had grown a solid carapace of civilians. Mostly traders who'd built up businesses supplying the legionaries, they rooted themselves to the land surrounding the fortress and brought up their own families there. This native shell eventually became the city of Chester, which still grows around its Roman base like barnacles clinging to shipwrecked ruins.

"It grew fat on the proceeds of industry," Eadric was saying, "before its importance as a trading port was overtaken by Liverpool."

"So, it's basically a mardy sibling?" I asked Eadric.

He frowned. "You could say that," he shrugged. "Although the reality is rather more complicated."

"Isn't everything?" I sighed. "You'd think being dead would simplify things. You know, not having to worry about, well, dying." I stared out of the window, which was high enough to show nothing but empty sky. "Above us only sky, and all that."

"That's a song lyric," said Eadric, "not a philosophy."

"Well, it should be," I retorted. "A philosophy, I mean. Cos there's nothing *but* sky—no gods, no heaven, no hell below us, no peaceful afterlife."

"Not for us," he said, "no. But maybe for others there is. We'll never know, because the dead generally lose the ability to communicate."

"Tell that to the undead idiots I spend most of my time with," I said. "Meant affectionately, of course."

"Of course," agreed Eadric. "So, what are you going to do about Chester?"

I thought about this for a minute, only half waiting for the city to pop up and give me some useful information. When it utterly failed to do so, I sighed and looked up at Eadric. "Write a list," I said.

"A list?"

"Yup. Lists are always a good start. Bad guys in one column, good in the other." I got up and stretched, my joints clicking most satisfyingly. Eadric winced.

"I do wish you wouldn't do that," he said. "It's a horrible sound."

"Says the man who personally destroyed my hometown," I said, eyeing him beadily. "Betcha know what the screams of burning peasants sounds like, don't you?"

"That was a very long time ago, Lilith," he said wearily, "and I didn't know any better. Besides," he got up to walk me to the door, "William had already done the same to plenty of my own people."

"Doesn't make it okay," I said. "You're as bad as each other."

"Not these days," said Eadric, a faint smile on his face. "I retired from burning and pillaging a long time ago." He pressed the button to call the private lift. "William, though, I'm not so sure about."

"He'd never get away with it these days," I said, mentally crossing my fingers. "People tend to gossip about that sort of thing." The doors opened and I stepped inside, turning to face Eadric. He tilted his head and regarded me thoughtfully.

"The thing is, Lilith," he said as the doors slid closed, "William never did care about gossip."

My phone rang as I was walking home along Brunswick Street. "Hey mum," I said, "how's things?"

"All good, love," she said. "Dad was just talking about you, so I thought I'd give you a ring." Mum visits regularly, but it's rare for Dad to make the journey. He makes do with Mum telling him I'm okay and seems happy to leave it at that. He's perfectly capable of travelling, I think it's more that he genuinely just can't be arsed. Dad's always been one of those 'I'll just assume everything's fine unless I hear otherwise' types, genuinely convinced I'm best left to my own devices. I couldn't help but love his blind faith, whilst also wondering if he even really knew me and my capacity for getting into scrapes. Mum, on the other hand, has been a regular visitor since I died. My initial worries about having to somehow hide my undead state were swept away almost immediately, on account of how my mother turned out to be a spooky little weirdo in her own right who was, apparently, utterly unfazed by her only daughter becoming a bona fide member of the living dead. And she still thinks I don't know about her occasional sneaky visits to Missy, who can be relied upon to fully spill the tea with no filter. And Mum's using Nik Silverton as a primary source for her PhD research, so she pops up regularly in order to go through her notes with him. We haven't quite figured out how she's going to cite her source—the source in question having been dead for almost two centuries—but she says PhDs take a long time and she'll worry about that bit when she gets to it.

"Is this to do with Lorcan, by any chance?" I said, turning into Harrington Street. When the ghost of my maternal grandmother had turned up in my flat earlier in the year, she'd accidentally outed Dad as being from a family of oddballs who thought nothing of their son's best friend occasionally transforming into a gigantic black cat called Lorcan. Yup—his own mother-in-law had known all along that he had a pet were-cat and not only did his family know all about it, they didn't even consider it to be anything out of the ordinary. The most surprising thing of all was that Gran somehow kept this information to herself, even when the boy with the were-cat began courting her own daughter. Those more generous than I might suggest Gran was simply good at keeping secrets, but I knew better. It was far more likely she simply considered the entire situation to be ridiculous and best ignored entirely. Gran had always been good at ignoring anything that didn't fit in with her own worldview.

Unbeknownst to anyone else, Dad had forced Lorcan to leave before he married Mum, in a misguided attempt at appearing normal. He'd regretted it ever since, and even more so since he'd discovered I now had a big cat of my own. I'd spent my entire life—both alive and dead—under the impression that my father was the most pragmatically non-spooky person I knew. So, the discovery that he had not only known about my newly minted immortality since the start but had also been party to some supernatural shenanigans of his own over the years had come as a bit of a shock. To put it mildly.

"I think Dad would like to meet your Finn one of these days," said Mum.

I snorted. "He's not *my* Finn," I said. "But I'll see what I can do. I'm sure he'll be happy to have a chat."

"Your dad knows it's a long shot," said Mum. "He won't prod Finn for too much information."

"The problem with Finn is not a lack of information," I said, "it's making sure it's *useful* information that's the difficult bit." When I'd first become acquainted with Finn, I'd spend hours quizzing him on the hows and whys of the were-cat life. Sadly for me, his general response was a shrug and vague mutterings about not really thinking about it. Get him talking about his beloved Sheffield Wednesday though, and he'd be there all night. I only made that mistake once. "I've got some more old paperwork from Eadric," I went on. "Going to look through it tonight." Eadric had found me as many relevant sections of his diaries as he could, in the hope I'd be able to find references to the Shropshire big cats. What information I had gleaned so far was scant. The 'wolves' in sixteenth-century Birmingham had, unsurprisingly—to me, at least—turned out to be of the feline rather than canine variety. Eadric had been at his family estate in Shropshire at the time, when the mediaeval grapevine had done its thing and alerted him. I'd been distracted by the realisation that Eadric's descendants appeared to have taken his visit in their stride, which was interesting in itself.

He'd informed me it wasn't anything like as interesting as it sounded. "They think I'm a distant cousin. I just leave a good century or so between visits, so no one figures it out."

"Why do you visit at all?" I'd asked. Eadric had pulled a strange expression that could only be described as a kind of tired sadness.

"I like to know they're doing okay," he said, and refused to elaborate any further.

"Oh good," said Mum happily. "Let us know if you find anything in the diaries. And I'm sure your dad could charm some information out of Finn, if we came to see him."

"You'll have to give me a couple of weeks," I said hurriedly. "I've got some stuff to sort out."

"It's nothing dangerous, is it?" asked Mum, immediately fretting.

"You know how I worry about all this responsibility you're taking on, Lil. Eadric really should be firmer about these things. You haven't been around nearly long enough to be taking charge." Cheers, Mum, I thought. Nice to know you've got such confidence in me.

"I keep telling you," I sighed, "I'm already dead. Anyway, I'll speak to Finn about having a chat with Dad." I let myself into the flat just as the afternoon sun wriggled through the small kitchen window. It illuminated the giant paw prints on the kitchen counters. "That's if I haven't turned him into a rug in the meantime."

"Oh Lil," said Mum, "You're so funny! Anyway, stay safe!" And with that, she rang off.

What's Going On

I got back to the flat to find Finn and Grimm in the living room, but still no sign of Kitty. "She popped up briefly," said Finn, who'd relaxed enough to return to his human form. "But then she went off to visit Jonny." He lay sprawled across the length of my battered sofa, dressed in tartan pyjamas and a pair of fluffy slippers. "Said she'll be back later." Clearly deciding it was my turn to take over babysitting duties, Grimm stalked past my legs and into the bedroom, where he bounced elegantly up onto my pillows and immediately curled up into a round ball of grey fluff.

"Huh," I said, heading back to the kitchen, "she said that last time." Jonny was Kitty's boyfriend back when she was human, and he reappeared on the scene when she reappeared as a ghost. It helps that Jonny himself has been dead since the early eighteen-hundreds, because ghost/human relationships aren't as easy as the movies make them out to be. It generally works out better if both parties are deceased, even if one's a ghost and the other a revenant like me. We might have landed in the afterlife via different routes, but there's an understanding within the undead community that living, breathing humans will never get their heads around. If you date a mortal, they tend to be surprised by things the rest of us take for granted. Disappearing into thin air unnerves people, especially when you reappear in a completely different place. That's just a ghost thing, though—I'd been very disappointed to discover revenants can't do it. We're too bloody solid. Some really clever ghosts can even take humans with them. Billy used to be able to do that —it's how he saved the day (and Liam) when Mab shot at Sean but hit Liam instead, up on the viewing platform of the Radio City tower. You'd assume someone as apparently powerful as a revenant could survive something as basic as a bullet wound, right? And we can—but we still have to heal from it first. Which means getting the bullet out and then sitting quietly for a few minutes while the tissues knit back together. Not easy when there's a deranged immortal with mama issues doing her best to destroy everything around her, including several major Liverpool landmarks. Anyway, Billy zipped Liam out of the tower and into the Liver Building, where Eadric got him fixed up and sent on his way as quickly as possible. He'd probably been concerned about the potential dramatics from yours truly if I'd arrived to find Liam injured, but I wasn't entirely sure how I'd have handled it. Like I say, me and Liam have history—the sort of history that involves taking off your clothes and getting to know the other person very well indeed. And that shit gets complicated. In my defence, I hadn't known at the time that I was shagging one of the most famous kings in British history, nor that he would turn out to be a Machiavellian bastard with an unexpected romantic streak. After a decade of terrible relationships and short-lived flings in the streets and clubs of Liverpool, it's quite the surprise to suddenly find yourself being courted by an ancient monarch with the face (and body) of a seriously fit and undeniably handsome bloke in his late thirties. Especially one whose idea of a passionate gesture is to drop the one true crown of the realm on your doorstep without warning, before leaving you to figure out for yourself what you're supposed to do with it.

And now Eadric was telling me he thought Liam might pick up the ol' burning and pillaging again. Why couldn't my love life just be *normal*, for fuck's sake? "Wasn't her fault Jonny dragged her off to that party," said Finn, interrupting my wandering thoughts. Jonny had indeed, a few weeks earlier, taken Kitty to what turned out to be less a party and more a fancy ball attended by the sort of people who send their kids to private school while claiming to be working class. "Because I still *work*, yah?" one of his friends had said to me when I'd had the misfortune to bump into them in the Bird's Nest Cafe in Shrewsbury market, whilst on a flying visit to my parents. I'd pointed out that taking selfies on various Caribbean beaches and posting them to Instagram with self-help jargon pasted over the top wasn't a job, and that she—and her well-educated kids—actually lived off her daddy's money. "It's not my fault Pops is an Earl?" the girl had said, with that 'rising at the end' intonation that's only not irritating when it's done by Australians, who can't help themselves. I'd asked Jonny how he got away with being friends with humans. Surely, they'd eventually realise he wasn't getting any older? He told me they took no real notice of anyone other than themselves, and anyway, he thought they were funny. Kitty, however, had found it all incredibly tedious and eventually forced Jonny into leaving said party by engaging a local hunt Master in a conversation about how he was an evil animal-murderer and deserved to be ripped apart by his own hounds. There are many reasons me and Kitty get on so well, and our mutual lack of filters is one of them.

"What are your plans for what's left of the day?" I asked the man-cat on the sofa.

Finn stretched out, his spine bending backwards in a way that made me feel slightly uncomfortable. "Gonna go down Sefton once it's dark," he said lazily. "See what's happening." He meant Sefton Park, the enormous green space just south of Liverpool city centre that comprises endless grass, a fancy palm house and, if the legends were true (and in my undead experience, they usually are) a sizeable community of shape-shifting cats.

"What *is* happening in Sefton?"

Finn turned to gaze lazily up at me. "Some say the dogs are back." He rolled his neck with an impressive crunch. "Needs sorting out, dunnit?"

"Yes," I said, "it bloody well does." I looked down at my semi-feral lodger and frowned. "Can't you go now? I've got the decorator coming and I need to decide on colours for the walls." I nodded at the shabby paintwork all around us. "He's going to think I've moved a toyboy in if he finds you here."

"Tell him I'm your nephew," suggested Finn. "Anyway, I can help!" He rolled himself upward and immediately put his feet on the coffee table. I pulled it away and glared as his heels hit the floor with a thud.

"Aren't cats colour blind?"

Finn shrugged. "I can tell you what shades look best together," he said. "It's only the reds and stuff I can't see."

"Well, I'm planning on doing this room bright pink," I said, "so you won't be any help. Shoo!" I flapped at him with a handy cushion. A cushion that was covered in cat hair, I noticed. "Go on, bugger off."

Finn groaned and slowly got to his feet. "You're a mean old woman," he said, even as he bounced forward to kiss me on the cheek. "Dunno how I put up with you." With that, he picked up his sneakers and headed for the door.

"Aren't you going to put those on before you go out?" I asked, looking at his bare feet.

Finn looked down at the sneakers in his hand as if he'd forgotten they were there. "Actually," he threw them back into the corner, narrowly missing me, "I'll just go cat. Quicker over the rooftops, innit."

"It's daylight," I pointed out. "You're going to be noticed."

"Not if I'm fast," he grinned, and shot out of the kitchen door.

"Fucking hell," huffed Missy, appearing at the top of the fire escape and ducking to avoid a hundred-odd pounds of flying cat, "that animal will be the death of me one of these days." She walked through the kitchen to the living room. "I thought he couldn't control the changing yet? Isn't that why he's always getting you to go to the shop for him?"

"Yup," I said. "I'm thinking it's probably time he went back to work." I'd discovered shortly after Finn's unexpected arrival on the scene that he was actually a roofer by the name of Finlay O'Shea. He owned his own company up in Wavertree and seemed to work whatever hours he chose. When I'd asked if customers ever complained, he'd said no. "They ignore the weirdness in return for lower quotes," he'd told me. "On account of how I don't charge for scaffolding. Easier when you can just climb up the wall, innit. And I'm a bloody good roofer."

"Why's he still staying here, anyway?" asked Missy, flopping down onto the sofa. She frowned. "There's hair all over these bloody cushions."

THE DREAM THIEF

"Oh, I don't mind," I said, "and I think Grimm likes the company. I guess it's more comfortable to be around your own kind."

"Finn's own kind are mostly down in the park," Missy pointed out. "*I* think you're just going soft in your old age." She put her feet up on the coffee table, but I didn't bother saying anything. Missy's a law unto herself and best left to do as she pleases. Eadric says she's got no manners, but she'd tell you it comes from spending her human life struggling under the patriarchy and there's no way she's going to be falling for that bollocks now she's dead. And as Missy's human life was based in sixteenth-century Italy, I'm inclined to believe her. Mapp once told me she was a painter back when she was alive, but she doesn't like to talk about it. Her house up in Anfield does have enormous oil paintings hung all over the place, though. And if their angry brush-strokes are anything to go by, she still bears a serious grudge. So yeah, Missy can do what she likes in my house. And she's fun company. Most of the time.

"I'm just learning to prioritise what's worth wasting mental energy on," I said, sitting in the chair opposite her and gazing pointedly at her feet.

"Decided on a colour scheme yet?" she asked, making a show of rearranging her boots on the table.

"Yup," I said, "I have. And it's driving Kitty mad already." Kitty's a hippy at heart, and would have liked pastels and flowers and natural everything. "This room's going pink, for a start."

"I didn't have you down as the pink sort." Missy gazed around her. "Peaceful though, I guess."

"Bright fuchsia," I said. "Probably with leopard print accents." Missy's eyes gleamed.

"Ooh," she said, "now that, I like the sound of. Are you replacing the furniture?"

"That sofa's going," I nodded to where she was half-lying on the ancient moth-eaten cushions, "but I'm keeping the chair. Eadric wanted me to choose everything from the John Lewis catalogue, but I've told him Mapp's on the case." Mapp likes nothing more than a treasure hunt, and even more so when someone else is paying the bills. "Old stuff, you know?" Missy nodded. "I've started a Pinterest board." I pulled my phone out of my waistband in order to show her, but Missy waved a hand.

"I'm not looking at that thing," she said, narrowing her eyes at the phone. "They're dark magic and no one will convince me otherwise."

I sighed and put the phone away. "What do you know about Chester?" I asked her.

"That's a sudden change of topic," said Missy, squinting at me. "Why do you ask?"

"Oh, I dunno," I said, "just wondering. I'm going to have to go over there, is all. Trying to be as prepared as possible."

"Surely you've been to Chester before?" said Missy. "Everyone's been to Chester, for gods' sake."

"Of course I've been to Chester," I said. "Dozens of times. But that was when I was still a standard human and the most I was expecting from it was better shops than it's actually got."

"You're not wrong there," she said. "I was well disappointed."

"You actually went shopping in Chester?" I found it hard to imagine Missy anywhere other than Liverpool. Which is stupid in itself, because having travelled to Britain from Italy—a big move, back then—she'd spent a long time living in London before finally ending up on the sunny shores of Merseyside.

"Yes," she said, "I went shopping. I do go shopping, you know."

"What for?" I couldn't hide my fascination.

"You've seen the size of my house," she said. I have, and it's huge. Missy's place sits in the cemetery off Priory Road and is a red-brick gothic vision perfectly suited to its location. "I enjoy redecorating it occasionally," she went on. "And Chester's good for furnishings." I'd never had cause to visit a different town purely to buy furnishings, but then until I'd died and ended up with my landlord's credit card, I hadn't had the funds to do so anyway. "And Alan keeps breaking things." Rachel's ghostly boyfriend is also Missy's lodger. She's banned him from practising his moves in the house and he'd been spotted in the cemetery too many times, so these days he can often be found dancing up and down the steps of my fire escape. Alan gave up the limelight long before he actually died back in the seventies, but death seemed to have given him his confidence back. I guess you don't have to worry about dying onstage if you're already dead to start with. Anyway, it doesn't hurt anyone and he's a nice bloke, so we mostly just leave him to get on with it.

"Tell me again," I said, "about how I'm the one going soft in my old age? Didn't Al put one of your windows through only last week?"

"It wasn't his fault the tree branch was so springy. Anyway, what do you want to know about Chester?" Fuck me, there's no one better at changing the subject than a revenant who's been put on the spot.

"Any of the spooky shit," I said. "Who haunts where, which spots are best for bumping into the local zombies with the gossip. That sort of thing."

"I wish you wouldn't use that word," said Missy.

"Dunno what you're talking about," I said. "Nothing wrong with being zombies. I seem to be doing okay out of it."

"It makes people think of flaking skin and weird eyes," she said. "Not really the best image, is it?"

"Given I only ever use the word with people who know what I mean," I said, "I wouldn't worry too much about it. So," I gave her an encouraging look, "tell me about Chester."

"First," she said, "I need to know what you're going there for."

"Why?"

"Because, Lilith," Missy got up and walked over to gaze out of the living room window, "I rather like my nice quiet life up here in Liverpool, and I'm not going to be happy if you disturb that."

"Not my fault I've been put in charge, is it?" I said. "You can take over, if you like." I looked at her hopefully.

"You can fuck off," she said, putting paid to my daydream of giving up the day job and retiring to spend all of eternity as nothing more than the manager of an inconsequential coffeeshop. "You're living proof enough that no one in charge ever gets any peace. Just with less of the living. Proof, anyway," she shrugged. Another thing about older revenants is they often seem to think grammar is for other people. "What's up with Chester, then?"

"Something's going on," I said. "More than usual, anyway."

"And you're going to sort it out?"

"Yup," I sighed. "But only if I know what I'm walking into. So, spill the spooky tea."

"Truth is, I don't actually know much," said Missy.

"Fucksake."

"There isn't much *to* know," she said. "At least, not as far as I've ever been aware. Yeah, it's a weird place, for sure—but then so's everywhere. Try visiting Colchester and then come back to me with how weird Chester is."

"What's wrong with Colchester?"

"What *isn't* wrong with Colchester, you mean. What can you expect, when one of the oldest settlements in the country is also the core of its warmongering?" I wasn't sure how the residents of Colchester could be considered warmongers. "No wonder it's permanently itchy, with that garrison giving it a permanent headache." I was tempted to point out that Colchester had been a garrison town since it was founded by the Romans and probably wouldn't still exist if it hadn't kept up the military tradition. But I've learned to my cost that she can argue a single point for hours, and appears to get huge enjoyment from doing so.

"You don't think Chester's *particularly* weird, then?" I asked, hoping to head her off. "Just our usual level of boring weird? Nicely non-dangerous weird?" Missy shrugged again. Some help she was being. "Why does everyone go on about it, then?"

"Oh, that's easy," she said, getting to her feet and walking over to the window. "Bit too close to home, see. We're here," she waved an arm around at the city in general, "and the city we replaced is just down the road, close enough to know what we're up to. I'd imagine it's had its Roman nose put out of joint over the centuries, wouldn't you?"

"You think it's jealous?" I couldn't imagine a city being envious of Liverpool's transformation over the years. Yeah, so maybe you'd be impressed if you were a city councillor in some dilapidated town in need of investment—the difference between Toxteth of the nineteen-seventies compared to the version you see today, for example, is incredible by any standards. And it's far from the only part of the city that's changed from a raggedy Cinderella to refurbished newcomer sweeping around like the queen of the ball. But a city itself? All it would see is the gouging of land and stealing of resources. Liverpool went from a small fishing village to the centre of filthy industrialisation in a terrifyingly short time, and still has the scars to prove it. Both the mental *and* physical kind.

"Not of the commercial development, I don't think," said Missy, as though reading my mind. "More the general importance. Chester used to be the centre of civilisation up this way, pretty much. It was where the cool kids were all at, you know?"

"If by 'cool kids' you mean Roman merchants and slave pedlars."

"Same thing, back then," she shrugged. "Anyway, it was huge and important, and everyone knew it. Then the Dee starts silting up just as the ships are getting bigger and suddenly Chester's on a road to nowhere, except as a staging post en route to the exciting new destination of Liverpool." Missy's flippant summary wasn't entirely incorrect. Liverpool was already taking over as the dominant port in the northwest by the seventeen-hundreds, and people do often assume it was the silt that cramped Chester's commercial style. But it was mostly just down to basic geology. Ships were indeed getting bigger, and the Mersey allowed for deeper hulls than the shallower Dee. It was the fast-growing shipping industry that did for Chester, not the city of Liverpool. And the overlap when both cities were competing for trade was a very long one.

"Surely things would have kicked off before now, if that was the reason?" I said. "And anyway, shipbuilding's declining pretty much everywhere—if anything, you'd think Chester would be calming its tits a bit."

"We're gendering cities now?"

"Don't need to be female to have tits," I pointed out.

Missy shrugged. "Whatever the status of its physical appearance," she said, "Chester has clearly not calmed anything. So, you're going over there to investigate, I assume?"

"Looks like it," I sighed.

"Let me know if the lighting shop's still on Eastgate. I need a new chandelier for the bottom stairwell."

"You could do all the shopping your little undead heart desires," I pointed out, "if you only got to grips with the internet." Missy shrugged. "Anyway, what's wrong with the chandelier you've got already?"

"Turns out," she sighed, "it wasn't strong enough for Al's trapeze act."

∼

Missy eventually sloped off home, presumably to check Al hadn't accidentally demolished the entire building in her absence. And the decorator called, apologetically cancelling our paint-choosing appointment. He'd gone out to his van to drive over to Harrington Street, only to discover that all four of its tyres had been slashed. "God knows what I've done to offend someone this time," he'd said. "It looks like Wolverine went at them with his claws." I carefully did not ask for any further details and put the phone down on him still grumbling about how it looked like interior design was becoming a dangerous profession, if this was the sort of lengths his competitors were prepared to go to in order to prevent him working. Heading into my bedroom, I decided to make the most of the rare peace and quiet. Picking the crown up carefully from its customary spot on my dressing table mirror, I lay down on the bed and stared up at the ceiling. The crown lay heavily on my stomach like a cat that's made itself comfortable and has no plans to move anytime soon. It even vibrated occasionally, a kind of weird metallic purr. At least, I assumed it was purring—it might have been building up to exploding in my face and destroying the known universe, for all I knew. But I was fairly sure it wouldn't put me at risk of injury. At least, not intentionally.

Come on then, I said silently to the city. *Tell me what you know.*
What we know about what?
Don't start arsing around, I said. *I'm not in the mood.*
Chester, then.
Yes, I said. *Chester.*
It's unhappy.
Why? There was a long pause, interrupted by occasional shuffling noises. I had no idea how many people made up the city in my head, but thought it must be thousands. Every last person from in and around Liverpool who'd died in the last few hundred years and felt they had a justifiable grievance against the world. Tens of thousands, then. Ugh.

Would you help it? it asked. ***If we asked nicely?***

Why do you want to help Chester out? I asked. *It's on the wrong side of the river, for one thing.*

It's part of our territory and we look after our own. I got the distinct impression it was shrugging. ***And Shrewsbury's on the wrong side as well, but that doesn't stop you from keeping an eye on it.***

Yes, I said, *but I'm* from *Shrewsbury, so it's different. Also, Shrewsbury isn't weird.*

Shows how long it's been since you've visited properly, then, said the city. ***That place is on the verge of going fully middle-class hippy and no one's stopping it.***

Should they? I asked. *Stop it, I mean.*

The city gave it some thought. ***Nah***, it said eventually, ***we're always in need of middle-class hippies. They're the only ones who can afford the artisanal hemp-based jelly sweets they're selling in the market hall these days.***

How do you know what they're selling in the market? I frowned. *Please tell me you don't follow me around?*

You should be so lucky, it snorted. ***Nah***, it went on, ***we just hitch a ride sometimes. When you're out on tour, like.***

I'm not sure that's entirely ethical. Shouldn't you ask my permission first?

Says the woman who bounced around a war zone without warning anyone she was going to do it.

Don't you start, I sighed. *I'm doing my best, for fuck's sake. And if it isn't good enough, then you'll just have to find another vehicle for your spooky meanderings.*

Nope, said the city. ***We're stuck with you. Nothing we can do about it. Probably best to think of us as Thelma to your Louise. Your ride or die, sort of thing.***

I'm already dead.

Can't have everything, it said brightly. ***So, are you going to help Chester or not?***

Depends what Chester's been up to, I said. *I might not want to risk it.*

Chester can't help what it is, said the city. ***It's been made that way by man.***

Sexist.

Literal, it said. ***It's mostly been men in charge of the country over the centuries. Been some spectacular women as well, mind. We quite liked the first Elizabeth. And Victoria was strange, but she meant well.***

Yeah, I said, *people used to say the same about Thatcher.*

That woman, the city snarked, ***is not in the same league as the Queens. And never was, however important she considered herself. 'We are a grandmother'***, it snorted. ***Honestly!***

My dad used to do impressions of that. I smiled at the memory—Dad sitting at the kitchen table with a brew in his hands, taking the piss out of the Tories and their grandiose hankering for the days of Empire. *He said nothing good ever came from self-importance, whether it was on a personal or national level.*

Wise man, your father.

Mostly, I said, thinking of poor, lost Lorcan.

Anyway, the city said, clearly getting impatient, ***what are we going to do about Chester?***

You need to tell me what's wrong with it before I can decide whether to help. If I even can.

Like we said before, something's winding it up. Or someone. We're not sure which.

Ivo? Chester was well within our territory, but Ivo's own lands bordered us to the north. Elizabeth was to the south, but too far away to bother with Chester, I thought. There was always the wild territory that had a tiny border with us to the east, but as far as I knew, that had been empty for centuries.

Not empty, said the city. ***It's lacking a monarch, which is a very different thing.***

It's doing okay as far as I can see, I said. *Maybe that's the way forward for all of us. Destroy the monarchy, down with the crown, that sort of thing.*

We suspect you'd feel differently if it was your crown at risk of being destroyed.

I thought about this for a minute. *No,* I said eventually, *I'd be fine with the hierarchy of the ol' netherweird being dismantled. But the crown itself is an actual, physical thing,* I patted it affectionately, *and it belongs to me.*

Some would argue the crown is symbolic of all that is wrong with the world. That we'd all be better without it.

Yeah, I muttered silently, *that's what Cromwell thought. Didn't stop him turning a protectorate into a monarchy by another name, did it?*

Everyone wants power in some form, Lilith.

No, they don't. Just because I'm attached to the crown doesn't mean I want to wear it. Anyway, I said, *can we get back to the actual conversation? You were telling me what's going on with Chester.*

We were telling you we weren't sure, it said. **But something is, indeed, going on. Has been for a long time. But it's getting worse. And now Chester's even weirder than usual.**

Yes, you all keep telling me that. I'm going to be needing a bit more to go on, in all honesty.

A sigh, and a faint shuffling noise that sounded like a small group of people settling themselves in, as they considered what to say. **It belongs**, the city said eventually, **but not in the same way as the rest of us. It is...other.**

Has it always been, I fumbled for a better word, but gave up, *other? Or is this a more recent development?*

Fairly recent, came the reply. **Last couple hundred years or so.**

I rolled my eyes at its definition of 'recent', but decided not to go down that particular rabbit hole. If you asked everyone in my immediate social circle to define what 'recent' meant to them, you'd get everything from 'last week' (Izzy) to 'anything since the death of Chaucer' (Ivo). Not that Ivo was in my immediate social circle anymore. He'd made himself scarce after the time slip chaos, for good reason. Half the inhabitants of spooky Scouse society would have happily kicked Ivo Laithlind right into the next millennium, and each had a different reason for wanting to do so. From his machinations with Eadric's duplicitous wife to triggering the chain of events that led to us losing Billy, let's just say Ivo hadn't gone out of his way to make friends and influence people.

But not knowing where Ivo was made me nervous, for very good reason. Not that I'd have admitted it to anyone else.

Nervous of what he might be up to, said the city, **or nervous of your own reaction when he does finally appear?**

I sighed, but didn't waste energy getting grumpy at the intrusion into my private thoughts. I'd long given up on trying to keep anything secret from my mental lodger. *Both*, I said. *I think, anyway.*

Better to be honest about it, said the city approvingly. **No point worrying about making yourself look stupid**. A pause. **That tends to happen anyway.**

Remind me again why I carry you around in my head?

Because you don't have a choice. We didn't ask to be here, any more than you wanted us with you. We're all stuck, and all we can do is make the best of it.

Yeah, I sighed, *you keep saying that. Anyway, stop distracting me. What's going on with Chester? By which I mean what do* you *think is wrong with it?*

There was silence for a long minute, broken only by the sound of Grimm's snoring wafting in from the living room. He leaves the room if I take the crown off the dressing table. I think it makes him nervous.

You've unnerved it, said the city, **we think. But we don't know why. There's no reason for Chester to have an issue with you personally. Unless it sees you as a direct representation of Liverpool, of course.**

Why would that bother it?

Liverpool is the reason Chester was demoted, it said. **Do you not remember anything from your history degree?**

No, it was not, I said. *And I remember plenty, thank you! It's not Liverpool's fault Chester dropped down the popularity list.*

Regardless of the reasons behind it, said the city, **there's no denying Liverpool took Chester's crown. Cities don't forgive that sort of thing.**

Then cities are mardy little brats, I said. *As if a city decides to spend centuries building itself up just to spite the next city down the road!*

You asked for our theory. It sounded huffy now. **And that's our**

theory—Chester's angry that Liverpool's surpassed it, and it's taken until now for things to reach a head.

You think someone's purposely winding it up?

And who would want to do that?

Anyone who might be out to cause trouble, I said, refusing to take the bait. *Doesn't have to be anyone specific.*

Well, we're assuming it's the Bastard or the Viking, it said. **If that helps.**

No, that doesn't help.

Someone's there who shouldn't be, and it's your job to find out who.

Our job, I think you'll find.

Nope, said the city, **this one's on you. But we'll come with you for moral support. We're well overdue an outing.**

I got up off the bed and carefully hung the crown back up on the mirror. There was the faintest of glimmers and then it settled down.

The weirdest thing round here isn't Chester, said the city. **It's that crown.** There was a distinct shuddering sensation that made the hairs on the back of my neck prickle.

I'd trust the crown before I'd trust most other people round here, I said. *All it wants is to be safe.*

And you know this how, exactly?

I can feel it, I said, giving the crown one last pat. *It's on my side.*

Strange Little Girl

I set out for Chester early the next morning, to avoid the worst of the rush hour. Basil might have an air-cooled engine, but he still complains if we have to crawl along in traffic for any length of time. It was sunny and the drive to Chester's an easy one, so I put Taylor Swift on the stereo and sang along (badly) as the little car trundled its way down the M53. And yeah, I listen to Taylor Swift, what of it? People need to stop being so stuck up about musical tastes, it's not a crime to put the Doors *and* Harry Styles on the same play list (despite what Izzy says to the contrary). So, I drove and sang and got to Chester far quicker than I'd have really liked. I parked Basil in the multi-storey carpark on Pepper Street and wandered slowly down to street level, wondering how on earth I was supposed to introduce myself to an entire city. I was pretty sure that, *'Hi, I'm Lilith, pleased to meet you. Why are you so mad?'* wasn't going to cut it. But it really would be nice to deal with just one minor issue without all hell being let loose.

That's asking a bit much. As it's you we're talking about.

I hadn't been expecting the city to speak while I was away from its geographical roots, and it startled me. Instinct kicked in and I was hopping onto a nearby wall before I even realised what I was doing—a learned reaction from too many vampire ambushes in the past.

*Are you **trying** to draw attention to yourself?* The city sighed. ***Get down, Lilith***, it said. ***You're going to scare people.***

I belatedly realised the wall I was currently perching on was a good fifteen feet off the ground and people on their way to work were beginning to gather to see what I did next. They presumably thought I was one of the endless street performers who busked on Chester's main streets every day, and just starting early.

Maybe you could strike a pose, said the city helpfully, ***and just stay there all afternoon. We might make some money***.

I dropped down so I was sitting on top of the wall, and made a show of turning round and lowering myself down slowly, as human-like as possible. Suddenly I felt a pair of firm hands on my waist and had to force myself not to kick out at my would-be helper. For one thing, they clearly thought they were being my knight in shining armour. And for another, if I kicked a human, I'd probably break their legs in the process. So I allowed them to hold my weight as I dropped to the pavement. I brushed my hands off on my jeans as I turned to thank them, a polite smile already pasted across my face. "Thank you so—" I stopped and glared. "What the fuck are *you* doing here?"

"Assisting a damsel in distress," said Ivo Laithlind, flashing a wicked grin, "obviously." The bystanders who were still loitering perked up at this potentially dramatic scenario. I'd have bet good money they were assuming we were a couple who'd had a row, and I'd stormed off to do something suitably theatrical for attention.

"Fucking patriarchal bullshit," I muttered to myself. "Not you," I said in response to Ivo's querying expression, "everyone else." I waved an arm towards the bystanders. A couple of them walked off looking sheepish, but at least three stayed to see what happened next. "Fuck off," I called helpfully. "There's nothing to see here." Ivo turned and smiled politely at them.

"We're fine," he said, "thank you. I'll make sure the young lady's safe." I gritted my teeth and forced myself to stay silent as the remaining nosy parkers finally got the hint and drifted off. As soon as they were out of hearing range, I turned on him.

"And again," I hissed at him, "why the fuck are *you* here?" He tilted his head and smiled. If I'd still needed to breathe, I'd have been holding my breath right now. There's no getting away from the fact that Ivo Laithlind is the sort of man who makes you just want to hop on and yell 'yee-haaaaaa!' whilst riding him like one of those fairground rodeo machines. He was dressed in his usual dark trousers and shiny, very expensive shoes, but as a nod to the warmer weather, he'd topped them with a cream linen shirt that was open at the collar. He'd rolled the sleeves up to his elbows and I was just suppressing an actual growl when he laughed and broke my train of distinctly grubby thoughts.

"Are you okay?" he asked. "It's just that you look rather…distracted." His eyes crinkled at the corners, and I wondered—not for the first time—how the fuck I'd ended up in bed with Liam O'-slimy-Connor the previous year, and not this…well. Let's just say Izzy isn't lying when she says he's the hottest man she's ever seen, and can I not just hump his supernatural brains out even if it's just so's she can hear about it and get her jollies at a slight remove. His blue eyes were like sapphires, and the flecks of grey in his stubble glinted in the sun. Presumably he'd had a good shave sometime back in the eighteenth century, and it had taken this long to grow back. Immortality would be far easier if I hadn't landed in the middle of the hottest collection of zombies the world had ever seen, I decided. "Red?" Ivo tilted his head and gazed at me in amusement. "Are you okay?"

"Just wondering how you've got the brass neck to turn up here," I snapped, to cover my blushes. "Aren't you supposed to let me know when you're in my territory?"

"Since when?" he asked. "We've always just got along without too many formalities. Of course, if you want to change things now you're in charge—"

"I'm just disappointed by your lack of manners." Ivo raised a questioning eyebrow. "Wouldn't it be polite to let other territories know when you're visiting," I went on, "instead of just turning up without warning?"

"Maybe," he shrugged. "But it's never bothered anyone in the past."

"You didn't have Liam O'Connor hanging around in the past," I pointed out. "Or if you did, he kept it on the down-low and didn't bother anyone."

"And he's bothering you now?" asked Ivo. "Want me to have a word?"

"You having a word with Liam is the last thing anyone needs," I said. If anything was going to herald the start of the zombie apocalypse, it would be Ivo and Liam coming to blows. "And you haven't answered my question. What are you doing in Chester?"

"Something felt a bit off," he shrugged. "I know the area well enough that I can usually feel when something isn't right. And something is very much not right around here, Red." He frowned, and I trod down hard on the urge to soothe his furrowed brow. "I just don't know what."

"That's why I'm here," I sighed, giving up on the stroppy act. I could never keep it up for long with Ivo, anyway. "Something isn't right, and I don't know what. It makes me itch. What's so funny?" Ivo's face was twitching into a lopsided smile.

"You're funny," he said. "That's all. And still very attractive, if you don't mind me saying."

"You can say what you like," I snapped. "It won't get you anywhere."

"We'll see," said Ivo. "Fate is fate, after all."

"Not when you've twisted it to suit yourself!" Ivo's ancient fiddling with time had nearly landed me permanently in an actual war zone a few months earlier, and no manner of flattering comments were going to make up for that. "You're like a kid who wants the shiny new toy," I went on. "It's not me you're after. It's the power."

"You're feeling powerful these days, then?" he said. "Excellent news. All I need now is to convince you I'm the good guy."

"There are no good guys in our world, Ivo. There's just us. Now, if you'll excuse me, I have to go."

"Where?" he said. "I'll come with you."

"No, you bloody well won't," I snapped. "You just cause trouble. Apart from anything else," I said, more calmly, "it will only rile the others if they discover I've been hanging out with you. Elizabeth will assume we're in cahoots or something. And gods only know what Liam would make of it."

"Not Eadric?"

"Eadric trusts my judgement." It was clearly my day for lying, because whatever Eadric might say to the contrary, I was pretty sure he wouldn't trust me as far as he could throw me. Although he could probably throw me quite a long way, to be fair. "He knows I'll end up taking over eventually, so we've learned to get along. The others, not so much."

"You've accepted it, then." Ivo's voice had taken on an interested tone. "Well done."

"Stop bloody patronising me," I said. "I'm not one of your mediaeval princesses who's thrilled by your every word."

"Clearly," he smiled. "So, you're not going to accept my offer of gentlemanly company? No strings attached?"

"Fuck off," I snapped, "and take your smarmy elbows with you." And with that, I stalked off, leaving Ivo looking down at his arms in confusion.

∽

Half an hour later, I was sitting on the stone base of the Chester Cross, wondering what to do next. A magpie landed on the cobbles nearby and stalked grandly around in front of a group of unimpressed pigeons before flapping away again. There had been nothing remotely strange about the city centre that I could feel, even as I walked along each of the Rows in turn. The Rows are the four main streets in Chester and famously built on two levels, with steps up to the first-floor properties and more steps down to those at just below street level. If you walked along them with no prior knowledge of the city, you could be forgiven for thinking you'd stumbled on a film set, the extravagantly timbered buildings all crowding together like something Shakespeare would have recognised from one of his own ridiculous plays. In fact, ol' Willy Shakes *would* have recognised Chester, because it's changed very little since the thirteenth century. Other than the shops now being occupied by artisan bakeries and branches of Waterstones, the heart of the city is relatively unchanged. Even back when I was still a boring breathing human, walking down Liverpool's old streets had given me the feeling of being part of something ancient—something alive in a way humans never were. And Chester was even older than Liverpool. So why couldn't I feel anything here?

You're looking in the wrong place, said the city. **Call yourself an historian**. There was a snorting noise from somewhere deep inside my head.

I've never called myself an historian, I said, *so you can cut out the snark.*

Says Madame Snark of Snarksville.

Have you been talking to Izzy? Cos that sounds like something she'd say.

We talk to no one but you, Lilith, it said. **But we hear what you hear, and can't help picking some of it up along the way**.

I told you to stay out of my private thoughts, for fuck's sake!

And we do. But you are most alive when you are with your companions. 'Alive' being a relative term, of course.

Of course, I sighed. *So where should I be looking?*

You really have to ask?

Well clearly, I was getting irritated now, *or I wouldn't be bloody well asking!*

No need to be grumpy, it said, in a tone so patronisingly annoying that I wished—not for the first time—that I could wash my brain out with bleach and start over without my [mental] companions. **You're missing the obvious**, it said in a more kindly tone. **Chester is older than any of us. You need to find its true heart.**

I leaned back against the blacked-out windows of one of the endless tattoo studios that seem to be constantly gathering like inked sheep in the city centre, and closed my eyes. Then I immediately opened them again, gave myself a mental kick for being so bloody *stupid*, and set off.

I stalked up Eastgate Street as far as Lush, then took a right down City Walls. By the time I got to the Wesley Church, with its red brick exterior glowing in the morning sun, I could feel...*something*. It wasn't anything I could identify as yet. But the faintest ghost of a tickle at the back of my neck suggested I was getting close. A quick skip across the road at the bottom—with an apologetic nod to the van driver I hadn't noticed and who'd had to perform a very bad-tempered emergency stop—and I was standing at the edge of the Roman amphitheatre. For some reason, it hadn't occurred to me that the problem might be as old as this. I'd naively expected Chester to be a smaller Liverpool—industrious and self-contained and maybe a little bit bolshy.

Mistakes are built on assumptions, said the city helpfully. Ignoring my onboard troll, I followed the line of the railings round to the entrance, where a gaggle of people were listening to a tour guide. The guide was a woman, in her mid-sixties at a guess, dressed in loose trousers with a smock over the top and comfortable lace-up shoes suitable for herding tourists around the city sights. She was telling them that yes, the amphitheatre was used for gladiator battles, but mostly for cock-fighting. I walked slowly into the amphitheatre itself. A group of schoolchildren were down on the lower level, some of them pretending to be gladiators fighting to the dramatic death. A boy brandished an invisible spear whilst a girl ran at him, her arms outstretched into bull horns. The boy dodged, laughing, as the girl tried to gore him with her spindly arms. A man who I assumed was their teacher stood nearby, with other children gathered around him. They were listening to a young woman who appeared to be explaining the archaeological layers of the dig that exposed the Roman remains to modern view. The back of my neck prickled again, as though I was being watched. I turned to look, but couldn't see anyone. It was a warm day and people sat in twos and threes on the grass, some reading, others chatting amongst themselves. A pair of women in office suits sat together with their eyes closed, faces lifted towards the sun. Walking across to where an empty area of grass grew up to the edge of the brickwork, I sat down with my legs dangling over the edge just a few inches above the amphitheatre floor. Putting my hands down beside me on the warm grass, I tried to empty my mind of everything other than pure sensation. The grass was ticklish under my palms as my fingertips burrowed through it, feeling for the soil beneath. The sun was warm on my closed eyelids and my heels bumped against ancient stone. As I moved my feet, the toes of my sneakers scuffed the shale surface. I could almost physically feel my mind wriggling as it tried to find a way into the soul of the city. Tentacles of thought probed walls that had nothing to do with bricks and mortar and everything to do with history and memories and ancient, rooted power. Romans had stood on the spot where I now sat, watching animals being forced to fight and listening to their leaders instruct how this newly formed citadel was going to expand and hold power on behalf of those even higher up the political food chain. Something was trying to keep me out, but I thought it was probably just the natural defences of a town old enough to remember what could *really* happen if you didn't keep yourself locked tightly away from incomers. I wriggled my fingers further down into the soil in the hope of getting a literal connection to the city I needed to speak to. I could feel something shifting, as though I'd accidentally pressed the button to open a secret door but didn't know how I'd done it, nor where the door actually was. *Come on*, I whispered silently, *I'm not going to hurt you.* There was a flutter, as light as a butterfly landing on the edge of my thoughts. *Speak to me*, I coaxed, *tell me what's wrong.*

Ten seconds later, I was hunched up with my arms wrapped around my head, desperately trying to stop the awful cacophony that was threatening to burst my eardrums. Chester—the real, ancient spirit of the city in which I sat—roared inside my head like a lion desperate to escape a trap but too panicked to see the way out. It was all I could do not to run screaming around the amphitheatre in an attempt to fling the monster out of my head. Instead, I gritted my teeth and concentrated on breathing—the sort of breathing therapists teach you to do in the hope of warding off panic attacks. I might have only been dead for just over a year, but it's amazing just how quickly you get out of the habit of breathing. The first panicked gulp of air had me choking and spluttering as my under-used lungs complained at being forced back to work with no warning. I managed to subdue it before anyone nearby attempted the Heimlich manoeuvre on me, concentrating on what my body was doing rather than listening to the noise that was filling my head. I could taste grass and air and sun and excitement and a deep, resonant anger that was flavoured with iron and sweat. An endless howl spinning on its own axis, an infinite spiral of pain and anguish and absolute raging fury. I wanted to run as far and as fast as I could away from whatever this was, but it wasn't an option. I had to get through it and out the other side, and hopefully not bash my own head open against the old stones whilst doing so. Gritting my teeth and keeping my eyes closed, I forced my arms to drop back down onto the grass. I did my best to look casual as I slowly lifted my face to the sun. Hopefully I'd look like an optimistic sunbather rather than someone who'd given their carers the slip. *I'm still here*, I said silently. *I'm not going to hurt you.* There was no direct response, but the noise gradually changed. It was still loud enough to make every muscle in my body tense up, but now there was an ebb and flow to it, as though whatever was making the noise was going round in circles. *Talk to me*, I said again. *Let me help you.* Without warning, the roar suddenly blew up into a tornado, ripping out of my head and throwing me backwards onto the grass.

~

"Hey lady?" The voice was young, and very close to me. "Lady? Are you okay?" I opened one eye carefully, squinting against both the light and any potential pain. The sun was bright, but the noise had gone. Whatever had been rattling around in my skull had clearly done a runner. And now I was lying flat out on the grass. A small girl was staring down at me, a worried expression on her face.

"Umm.." I struggled up onto my elbows. What the *fuck* had just happened? Before I could give it any further thought, the girl coughed loudly, and I turned to look at her. "Right," I said. "Yeah, I'm fine. Thank you." She was about eight years old and dressed in a grey pinafore over a long-sleeved shirt that had started out as white, a very long time ago. Her blonde hair was tied up in wonky bunches with those hairbands that have heavy plastic balls on them. My brother Cally had once pinged a very similar hairband at me when we were kids and the plastic marble hit me straight in the face, chipping one of my teeth. Luckily, it had been a baby tooth that was already wriggling itself loose, but that hadn't stopped Mum from losing her absolute shit with the pair of us. I could still remember the feeling of outraged fury at being included in the scolding.

"You fell over." The girl's tone was serious, as though she wasn't sure whether to call a grownup for help. "Like something hit you."

"I think I must have dropped off to sleep," I said, smiling in what I hoped was a reassuring manner. "Perhaps I should go to bed early tonight."

"Yes," said the girl. She put her hand out towards me and opened her fingers to reveal a rounded and polished quartz stone nestled in her palm. "This is for you," she said, and dropped it into my lap. It was small, but surprisingly heavy. "You can stroke it." It was a beautiful stone, pinky-silver with crystalline fissures running through it. I picked it up and gave it the attention its donor clearly thought it deserved.

"That's very kind of you," I said eventually, handing the stone back, "but you keep it. It's too pretty to give away."

"Nope," said the girl, stepping backwards out of reach before I could give it back. "It's for you. I have to go now. Bye!" Turning, she skipped off towards her school friends, pigtails bouncing as she went. I watched until she rejoined the group, then looked back at the stone. Now she was gone, I could see it really was just a plain old stone—the sort you find on beaches, worn smooth by the water and banked up the shorelines in their thousands. If I dropped it onto the floor of the amphitheatre, no one would notice. I slid it into my pocket. A gift was a gift, after all. And at least the noise had stopped.

Has it gone? asked the city.

Looks like it, I said silently, getting to my feet and brushing bits of dried grass off my jeans. I slid the stone into my pocket and looked around. Everything was the same as before. The school group had moved along to the next information board. I looked for the girl who'd given me the stone, but she'd disappeared in amongst her friends.

We told you it wouldn't like you poking your nose in. The city sounded hurt, as though it was upset I hadn't believed it.

Well you're the one who asked me to help, I said. *And it needn't have tried to bloody well deafen me! It could have just not let me in, and I'd have given up and gone away, eventually. No need to pull that sort of trick, is there? Bit bloody rude, if you ask me.*

No one asked you anything. Also, cities rarely worry about whether they're being rude. Did you get the information you needed?

Nope. It gave me nothing other than a banging headache.

You can't get headaches, the city pointed out. ***You just* think *your head hurts*.**

It certainly feels like it hurts. I had one last look around me in the vague hope I might find an answer amongst the ruins, but Chester was long gone. The city was still around me, complete with cars and people and all the accoutrements of humanity going about its daily business, but the spirit had absolutely disappeared. *Come on*, I said. *Let's go home.*

Family Ties

I'd stayed up all night looking through Eadric's books, but there was no mention of the were-cats after the nineteen-fifties. I'd even rung him to ask why he thought that might be and had been surprised by his theory. "It was all about space travel by then," he'd said. "People wanted to scare themselves with the possibility of little green men coming down in spaceships. They'd just come out of yet another world war and probably had enough of the dark gloomy gothic stuff." I remembered the goths at school, desperately trying to look spooky and intimidating under a thick layer of white foundation and acne cream. I'd got on with most of them—a therapist would probably mark it down as an early sign of identifying with outsiders—and couldn't help but wonder what they'd think if they saw me now and knew the truth of my life in Liverpool. On paper, I was living the gothic dream—undead, no money worries and sharing my flat with a giant puma. My school friends would be disappointed with the reality, though. For one thing, it involved far more admin than they ever showed in Christopher Lee movies.

Not even a good couple of hour's googling found me anything more than a clutch of reports of attacks on sheep in the Powys area during the previous summer. By the time I could hear Izzy opening Flora's downstairs, I had to admit I was at a loss about what to try next in the search for Lorcan. I decided to visit Mapp. He was an endless source of randomly esoteric knowledge and had the best second-hand book collection of anyone I knew. There might be something about the cats in one of the many dusty old volumes crammed on his shelves. Besides, he owed me one for having sent me to be shouted at by Chester. When I checked the living room, there appeared to be no one else in the flat other than Grimm, so I told him my plans just to be polite. He studiously ignored me, even when I promised to stock up on tuna while I was out.

I was walking along Church Street when the yelling started. Turning to look down the alley that leads to the Bluecoat, I could see people scuffling in the distance. There was something familiar about one of the voices that made me turn and head towards the drama. A pair of frazzled-looking waitresses from the cafe were manhandling someone out through the front doors, but he was putting up a fight. Assuming it was just a random drunk or an unhappy customer, I turned and began walking away down School Lane, on the sound reasoning that my life involves enough drama as it is, without intentionally looking for more. Then the shouting started up again. "You need to listen to me!" yelled the man being evicted. "I'm not breathing, for chrissakes! Do you not think that's weird?" I stopped walking and turned to look back just in time to see the smaller of the women being thrown right across the courtyard. She thumped into the wall and slid down and for a second I panicked, but she immediately scrambled to her feet to help her friend, who was still hanging onto the man. He had his back to me, and I couldn't see much more than a mop of black hair above the white colour of a waiter's uniform, but I'd have recognised that voice anywhere. Devin Reynolds had been a colleague of mine when I'd worked at the Bluecoat years earlier. He was politely left-wing and painted Dungeons and Dragons miniatures in his spare time. We'd had a brief relationship which fizzled out with zero drama, and both got on with our lives.

"Calm down," said the woman who was still hanging onto his arm, "you've had a shock, is all."

"And you'd be shocked if you woke up dead one of these days, wouldn't you?"

Fucksake. Could I not have *one* afternoon without something ridiculous happening? Onlookers were gathering and the woman who'd been thrown was pulling her phone out and dialling. The police, probably—or possibly an ambulance. Because their colleague had clearly lost his mind. I ran over as fast as I dared and pulled the man away from the women, gripping his arms behind his back.

"I am *so* sorry," I said. "I'll look after him, don't you worry."

"And who might you be?" asked the woman with the phone. I recognised her as someone who started working in the Bluecoat's cafe just before I left to start Flora's. I was pretty sure her name was Jasmin, but couldn't have sworn to it. She put the phone back in her pocket, which was a good sign.

"Lilith?" The man craned his neck round to look at me, an expression of utter confusion on his face. "What are you doing here? Look," he sagged against me, "I didn't mean to hurt anyone, you know that."

"I know, Devin," I said. "Come back to the cafe with me and we'll have a chat."

"I know you," said Jasmin. "You used to work here."

"Yeah," I said, "I did. How's it going?"

"Oh, you know," said Jasmin. "Nice enough, but I'm sick of the sight of soup." Soup was the Bluecoat's main menu option back when I'd been working there. Things clearly hadn't changed much. "Look," she went on, "we know Devin, and this isn't like him at all. He's been, well, I don't know…" she trailed off.

"Weird," said her colleague. "Really bloody weird, is what Jas is trying to say. Haven't you, Dev?"

"I keep telling you—"

"Shush," I interrupted him. "Tell me about it when we get back to Flora's. Honestly," I said to the women, "just leave him with me. I know him well enough; I can call people if needs be." Devin opened his mouth to speak again, but I gave his arm a squeeze. He flinched with surprise, but thankfully kept his mouth shut. "Maybe he's just overtired." The women looked equally unconvinced, but didn't argue. "Come on, then," I said to him, "let's go."

"Hang on," said Jasmin, "let me get his things." She disappeared back into the building.

"He threw his bag across the cafe," said the other woman. "Right at a customer."

"I keep telling you I didn't mean to," Devin said. "It's like I don't know my own strength right now."

"Been at the scouse again?" I joked. "You always did like that stuff."

"Can't eat it anymore," he said. "Makes me sick."

"Here you go," Jasmin came back out with Devin's jacket and a rucksack. "I've made sure his phone's in it. I don't think there's anything else."

"Thank you so much." I flashed them both what I hoped was a winning smile, and not the stricken grimace of someone who's just been dealt a really crap hand and has no idea how to escape without losing everything. "Like I said, I'll look after him. Maybe don't expect him back into work for a while, though." *Or forever*, I thought. Because what I knew and they didn't was that Devin was, in fact, dead.

∽

"Dead as the proverbial dodo," I said. "Brown bread. Deceased. No longer of this earthly plane. An ex—"

"Okay!" said Devin, "that's enough." He was sitting on the sofa in my flat, no longer hysterical but definitely very confused. Mostly by the fact that a gigantic cat was snoring in the middle of the living room floor. He'd screeched in fright when I'd first coaxed him into the flat, only to discover that Finn had returned while I was out and made himself comfortable on the rug. As I watched, the cat stretched and rolled until he was lying flat on his back with his legs flung out like a starfish. Sighing, I picked up a blanket from the sofa and draped it carefully over the bits I didn't want to be looking at when he changed back into his human form. "And this," he said, pointing to Finn, "is your *pet*?"

"God, no," I said. "That's a roofer from Wavertree. Anyway, he's not important right now."

"I think you'll find," began Devin, but I shushed him.

"Honestly," I said, "the sooner you give in and start accepting the weirdness, the sooner you'll get your head round it."

"How long has it taken you to get your head around it?" he asked.

"A year or so."

"And you've been," Devin struggled to say the word, "dead, all this time? Like, properly, fully dead?" I nodded. "Wow," he said, "that's heavy."

"Like I said," I shrugged. "You get used to it."

"Will you take me running?" I stared at him, confused by the change of subject. "You said you—we—can run really fast," said Devin. "Like superheroes." I was really beginning to regret having told Devin quite so much about his newly undead status. I'd foolishly assumed he'd react in the same way I had—brief hysterical panic followed by trying to carry on in as normal a fashion as possible—but it wasn't working so far. I'd forgotten just what an absolute nerd Devin was. And I don't mean that in a derogatory sense—some of my favourite people are terminally geeky. Mapp's friend Owain looks like an ageing crusty—you know, one those blokes who haven't washed their jeans since the early nineties and still drink snakebite and black cos it reminds them of their youth—but was actually a talented lace-maker. He loved nothing better than to lecture me on which patterns held specific ancient meanings, and could tell you anything you might ever wish to know about the history of bobbins. Owain never puts blackcurrant in his snakebite, mind. He says it's too risky while working with white lace. But Owain had been dead for a very long time and if he'd had any teething troubles with the undead lifestyle, he'd worked through them long before I came on the scene. Devin was another matter. I reckoned I had a couple hours to keep him distracted whilst I got Eadric's input about what to do next. In the meantime, he was mesmerised by the sheer, brain-melting insanity of realising he really was a dead man walking. I remembered that bit well enough. Back when I was the new girl in town, I'd spent hours running at full speed down the promenade to Otterspool, mostly in the middle of the night, when there wasn't anyone around to see me. I could still feel the thrill of pure adrenaline that ran through me as I parkoured my way up the roofs of Lark Lane, before taking a detour home for the sheer joy of launching myself into the lake in Princes Park and scaring the fish.

"We can," I said, "but not today."

"Why not?"

"Because I said so." Christ, it was like having a toddler in the house. Devin opened his mouth to argue, but I stopped him. "Look," I said, "I get it. Everything's weird but also exciting at the same time. And you know you can't really be dead, because the supernatural isn't real."

"Oh, but I know it is," said Devin, to my surprise. "I still speak to my mum sometimes."

"We all speak to people we've lost," I said in my most sympathetic voice. "It's comforting. But we know we're not *actually* speaking to them, don't we?"

"You can tell Mum that if you like," said Devin. He nodded to something behind me. "She's listening to you." I spun around so fast that the draught sent magazines sliding off the table and ruffled the curtains in the window. A woman stood behind me with a confused expression on her face. She was in her mid-forties, and had short brown hair and kind eyes that were fixed on Devin.

"Oh," she said, completely ignoring me. "Oh, my boy. My boy!" She flitted past me and I turned back round to see her clinging onto Devin, who was clearly trying to figure out how to hug a ghost.

"You just have to tell yourself she's solid," I said helpfully. "You'll be able to touch her then." I'd been the same with Kitty when she first appeared in the flat. It's difficult to accept the existence of a real—and fully sentient—ghost who can move and talk like a human, whilst at the same time also being unnervingly transparent. Mapp had eventually taken pity and explained that much of the issues involved with finding oneself unexpectedly dead were down to sheer cognitive dissonance. If you can persuade yourself to make the mental leap across to believing what you're seeing, it becomes a lot easier. "Just believe what you're seeing," I dutifully told Devin. "It gets easier, I promise." He patted his mother's back nervously, and looked surprised when his hand connected, rather than going straight through her. Tears glinted in his eyes. I stood up, planning to head into the bedroom and leave them to it for a while. Just then, Devin's mum took a step backwards away from him and looked around at me and the flat as if suddenly becoming aware of her surroundings. Then she turned back to her son.

"What a *stupid* thing to do!" she yelled. To my astonishment, she slapped Devin hard across the face. "What on earth did you think you were doing, climbing on that stupid statue?" I had no idea what she was talking about, but decided discretion might be the better part of valour and began sliding myself carefully backwards towards the bedroom door. "And you've got some explaining to do as well, young lady!" She turned to give me a fierce glare. "Why is my son—my *dead* son—in your flat? More to the point," she stepped towards me, "why can I see you? Lilith, isn't it?" I nodded. "I haven't seen you since, well, I can't quite remember..."

"It's Valerie, isn't it?" I asked her. She nodded. "The thing is, Valerie," I started slowly, having no idea how to word things, "I've been dead a while. Devin didn't know I was dead until he was dead as well."

"Did you fall off a statue as well?" asked Valerie, sniffing slightly.

"I fell off the fire escape," I said. "The one outside this flat."

"Is that why you're still here?" she asked. "Are you stuck? Is this flat," she looked around at the shabby furniture alongside bare walls that had been stripped of their paper ahead of redecorating, "actually empty, and we're all just haunting it?"

"No," I said, "I live here. Properly, I mean. I've got friends and a cat, and I still own the cafe downstairs."

"But you said you're dead," said Valerie. "How can you be standing there in front of me if you're dead?"

"You're dead as well," I said. "Don't you remember?"

"Off course I remember," she said. "How could I not? I've been waiting to see my Devin again for what seems like forever. But I expected him to be an old man," she went on, "not this. Not someone who should still have their whole life ahead of them."

"Well, now he's got his entire afterlife ahead of him," I said cheerfully. "And so have you."

"And we're supposed to just stay here with you?"

"NO!" I practically shouted. "There's not enough room," I went on, trying to cover my panic. "I've got too many people coming and going as it is."

"There's no one else here," said Valerie, looking around.

"Yes there is," said Kitty, materialising next to me. "Got visitors, Lil?" She smiled brightly. "I do love meeting Lil's friends."

"Kitty," I sighed, "this is Devin." I gestured to him. In return, Devin gawped in astonishment at Kitty's sudden appearance. "And this is Dev's mum, Valerie."

Kitty stepped forward and politely shook hands with each of them in turn. "It's lovely to meet you," she said. "Have you seen *True Blood*? Only I was just about to settle down and start on the third series."

"Oh, I've only seen the first series," said Devin enthusiastically. "Could we start from the second one?"

"Of course," said Kitty. She sat down on the sofa and patted the empty seat until Valerie took the hint and sat next to her. Devin dropped into the armchair and looked at me.

"Going to join us, Lil?" he asked. "You can sit on my knee if you like."

"She'd rather sit on my knee," said Finn, from down on the floor. He must have changed back into human form while I was distracted. Luckily the blanket was still over him. "She just won't admit it." He pulled a plastic box out from underneath the sofa and I saw it was filled with prawns. "What are we watching?" He stretched lazily, before popping open the tub. Considering its contents must have been at room temperature for a good while, I was very glad I didn't need to breathe. "Anyone?" he asked, offering the box of sweaty shellfish around the room. "Awesome," he said, as everyone shook their heads. "More for me."

Unexpected Ghost In The Bagging Area

"Morning, Lil," said Missy as I stepped through the front door into Flora's. "Business or pleasure?" She was busily wiping down tables with what looked distinctly like my London Dungeon souvenir tea towel. It had been hanging in the back room of Flora's since the day we'd opened, after I'd somehow got it into my head it was a good luck charm. "Hey!" I whipped the towel out of her hand as I walked past.

"Both," I said, heading behind the counter. "And this is my *special* tea towel, you heathen!"

"Well it was the only one I could find," said Missy, following me through. "God knows what Izzy's done with them all. I was just making do til she comes in." Missy opened up some mornings, to give Izzy a break. Todd was still working regular shifts, but he'd never quite got to grips with starting up the till system. And the one time he'd been left to shut it down after closing time, he'd somehow locked the bloody thing completely and we'd had to make do with writing lists on paper and begging change from the newsagents around the corner until I'd got an engineer out to fix it. So we kept Todd on afternoon shifts only, and either Missy or Izzy opened and closed each day. Sometimes they even let me do it, but only if they were *really* desperate. I'd pointed out that

Missy was as dead as me and *she* was allowed to look after Flora's without supervision. Izzy had just rolled her eyes and pointed out that Missy could be relied on not to accidentally throw a chair through the window. I'd explained for the millionth time that I'd merely been putting it up on the table so I could mop the floor and it wasn't my fault I had superpowers, but Izzy had reminded me Missy had been dead a lot longer than me and had learned to control herself, and 'maybe you could learn a thing or two from her, huh?' At which point I'd stropped off upstairs and sulked for twenty minutes, before Izzy stomped up after me and told me to stop being such a bloody drama queen. Which all went to prove just how exhausted Izzy must have been after the vampire-murdering drama, to have let me open up on my own. And I didn't even accidentally burn it down, yay me.

I really did miss the cafe though, so whenever I had paperwork to do, I went down to the little staff room behind the counter and worked from the table in there. I'd tried looking through Eadric's notes for information about Chester in my bedroom the night before, but hadn't been able to concentrate over the noise of ghostly shrieking and Finn's high-pitched cackling. Kitty had even popped downstairs at one point to see if Rachel wanted to join them, but Al had been with her and they were apparently planning a quiet night in. It was a bloody good job I didn't have any other neighbours, because anyone coming up to complain about the noise would get a very unusual reception. I'd eventually given in and gone through to watch television with the netherworld's answer to the Brady Bunch. Devin hadn't been impressed when I'd reclaimed the armchair, but Finn gave him a warning look before I had time to lose my temper and Valerie told him off for having no manners. As he flopped onto the floor like a grumpy toddler Dev had looked like he might be regretting this particular family reunion.

So no, nothing practical had been achieved overnight. Which meant that today's project was to find out what was wrong with Chester. No biggie, then. I hung the tea towel up on its hook and turned to give Missy what I liked to think was a hard stare. Which, of course, she ignored entirely. "There are literally dozens of tea towels in this place," I said to her. "We've never run out in all the time I've been here."

"Well, we've run out now," Missy said, folding her arms and leaning against the doorframe that separated the back room from the cafe counter. "Look for yourself."

"Christ," I sighed, opening the door of the cupboard I knew damn fine held the stash of clean tea towels, "are you losing your eyesight? Here they—oh!" The cupboard contained packs of paper towels for the customer loo, as it always had. We'd learned to keep them hidden away, because otherwise they ran out at a terrifying rate. Izzy was convinced the customers must be secretly eating them. There was also a roll of bin bags and a spare box of teaspoons. But no tea towels. "Where have they gone?" I asked, straightening up to look at Missy.

"Like I said," she shrugged, "no tea towels." There was a clatter behind her as the front door to the cafe opened. "Gimme," said Missy, holding her hand out. "I've got customers to see to." I threw the Dungeon tea towel at her with as much force as I dared, and she caught it in mid-air with annoying casualness. "Gotta get up early to get past me," she grinned, before turning to head back into the cafe. "Oh, hi Sean! It's Sean," she said unnecessarily, whipping back round to me. "Want to make his coffee?"

"You left these out," said Izzy, coming in behind Sean. She was waving what looked distinctly like a stack of tea-towels. Missy turned to look at me.

"Didn't you see those when you came in?" she asked.

"Obviously not," I said. "If I had, we wouldn't have just had an argument about tea towels, would we?"

"They weren't there five minutes ago," she said. "I'm sure of it."

"Good job Izzy found them then, isn't it," said Sean happily. We all turned to stare at him, but he was oblivious. "Usual please, Missy. Or are you going to grace me with your delightful presence this morning, Lil?" God, he was literally the walking definition of irrepressible. Those cute puppies who sell toilet rolls have got nothing on Sean for sheer joie de vivre.

"I'll do it," I said. "Go sit yourself down and I'll bring it over."

"Try not to break anything on the way," said Izzy, as she came past me into the back room in order to dump her coat and bag.

I glared at Missy, who was trying not to laugh. "What happened to respecting your leaders?" I said to her as I started pouring Sean's Americano. "A bit of casual worshipping of my queenly status wouldn't go amiss occasionally, you know."

"I can find a guillotine if you like?" Izzy offered. "Stick with tradition?"

"You are all *entirely* mad," I muttered.

"And that," said Missy, "is how we cope."

∽

"Aaaaaaaaarrrrrrrggghhhh!!!!" I was just putting Sean's second coffee down on the table in front of him when a scream from behind the counter made me lurch in panic, spilling it all over most of his paperwork and down into his lap.

"Oh god I'm sorry," I said, flapping at him with a tea towel whilst also craning my neck round to see what was going on.

"I'm fine," said Sean, taking the cloth off me. "Go see what's occurring." I left him to mop up the mess and ran behind the counter to find Izzy staring at what, to me, looked like a perfectly normal plate, on which sat a fresh scone with its portions of jam and cream to the side.

"What on earth's the matter?" I said, putting a hand on Izzy's arm. She jumped as though I'd given her an electric shock and turned to stare at me with wide eyes.

"It moved," she said, pointing towards the plate. "The plate moved."

"Don't be daft," I frowned. "Plates don't move themselves around like that. Anyway, we're the only ones here." Missy had headed home just after ten, saying it would do me good to keep my hand in. And I'd been enjoying myself, I couldn't deny it. Working in Flora's was a nice dose of normality amidst the insanity of the rest of my life. Or at least it had been until now.

"It did," came a voice from behind me. A woman who had presumably been the intended recipient of the scones was standing at the other side of the counter, looking equally shell-shocked. "I saw it happen." A couple of other people were standing to the side of her. "So did Judith, here." She nodded her head at the woman next to her. Both women looked to be somewhere around retirement age, and they both eyed me beadily.

"I saw *something* happen," said Judith, "but I'm not really sure what it was, exactly."

"It was a bloody ghost, Judith!" Her friend was indignant. "How could it be anything else?"

"Flora's isn't haunted," I said, hoping Kitty wouldn't choose that moment to walk through the cafe wall, or anything ridiculous like that. "Never had so much as a bump in the night."

"Is this what you're looking for?" Sean stood behind me with a small plate in his hand, the contents of which were identical to the one by the sink. "You work so fast, Izzy," he went on, "maybe you put it down and forgot, so just instinctively made up a new one?" He was waggling his eyebrows at her alarmingly, and for a second, I thought I might burst out laughing. It did the trick, though. Izzy exhaled loudly, patted down her skirt and held her hand out to him.

"Thanks Sean," she said. "I'd forget my own head some days. Sorry for the scare." she turned to where Scone Lady and Judith were both gazing at us in silent bewilderment. "This one's on us. In fact," she turned to the coffee machine, "why don't you go sit down and I'll bring you both a cappuccino and some of our new fruit cake. A little apology for the drama, sort of thing."

"But I *saw* it move!" said the first woman. "Judith, you saw it too. Don't deny it now."

"Like I said," Judith was already heading to the corner table in the window, clearly knowing a good offer when she heard it, "I don't know what it was I saw. Maybe a cuppa and a nice bit of cake will help."

"For god's sake, Judith," grumbled the first woman, "you only think of your bloody stomach! How can you ignore something as ridiculous as a plate moving around on its own?"

"I can ignore a lot of things when there's cake involved," said Judith, already settling into her seat. "Aah thanks, love," Izzy was placing a ridiculously generous variety plate of cakes on the table. "You're a diamond."

"It bloody well *moved*," hissed Izzy under her breath, as she came back behind the counter for the women's coffees. "Right in front of my bloody sodding eyes!" She delivered the drinks, then stalked back to me, a grim expression on her face. "There are already way too many weird..."

she struggled for an appropriate word, "...*things* in this building as it is, Lil. I can't be doing with them bouncing round the café as well as upstairs!"

"It isn't one of mine," I said. "At least, I don't think so."

"What do you mean," said Sean, "not one of yours?" Fucking hell, I'd forgotten Sean was even there. Okay, so he knows most of my immortal secrets, but I try not to involve him. Like I said, he's nearly died twice already because of me, and I didn't fancy someone—something, possibly—hitting third time lucky.

"I mean," I thought quickly, "it's nothing to do with the usual weirdness around here. Maybe Izzy really did just make up another plate of scones without thinking."

"That was me," said Sean, before Izzy could open her mouth to say something. She settled for glaring at me instead. "I mean, everyone knows what a plate of jam and cream scones looks like, right? I just leaned over the far end of the counter while you were all distracted and put a new one together." Me and Izzy both turned at the same time to look across at where the serving counter butted up against the wall of the cafe. There was indeed just enough space down the side of the till for someone to reach an arm down and round into the cake display, if they stretched. "It worked, didn't it?" he said, grinning. "And now we have to figure out who it really was."

"*We* don't need to figure anything out," I said firmly. "This one's on me and Iz. Okay," I saw the look on her face, "it's on me. I'm used to dealing with this shit. One more weirdo on the premises won't make much difference." It was at that point that the tap in the back room shot off its fixing and hit the ceiling with a loud bang, leaving water spurting vertically out of the pipe. And then the lights went out.

∽

"Well, it's certainly been an interesting afternoon," said Izzy. We were sitting in the window of Flora's with our feet up on chairs, waiting for the floor to dry. It was lucky it had been a quiet afternoon, because we'd only had the four screaming customers to deal with when the lights blew. Had it been a Saturday lunchtime there might have been injuries, but thankfully a bright weekday with few customers had meant we could at least see what we were doing as we ushered people outside. Scone Lady—who'd turned out to be called Delphine, which was most unexpected—had clearly decided that discretion was the better part of valour, and had scarpered down the street as fast as Judith could manage. The remaining two customers were postmen who'd not long come off shift and were having a civilised coffee before giving in to the inevitable and heading off to the pub. One of them had gallantly offered to look at the pipes, but by that time Sean had already switched the water off at the mains and retrieved the tap from underneath a storage cupboard. I thanked them for being so understanding and sent them on their way, before ringing Eadric. Nik answered the phone.

"What's today's drama?" he asked when he picked up. "Do I need to call in any favours, or is it just a standard Interpol job this time?"

"Ha bloody ha," I said. "And whatever happened to 'Hello Lilith, how are you today?'?"

"Lilith," Nik said kindly, "we both know that if you didn't have something dramatic going on, you wouldn't have called in the first place. I'm sorry, darling, but you really are *terribly* predictable."

"Oh, shut up," I said, too distracted to even bother insulting him back. "Where's our lord and master? I need to speak to him."

"I'm not sure Eadric is anyone's lord and master," said Nik. "It's hardly as though—"

"Good afternoon, Lilith," said Eadric smoothly. "I have no idea what Nikolaus was talking about, and I think it's almost certainly better if we leave it that way. What can I do for you?"

"There's a poltergeist in the cafe," I said. "And it's not one of ours."

"How do you know? That it's not…ours, I mean?"

"Because it is an annoying asshat that needs to get its shit together before I exorcise it into the middle of next bloody week," I snapped, just as a box of paper straws came sailing out from behind the counter. "For fuck's *sake*!"

"And why do you need me?" asked Eadric.

"I was hoping you'd know how to deal with this sort of thing," I said, ducking again as a custard slice came flying at us and hit the window. Izzy and I both turned to look at where shards of creamy pastry were sliding down the glass. A group of teenage boys were standing outside and watching in amazement. "Go out and close the shutters," I said to Izzy. "Sean, you go with her."

"Shit," said Izzy, patting the pockets of her apron, "the keys are behind the counter." Even as she said it, the keys came sailing over and landed at her feet. We looked at each other in stunned silence for a second, then she bent to pick them up. "Thank you," she said in the direction of the invisible force. A mug dropped off the shelf in response, shattering loudly on the hard floor. "Mardy twat," muttered Izzy.

"I'm not leaving you to deal with this on your own," said Sean. "You might need backup."

"Sean," I said patiently, "we both know I am not your average human."

"Exactly," he grinned. "I'm hoping to see your true nature! Witness the paranormal powers, that sort of thing." I raised an eyebrow at him sharply. "Might even take some notes," he went on. "It could be useful research."

"Get out," I said firmly, already pushing him towards the exit. Izzy unbolted the front door and stepped outside. Sean hesitated, but finally followed her. "The back door's open," I said to Izzy. "You can come back in that way." Her expression suggested that coming back into the cafe was the last thing she wanted to do. "Not you," I said to Sean. "You are to stay out of the way. Come back tomorrow and help us clear up, if you like."

Sean looked crestfallen. "Why do you keep shutting me out of things?" A shower of pepper sachets hit the back of my head with surprising force. "Out," I said firmly. "Out, out, out!" I gave him one last push, then closed the door and pulled the bolts across. Sean stepped reluctantly backwards, keeping his gaze on me. I could hear the creaking low rumble of the aged shutters slowly rolling themselves down and stayed where I was until they'd hidden the outside world from view.

"Are you still there, Lilith?" said a concerned voice. I looked down at my hand, almost surprised to discover my phone was still in it. As the cafe darkened in front of me, I sighed and put it to my ear.

"Yeah," I said to Eadric, "I'm still here. And so is the most annoying ghost in history. Don't worry," I turned to look at the dark room, "I'll deal with it."

"Good work," said Eadric, sounding relieved. "Let me know how you get on."

"I'll be sending you the cleaning bill," I said, and cut the call before he could reply. Wedging the phone back into my pocket, I stepped forward into the centre of the room and turned slowly to look around. "Come on then," I said to the empty space, "out with it. What the fuck have I done to deserve this bullshit behaviour?" Silence. I walked slowly up to the counter and peered around. The floor was strewn with broken crockery and splattered cake. "I'm trying to run a business here, for fuck's sake. And I've already got more spooky residents than any building really needs. So, you're not wanted." Silence. "Do you hear me?" I said, raising my voice. "You're not wanted!" Something small and round hit me in the forehead so hard that I fell backwards onto the floor. As I sat on the tiles rubbing my head, bits of white paper began fluttering around me as though I was sitting inside a giant snow globe. It was raining paper napkins. I sat in the middle of the ruins of my beloved cafe with tissue paper wafting around my ears and something snapped. I'd been dealing with other people's bullshit ever since I'd woken up dead and, for some unknown reason, this ridiculous poltergeist was absolutely the last straw. I got to my feet and looked around.

STOP. I didn't even need to speak loudly—my voice had a resonance that I could feel deep inside my chest and it carried to every corner of the building. A crash from upstairs confirmed that Rachel had also heard it. Christ, now I was going to have to deal with a panicked vampire on top of everything else. With any luck she'd be too scared to come out and I could go speak to her later. MAKE YOURSELF VISIBLE, I said slowly, each syllable rumbling outwards like a wave crashing into the shore. The silence around me grew emptier, as though something was doing its very best to pretend they'd never been here in the first place. Good. It was about time I used whatever stupid bloody powers I had to make my own life easier. The rest of it could be dealt with once I'd got my own house in order. I'M WAITING. A shape slowly formed in the corner next to the sink. It flickered as though it was trying its hardest not to be seen, but its edges were developing into a recognisable form whether it liked it or not. DO IT NOW. The formless shape disappeared. I wondered whether I'd scared it off entirely. That wouldn't be the worst outcome, although it would still be annoying. I was proud of that voice, even if it did make Kitty retch with fear when I used it. *Maybe that was the problem*, I thought to myself. *I haven't been using it enough to learn how to control it.* Well, that was going to change right now. LISTEN TO—

"I'm here," said a voice from behind me. I spun around and saw a young white woman standing between me and the cafe door. Tall and slender, she had long brown hair that hung down past her shoulders and wore a beige woollen shift over an off-white linen shirt that was tied at the neck and wrists. Her feet were bare. I'd have put her age at around seventeen or eighteen, but I'd have bet good money she wasn't entirely what she seemed. Mostly because, despite her height and distinctly female figure, her face was that of the little schoolgirl from Chester amphitheatre.

"What the fuck was all that in aid of?" I waved an arm vaguely at the mess. "Did mummy not give you enough attention when you were little? Is that how you learned to throw tantrums? For the attention?"

"Don't you dare bring my mother into this," said the girl. Her voice was subdued but steely. "Don't you *dare*."

"I dare do anything I bloody well please, missy," I snapped. "You're the one who's been terrorising my staff and frightening off the customers."

"Help me," she said. I saw for the first time that her ghostly face was streaked with tears, and she was white as a—well. She really was white as the proverbial ghost. If the ghost in question had had a really rough night and hadn't slept for weeks. "I need you to—" she stopped talking as we both heard the back door open. I spun around to stop Izzy from coming inside, but it was too late.

"Has it calmed down yet?" Izzy asked, nervously poking her head around the door into the cafe.

"She can tell you about it herself," I said, turning to the ghost. "Oh!" The girl had disappeared. "Cover your ears a minute, Iz." Izzy complied. COME BACK OUT THIS INSTANT, YOU LITTLE BRAT. Nothing. I swung back round to where Izzy stood with her fingers wedged firmly in her ears. "You're safe again now," I said. Izzy didn't move. "*I said you're—*"

"Okay, okay," said Izzy, rubbing her ears, "no need to shout. Who was the phantom flan-flinger of old Liverpool town, then?"

"No idea," I said truthfully. "But she clearly has issues."

"You don't say." Izzy gazed around at the mess. "That's an entire bakery delivery of cakes that she's ruined. I'll have to get extra dropped off tomorrow." She sighed. "I'll go get the mop."

"No," I said, "this is where my mostly pointless superpowers actually come in handy. You go sit in the back room and leave me to it. I'll be ten minutes, tops."

In the end, it took me less than eight minutes to clean the cafe, literally from top to bottom. I washed the walls down where they were splattered with cake, then stacked the tables so I could sweep and mop the floor. Then the tables went back in their rightful places, and I cleaned the glass panes in the front window. They'd needed doing, anyway. Students have a long-standing tradition of writing in the condensation on the window and random words were still faintly legible. *'Dom is a b —'* read one of them. I got the vinegar spray out from under the sink in the back room and did that pane again, just to be on the safe side. I didn't care what Dom might be, I just didn't want it announced on my nice clean cafe windows. Finally, I topped up the salt and sugar sachets and re-hung the little sign Izzy had had made as a joke a few weeks earlier. It read *'FRESH SARCASM SERVED DAILY'* and usually swung from a hook on the wall next to the till. "Whaddya reckon?" I said when I was finally done. "Not a bad job, even if I say so myself." There was no response, so I turned to look at Izzy and found her hunched into a ball on one of the rickety chairs in the back kitchen. "Are you okay?" I said, getting over to her in record time. "What's the matter?" I put a hand on her shoulder and was shocked to realise she was shaking. "Iz?" I asked. "Are you okay?" I gave her arm a squeeze, and she slowly unfolded herself. It was only when I saw her face that I realised she was laughing, tears running down her face as she tried to regain control of herself.

"Oh my god, Lil," she said, clearly struggling to breathe, "this is all *entirely* insane, you do realise that?" Without warning, the laughter turned to tears—huge, gasping sobs that had her choking for breath and scrabbling around for something to wipe her face. All the napkins were now in the bin, so I passed her a clean tea towel and she mopped her eyes.

"What's insane?" I said, kneeling down beside her and putting a hand on her arm. I could feel her shuddering as she tried to control her breathing. "I mean, apart from the whole 'rogue poltergeist dropping in for a cuppa' thing, obvs."

"Obvs," snorted Izzy. "And the fact you felt the need to state that shows just how mad it all is. Fucking hell, Lil," she took a deep breath, and I could see the effort she was putting into letting it back out slowly, "who'd have thought, eh? All those years back, when I was the new kid at your school, and you were the only one who'd speak to me."

"I seem to remember it was more that I didn't have any friends and you felt sorry for me," I said.

"Bit of both, I'd say," said Izzy with a weak smile. "And both as weird as each other. Now here we are, over twenty years later, and the weirdness is off the bloody scale." She hiccupped and I thought she might start crying again, but she took another deep breath and swallowed hard. "Thing is," she said, "it's not actually that difficult to cope with. The whole 'my bestie's a zombie' thing, you know? It's easy, when the alternative would have been losing you completely." Tears were running down her face again. "Sometimes...you do things like this," she gestured around the clean cafe, "and all I can do is sit here gazing in wonderment. I have this mad desire to grab people and make them look at you and shout 'that's my best friend, isn't she cool?' in their faces."

I didn't know what to say to that. "I'm really not very cool," I managed eventually, "and we both know it."

"Yeah, I know," said Iz, smiling at me through her tears. "Dork of the century, so you are."

"Yup." We sat quietly like that for a few minutes, both lost in thought.

"It's a handy talent though," said Iz eventually. "Nobody could deny that." I looked around at Flora's, which was now cleaner than it had ever been. "Do you think it's gone?" She looked around warily. "The poltergeist, I mean."

"Honestly?" Izzy nodded. "I think it's still here," I said. "I can feel it, somehow. It won't mess us around anymore though. WILL YOU? Oh god, I'm sorry!" Iz was holding her hands over her ears in what looked like genuine pain. "I'm not even talking loudly, though! What is it that's so horrible about the voice?"

Izzy squinted at me. "It's as if, I don't know, like you're talking from another dimension. A really dark and dangerous dimension that might suck people in and chew them up. It scares me." She saw my face. "Sorry."

"Don't be sorry," I said, patting her shoulder, "it's not as though—" I was interrupted by loud banging from the shutters. "Fucksake," I muttered, getting to my feet. "Can't anyone leave us in peace today?" I walked back into the cafe proper and went up to the window. "Who is it?" I called, not sure whether they'd even be able to hear me through the glass and shutters.

"It's Damon," came the muffled response. "What the *fuck* has been going on?"

"Hang on," I shouted, then turned back to Izzy. "Your man's come to save you from the big bad wolf."

"Christ," she said, "talk about arriving after the fact." She grinned.

"Come round the back," I shouted through the glass. "You can carry your swooning princess home."

To my horror, when Izzy opened the back door, Sean was standing next to Damon. "Did you really expect me to just leave?" he shrugged, as he followed Damon into the back room of Flora's.

"Yes!" We stood glaring at each other across the table, Izzy and Damon standing awkwardly to one side. "I asked you to *leave*, Sean," I went on. "That doesn't mean hanging out round the back like a reporter trying to get a bloody scoop on things."

"You're assuming that's why I stayed?" asked Sean. "Out of professional curiosity?"

"You literally said you wanted to see what would happen," I snapped. "There was no assumption about it."

"We're going to leave you to it," said Izzy, already pulling a reluctant Damon towards the door. "Please don't break anything."

"Sure you're okay, Lil?" asked Damon. Sean and I both turned to look at him.

"I'm not going to hurt her, for fuck's sake," snapped Sean.

"Never said you were, mate," said Damon. "Cos you know I'd break your legs if you did." Well, there went any chance of me and Izzy ever double-dating. Not that I was going to date Sean.

"We're off," said Izzy firmly. "Come on," she tugged Damon's arm, "you can pour me an exceptionally large gin and tonic and I'll fill you in on our *very* interesting afternoon." I gave Izzy a sharp look. But Damon was one of the growing number of people who already knew the truth about me, so I couldn't really argue. He couldn't *not* know, because he'd been with us at the top of the Radio City tower when Izzy had been thrown through the plate glass window, only to be saved by the flying form of William the bloody Conqueror. And he'd also witnessed Mab trying to kill me and shooting Liam by mistake. So, yeah. Damon knew all the secrets. As did Sean. "Bye then," said Izzy, looking uncertainly from one of us to the other. "Try not to hurt each other, aye."

"Of course," said Sean. He stood firmly planted in front of the sink with a determined expression on his face.

"You'd better come upstairs," I said to him. "We can talk more easily up there." Izzy grinned and gave me a thumbs up, before dragging Damon away while the going was good.

"Do you have any rabid mermaids living up there?" He sounded nervous, despite his earlier bravado.

"Nope," I said, stepping outside into the car park and waiting for him to follow me so I could lock up. "But what are you like with cats?"

Romance Is, Apparently, Dead

AND I DO THIS VOICE, I said, WITHOUT EVEN MEANING TO. A pigeon that had been flying across the car park veered sideways and hit the wall in shock. I watched as it landed heavily on the ground and shook itself, before flapping off again. Sean, who had been patiently listening to me list the many and varied ways I thought it was a terrible idea for us to try dating again, just smiled. We were sitting on the fire escape outside the kitchen door, leaning on the rails and swinging our legs over the car park below. "What's so funny?" I said indignantly. EVERYONE HATES THE VOICE. In the distance, a dog began to howl.

"It's just a voice, Lil," he said. "Yeah, it's a..." he trailed off, clearly struggling to find the words, "it's weird. Yeah. Weird." He grinned. "But it's kind of sexy at the same time, you know?"

"No, I don't bloody know!" I could feel myself blushing, and what should have been my carefully normal voice went up an octave at the same time. "What's sexy about someone commanding people like they're irrelevant minions in her own personal universe?" I narrowed my eyes at him. "Please don't tell me you have some kind of humiliation kink," I said. "Because I had to deal with that once, and let me tell you it is *not* my thing. At all."

"Christ," said Sean, "I don't think I've met anyone as cynical as you in my entire life. And believe me, I've met some cynics. Why is it so hard for you to believe that I just, well." He looked sheepish. "I just *like* you, Lil. That's pretty much all there is." I didn't know what to say to that, so made do with gaping at him like a fish out of water. Never let it be said that I don't know how to be seductive.

"Have you considered," I said eventually, for no other reason than to break the awkward silence, "that you're possibly just a really poor judge of character?"

"Could be," said Sean amiably, "but I don't think so."

"You've narrowly avoided being killed on several occasions—"

"Twice," he interrupted. "Not several. Only twice."

"You've narrowly avoided being killed on *only* two occasions," I said, scowling at him, "which makes me think you're already pushing your luck. Because there will be more occasions, Sean. And that's a promise."

"How do you know?"

"Because I am the head of an undead territory in a country where no one appears capable of behaving like anything other than a bratty toddler," I said. "And at some point, it's going to be down to me to knock their stupid undead heads together and make them play nicely."

"And that's connected to me how?"

"Sean," I said slowly, "you are clearly not listening to me. I am immortal. Do you understand what that means?"

"Are you actually expecting me to answer that?"

"Yeah," I said, "I am. Because quite frankly, I really don't think you're understanding this situation at all."

"You're dead," said Sean. "But you're still here and still living and working in your cafe, as if that isn't really fucking weird in itself. And you think other people—other undead people—are going to fight you for power at some point. Am I getting it right so far?"

"Pretty much," I shrugged.

"And you think this very unusual lifestyle of yours requires you to sacrifice your own personal life in favour of the good of your lands. Land. Lands?" He frowned. "Whatever. The bit you're in charge of, anyway."

"Well," I said, "not technically. Eadric was married, and being dead certainly doesn't appear to have stopped Nik or Mapp playing the field. I just think it's safer, is all."

"Safer for who?" asked Sean. "Cos I don't think I'm the one who's the scaredy-cat here, Lil."

"Oh, this is ridiculous. Sean," I said, "I like you. A lot. Is that what you wanted to hear?"

"Yes." He grinned. "So, we're agreed on one thing, at least."

"But we really can't do anything about it," I said. "And I'm sorry. I really am." I meant it, as well. Sean was, well—there wasn't anything about Sean that didn't tick all my romantically inclined boxes. He was sweet and funny and clever and cute, and I could still remember in terrifying clarity just how good a kisser he was. But I was a dead girl in a living world, and I had way too much on my plate to let myself get sidetracked by a pretty face.

"Cooooeeeee!" Mapp, the prettiest face of them all, was bouncing his way up the fire escape. He had a wicked grin on his face. "I hope I'm not interrupting anything deliciously exciting, my darlings? Budge up, Lil, there's a good girl." Without waiting for a response—or even for me to move—he swung himself on the rails and dropped down to wedge himself in next to me. "May I enquire as to today's topic of no doubt fascinating conversation?" I shook my head in mock despair, but Sean leaned forward in order to look at him.

"Lilith here thinks she's too dangerous for me," he said.

Mapp arched a neatly plucked brow. "Oh, does she now?" His lips twitched in amusement. "Of course, she *is* known throughout the land for her tempestuous nature and tendency to get the raging hor—"

"*Mapp!*" I hissed, thumping him hard. "Pack it in, for fuck's sake."

"No need to resort to violence, my dear," he said. "But you really shouldn't be embarrassed about your true nature, you know." Sean snorted quietly.

"Are you here for anything in particular?" I asked. "Or do you just like winding me up for fun?"

"Both," he said happily. "Nah, I heard about your visitor, is all. Came from Chester, did it?" I twisted to look at him.

"How did you know that?"

"Because there's been something...extra around here since you got back," he said. "Thought I was imagining it at first. Doubted my own spooky senses, can you believe that?" I could not believe that, as it happened. I was pretty sure Gaultier Mapp hadn't had a single doubt about his own abilities in his entire, everlasting life.

"Well, you were right," I said. Even without looking at him, I knew he was preening. "There's something—someone—in Flora's, and they're from Chester."

"How did they know where to find you?" asked Sean. "It's not like you're listed in the phone book, is it? 'Lilith O'Reilly, professional dead girl'?"

"Oh, I suspect our Lilith here knows exactly how it found her," said Mapp.

"It's a she," I sighed. "She gave me a pebble when I was in Chester."

"So, you brought it back with you," said Mapp. "And put it down somewhere in Flora's, I'll wager."

"Yup," I sighed. "It's on the shelf that holds the glasses. Next to the sink."

"Then we must discover the root of the problem," said Mapp firmly, "and free the little mite."

"That little mite ruined an entire display counter of cakes," I snapped, "and lost me an afternoon's trade." I remembered the girl's expression as she pleaded with me to help her, only to disappear at the sound of Izzy's voice. "She seemed really sad, though."

"Ooh," said Sean, "are we going to do an exorcism?"

"Absolutely not," I said. "We are going to leave her be and I am going to worry about it all tomorrow instead."

"And you two can have a lovely cosy evening in together," said Mapp, "just the two of you. Won't that be nice?" Right then, Finn came bouncing over the rooftops and down into the carpark, before sauntering over to the fire escape. "Three of you, then," said Mapp.

"Is that," said Sean, "a *cat*?" As he spoke, Finn peered round the bend of the fire escape in his human form. In his *naked* human form, I realised.

"Throw me a towel, eh Lil?" he said sheepishly. "Got me timing a bit wrong, innit. Hi, Mapp!" He grinned up at us. "No Heggie today?"

"He's gone to visit his nan," said Mapp. "Over in Skelmersdale."

"Heggie's got a grandmother?" I knew Heggie was human, but it was still somehow strange to imagine him with something as boringly normal as a family. "Awww, that's lovely!"

"She is an absolute *menace*," shuddered Mapp. "Honestly, your own family witch has nothing on that woman."

"Don't talk about my gran like that," I said. "It's rude." A coughing noise from further down made me turn back to Finn. "Yes, yes," I sighed, "hang on." I went into the flat and found an old dressing gown in one of the storage boxes underneath my bed. It was pale blue with flowers all over it, and I'd picked it up in a charity shop one winter when it was especially cold and the heating wasn't working properly in the shared house I lived in before moving to Flora's. God knows why I even still had it—it wasn't as though I felt cold anymore. When I went back outside, Sean was standing at the top of the stairs.

"I'm going to head off," he said. "You've got enough company, I think."

"No, no," said Finn, coming round the corner so he could look up at us. Me, Sean and Mapp all made a point of staring off into the distance.

"Here," I said, throwing the dressing gown in what I hoped was Finn's direction. "You forgot this. Look," I said to Sean, "shit like this is why it's impossible for me to date a human."

"Don't be silly," said Finn, tying the dressing gown closed as he finally came up the last flight of stairs. "You two can have the living room to yourselves. The rest of us will just go hide out in your bedroom or something."

"No, you bloody won't," I said.

"You go in the bedroom then, and we'll stay in the kitchen," said Finn helpfully. Just as I was opening my mouth to argue, there was a thudding noise above us. I looked up to see my delightfully grumpy vampire guard settling himself in on the roof for the evening. I smiled up at him and he hissed in return.

"Okay," said Sean, "I'm definitely going now."

"Cool," said Finn, "see you, Sean." With that, he headed into the flat, followed almost immediately by the sound of the fridge door opening. There was a happy yowl as Finn found the packet of prawns I'd bought for Grimm.

"I'm going to have to go referee," I said apologetically. "If he steals Grimm's food there'll be hell to pay."

"Come on, Sean," said Mapp, "let me take you for a drink. What?" My face had never been good at hiding my true feelings, and I clearly wasn't managing it now. "You have enough to deal with, your highness," he bowed deeply. "Allow me to escort your bereft suitor toward some alcohol-based solace."

"Stop being ridiculous," I said. "It's not as if—"

"Thank you, Mapp," Sean interrupted, "that's very kind of you. You heard the man, Lil," he grinned at me. "Boys' night out." Mapp winked in an unnervingly lascivious manner, and I wondered if Sean had any idea what he was letting himself in for.

"But," I started, "you can't—"

"Oh," said Sean, "I think you'll find we can." He started down the stairs. "Coming, Mapp?"

Mapp looked at me and shrugged. "Who am I to argue?" he said. "Good luck with the cat fight." I stood at the top of the staircase and watched as Sean and Mapp headed down to street level. I could hear them chatting about which pub to head for first. Sean suggested heading up to Ma Egerton's over on Pudsey Street, but Mapp thought they should start closer to home. As they headed off toward Mathew Street, I saw Sean giving Mapp a playful shove as the older man said something that made Sean laugh. Sighing, I headed back indoors just as the fur began to fly. I was pretty sure I heard sniggering coming from the vampire on the roof.

Consider The Wig

"So, what I think you're saying," said the man sitting opposite me, "is that you know you have to deal with, aaah," He trailed off.

"All this shit," I said helpfully. "I have to deal with all this shit."

"Yes," he said. "All this...whatever. And you think you need my permission for that?"

"I don't need your permission for anything," I said. "I need your information. What I need, Joe, is any knowledge you might have about cats." Joe Williamson—aka the Mole of Edge Hill—gazed placidly at me through his thick, pebble-lensed glasses, the firelight between us reflecting off them so I could only just make out his dark eyes peering out. We were sitting by the fire in the Great Cavern, many metres below the city's modern surface. "Oh, we don't like cats down here," said the little man, shuffling uncomfortably. "No, no, no." He shuddered. "Cats are not very nice, Lilith. You should avoid them at all costs."

"What have cats ever done to you?"

"They like to pounce on my charges," he said, "and chase them. For fun, it seems like." I could believe that. It took very little imagination to picture Finn and his cronies racing after one of Joe's rodent-like vampires in order to see how loudly they could make it squeak.

"Haven't seen one for a long time now, thankfully." He pressed a hand to his chest, roughly where his heart would be. "Terrible creatures, all of them."

"Well, I wouldn't put it quite like that," I said. "My Grimm's only little, he couldn't hurt any of your..." I struggled for a suitable word, "people."

"He is the worst of the lot," said Joe darkly. "You don't know the half of it."

"What don't I know?" There'd been a lot of mysterious comments about Grimm over the last year, all from people I hadn't even met until I was dead as the proverbial doornail. I'd asked all of them what they meant, and every last one had refused to elaborate. I was beginning to think they were just uncomfortable around anything that wasn't intrinsically paranormal. "He's just a cat, Joe."

"That's what you think."

"Yes," I said firmly, "I do think. Actually, what I mostly think is that you're all a bunch of drama queens who need to get out more. Look," I changed the subject, "do you know anyone called Jonathan? He isn't—wasn't—from here, I don't think. But he's been hanging around recently."

"So, he has departed this vale of tears?"

"If you mean 'is he dead'," I said, "then yes. But still around. He's a ghost," I added helpfully, just in case that possibility hadn't occurred to the two-hundred-and-fifty-year-old man in front of me. "I met him in Toxteth," I went on. "When the time-slips were playing up."

"That was an interesting time," said Joe. I narrowed my eyes suspiciously, but he appeared to be absolutely serious. "Rather exciting for some, I hear."

"Depends how dangerous you like your excitement, I guess. Anyway," I leaned forward encouragingly, "I met Jonathan, and he said he was from Chester. But I've no idea who he actually was."

"Did he have a wig?" asked Joe. "The type a magistrate might wear, rather than one of those strange hairpieces for those who are lacking in the tonsorial department."

"Have you been speaking to Mapp recently?" I asked suspiciously.

"Because I'm pretty sure that 'tonsorial department' is not a phrase that generally springs from your lips, Joseph Williamson."

"I enjoy a debate with the delightful Gaultier, I must admit," said Joe. "His presence is always so uplifting. Although it does also make one slightly embarrassed by one's own rather dull appearance. Perhaps I should ask him to assist me in updating my wardrobe?"

"Only if you want to wander the tunnels wearing chiffon trousers and satin capes."

"Hmmm," said Joe thoughtfully. "Perhaps not. Although some of my charges are very envious of his dress sense, I must say. I hear them talking when they think I'm not paying attention. I suspect they consider me rather old-fashioned."

No shit, Sherlock. "I'm sure they think you're super cool," I reassured him.

"And I'm sure you sometimes take the—what's the word?" He frowned. "Micky? Taking the micky. Are you taking the micky out of me, Lilith?"

"As if I'd do that," I said, the picture of innocence. "So, you know Jonathan?" I remembered walking through ancient Toxteth with the strange man in his once-impressive clothes, an almost physical air of sadness floating around him like a cloud.

"I met him once," Joe said. He looked thoughtful. "Many years ago, I think. I might even have still been alive."

"Was he alive at the time?"

"I doubt it," said Joe. "He walked in through my parlour wall as though it wasn't even there. Gave poor Sally the maid such a fright! So yes, yes," he brightened up, "I must have been alive. Such a long time ago!"

"So he was already a ghost back then."

"Yes," said Joe, "that would be the most likely option, I think. And that would have been, well..." he trailed off. "A century or so past, I would say."

"You've been dead nearly two centuries now, Joe." I said gently. "So if it happened when you were still alive, that means Jonathan is from the late eighteenth-century. Early nineteenth, maybe."

"Eighteenth, I suspect," said Joe, "when one considers the wig."

"Did he tell you why he'd decided to pop up in your parlour?" I asked.

"He didn't speak," said Joe, "just stood in the middle of the room, looking rather confused. Not as confused as we were, mark you. I asked him how I could help, but there was no response as far as I could see."

"How do you know it was Jonathan, then?" I asked. "Surely a lot of ghosts from back then would be wearing wigs?"

"I recognised him," said Joe, as though it was obvious. "From his portrait."

"Okay, now you've lost me entirely." I squinted at Joe in confusion. "You're saying you knew him from his *portrait*?" Joe nodded. "Firstly," I went on, "how? Where did you see this portrait? And secondly, why did he have his portrait done? Is he someone important and I'm just being dense again? 'Cos it does happen." I squinted at him. "Occasionally."

"Everybody is important in their own way, Lilith," said Joe.

"But not everyone's important enough to have their portrait commissioned," I pointed out. "Especially not back then."

"I'd always recognise a fellow engineer," said Joe. "Even an unsuccessful one. Hulls, his name was. Yes, that's it. I'm remembering now. Jonathan Hulls. I'd actually been researching his work at the time, wondering if any of it could be put to use in my little project." Joe's 'little project' is actually an enormous network of tunnels that sprawl underneath the city and no one knows exactly how far they go. The Great Cavern, the enormous underground space we were currently sitting in, was the largest of his underground excavations. At least, he thinks it might be. Even Joe himself isn't sure just how far or deep the tunnelling extends. Several of the largest tunnels up at the Edge Hill end —the ones that were dug when Joe was still alive—are now open to the public, having been carefully unearthed by a team of enthusiastic volunteers. These modern excavations have been going on for almost thirty years now, and they're still nowhere near Joe's current location. The Great Cavern is actually closer to Flora's than to its birthplace in L7, and it's connected to enough further secret tunnels to give the average town planner a nervous breakdown. The tunnel that connects the Great Cavern to Harrington Street originally continued on into the *original* cavern—the one that lies underneath the Cavern Club on Mathew

Street. But that was blocked off when Maria Silverton lost her unholy shit and dumped several tonnes of rubble down into it. Not that it was necessarily a bad thing. At least now I could use the link as a quick way of visiting Joe, without also having to worry about what might be slithering its way up from the Mersey end. Although to be fair, what was left of the Mersey end was now patrolled by a pod of feral water creatures. And their leader had been loyal to me since I'd rescued her from these very caves shortly after I'd died, so I was probably safe anyway.

"To be absolutely honest, Lilith," Joe's voice dragged me back from my wandering thoughts, "I assumed I was perhaps a little overtired and just imagining it. But poor Sally was screeching like a banshee, so I had to assume she was also witnessing our unexpected guest."

"What happened next?" I asked. "Did you pry his trade secrets from him?"

"If only," said Joe wistfully. "No, Lilith, I'm afraid I failed in that task. Mr Hulls faded away in front of my eyes, as though he was mist dispersing on the wind. And then Sally herself faded into a dead faint, and I was distracted with trying to catch her. By the time she was settled on the window seat and my wife was seeing to her, my visitor was nothing but a memory." I thought for a moment about Joe's occasionally sentimental side, and how it must chafe against the necessity of keeping order underground.

"What would you have done with Daisy if I hadn't taken her on?"

Joe blinked slowly. "My apologies," he said finally. "I had sailed away on old memories for a moment, there. I'm sure I don't know what it is you want to know, Lilith," he said, looking up at me. "Are you asking if I might have...*disposed* of her?"

"Yeah," I said. "That's what I want to know." Daisy was the Asrai I'd taken pity on down here in the tunnels. Asrai are a type of water creature similar to mermaids, but with legs rather than tails. This difference does not stop pretty much everyone—myself included—describing the Asrai as mermaids, humans being inherently lazy in speech as well as action. Curiosity had led me down into this same cavern, right at the start of my undead adventures. Just when I'd been thinking that the discovery of an underground commune run by a long-dead philanthropist in order to house feral vampires had to be up there with the weirdest things that had ever happened to me, I'd turned round and spotted Daisy. She didn't have a name back then, and it was me who named her Daisy. I've told her she's welcome to change it if she wants to, but she never has. All I'd seen at the time was a ragged figure hunched up behind the heavy iron gate that closed off a small cell in the cavern's darkest corner. These days the cell was empty, and the gate stood open. But when I'd first ventured down here, it had held a sick and fragile Asrai. I didn't know what she was then, of course. Kitty had told me that later on, after I'd found Daisy eating mackerel on top of my television (yes, it was quite the experience, thanks for asking) and didn't know what to do with her. Whoever and whatever she might have been, Daisy knew a friend when she saw one, and she's been with me ever since. Most of the time she stays safely tucked away in the depths of the Mersey, but she still likes to pop in on Eadric occasionally. He's taken to keeping plastic tablecloths on his desk underneath his paperwork, just in case she brings him an unexpected gift. Turns out the smell of trout is really difficult to get out of even the most highly polished mahogany, especially after a couple of them have been left to flap themselves to death on it for a couple of hours.

"My word," said Joe, "you really think I might have caused harm to the creature, don't you." He chuckled quietly. "As if I would ever hurt something like that."

"Daisy's a she, not an it," I said indignantly.

"Is she, though?" Joe's gaze was measured. Some days he seems away with the fairies, and you can barely prise two words of sense out of him, but at other times he's as sharp as a flick-knife and twice as dangerous. And you never know which one you're going to get. "Rather presumptuous of you to choose a wild creature's gender based only on your very human powers of deduction, wouldn't you say?"

"So, what *would* you have done with her?"

Joe sighed. "Who knows?" he said. "Probably worried about her until her death came to pass, before disposing of the body and pretending nothing untoward had happened. Please don't scowl at me like that, Lilith. It's the circle of life. And also of death, of course." A brief pause. "She's very lucky to have found you," he said eventually. "And you her."

"Yup."

We sat in silence for a few long moments. "Well," said Joe eventually, "if it helps, I don't think anyone is going to rise against you. That might just be because they're too scared to attempt it, of course." His eyes twinkled. "May I ask how the elocution practise is going?"

"YES YOU MAY." I grinned as Joe's eyebrows shot up into his receding hairline. Two could play at being a smart-arse.

"Well now," he said, recovering himself, "isn't that just marvellous? Just be careful how you use it, Lilith."

"Always careful, Joe," I said, standing up just as a tall young man with lanky hair dropped into the cavern through a small access tunnel halfway up the wall. "Hey Tomasz," I said, "how's tricks?" Tomasz smiled shyly and said nothing. He was one of Joe's newest residents, and still nervous around outsiders. Which was better than wanting to attack me, which was what had happened with some of Joe's earlier vamps (and the reason I ended up dead in the first place). "I'll leave you to it, Joe," I said to the little man. "Got stuff to do. Undead worlds to run, you know how it is." Joe smiled at me from his seat by the fire. The cavern was so deep underground—and so well-insulated by the sandstone from which it had been dug—that it was always chilly down here, regardless of the weather in the outside world. I wondered why Joe felt the need for a fire. He was long dead, and therefore presumably unaffected by the cold. Maybe he just liked the look of it. I'd popped into a new bookshop over in the Baltic Triangle a couple of weeks earlier and been amused by the enormous flat-screen television that was fixed to the wall roughly where a fireplace would be, playing firelight videos on a flickering loop. The shop owner had told me it was psychological. Apparently, his marketing advisor thought people associated books with comfort and warmth. Perhaps Joe was the same. Not that a cavern the size of a small cathedral would ever feel cosy.

"Do appraise me of how you get on with it all," he said, getting to his feet. He always got up to greet me or say goodbye—if he was wearing a hat I was pretty sure he'd have doffed it. "I really am quite fascinated by all these new layers of our, heh, world that you seem to be uncovering."

"Lilith!" Joe and I both spun round to stare at the newcomer. Devin was stepping hesitantly through the entrance to the cavern, his eyes wide. "Oh my *god*," he said, "this is incredible! Just wait 'til I tell the urbex lot about this, they'll lose their minds!"

"What are you talking about?" I snapped. "You can't tell anyone about it, Devin. We discussed this."

"Yeah," he said vaguely, still gaping at the cathedral-like space around him. "But look at it!"

"I am assuming I can leave you to deal with this, Lilith?" Joe sounded worried, as well he might. It was one thing having one or two sympathetic council workers in on the secret, but an influx of urban explorers would blow the netherweird's secrets right out into the open. Although maybe Joe's children of the night could just eat them, that would solve the problem. And it was definitely a tempting option right now.

"Yes," I sighed. "I'll sort it out. You go tell the others to stay out of the way for a bit, and I'll deal with Devin here."

"You know him then?"

"Nope," I said firmly. "Never seen him before in my life. Now chop chop, there's a good little philanthropist. I've got admin to deal with."

∾

"He's got to go," I said. "I need that man out of town a.s.a-fucking-p and I need you to help me sort it."

"Which particular man are we talking about?" asked Nik, coming into the room. I'd dragged Devin back to the flat and informed Kitty and Grimm they were on babysitting duty. Neither of them had looked happy at the prospect, but I'd threatened exorcism and cessation of tuna privileges—in that order—and had eventually left the two of them sitting on the sofa glaring determinedly at a now very nervous Devin, who was hunched in the armchair. "Have you been getting into trouble again, Lil?" I narrowed my eyes. "No offence," he said, holding up a hand, "I've just learned to ask. I mean," he picked up a book from a side table and flopped into an armchair, "it is the usual reason."

"Go fuck yourself," I said mildly.

"If only," said Nik with a grin. "Do carry on." He waved the book at us regally. "Don't let me interrupt matters of state."

"I'm assuming this is your...friend, we're talking about?" Eadric said, shaking his head at Nik. "From the Bluecoat?"

"Yeah," I said. "Devin. My friend."

"And ex-boyfriend," offered Nik helpfully. "Don't forget that bit."

"That was a long time ago," I snapped.

"And now you want him removed from the city?" asked Eadric. "When you yourself refused to do the very same just a few short years ago?"

"That was different."

"Why?" Eadric looked genuinely curious. "Why is this any different to what happened to you?"

"Actually," interrupted Nik, "what did happen to Devin? Have you found out yet?"

"Turns out he decided to climb the Lambanana up on Tithebarn Street in the middle of the night," I sighed. "You know, that big blue and yellow one? Because he is an idiot who has never been able to handle his booze." I knew this from personal experience, having once had to drag him home from a staff party after he'd had one too many shandies and started singing Boney M's *Rasputin* at full volume. Which would have been fine had it been a karaoke night, but it wasn't. "Last thing he says he remembers is standing up on its back pretending to be a rodeo rider. Reckons he must have slipped and landed on his head, because there was a big lump on his temple when he woke up. So, he went home to sleep it off, only to wake up with no lump, zero apparent aftereffects and the brand new ability to run faster than the *Flash*."

"That must have been confusing for him," said Eadric.

"It was certainly confusing for the customers in the Bluecoat," I said, "when he tried to go to work as normal. Apparently, he really didn't have any idea what had happened, and couldn't understand why people were getting cross at him for doing things so fast. Then one of the waitresses caught hold of his arm to ask if he was okay and he shook her off, only she got thrown across the room and all hell broke loose." I knew this last bit because I'd been back into the Bluecoat earlier in the day, to tell them Devin wouldn't be back into work. They'd asked for a forwarding address—ostensibly to send a 'get well soon' card, but more likely for his P45—which I hadn't been able to give them. Mostly because Devin's only family had been his mum, and she'd died back when I first knew him. So, I gave them my own address instead and just hoped Eadric could come up with enough supporting paperwork for me not to end up being investigated by the *Post*. "Look," I said, "this is different. Don't you dare give me that look," this was to Nik, who raised an eyebrow and went back to his book, "because you haven't seen what he's like." In fact, I hadn't dared let Devin do anything unsupervised since I first rescued him from outside the Bluecoat, because he really was a liability. If he so much as went to pee, Finn or Grimm had to sit outside the bathroom door, waiting to make sure he came back out within a reasonable timeframe. If he didn't, they had instructions to break in and make sure he wasn't trying to escape through the tiny window. Again. It was as though he simply couldn't comprehend what had happened and forcing him to do so just made him even more confused. "Do you think that this," I waved my arms around to encompass me, Eadric and Nik, "is really just accidental? Cos I don't mind saying that it's clearly wasted on some people."

"And you're taking it upon yourself to decide who's worthy and who isn't?" Eadric looked amused. "When you yourself refused to accept your new state for some time?"

"Yes, yes," I said impatiently, "I was a mardy little cow who didn't want to be told what to do, and you were probably really pissed off with me."

"You could say that," said Nik. "There was certainly some lively conversation regarding quite what we should do with you."

"Well, it's a good job you didn't make any rash decisions," I snapped, "innit? Seeing as how I turned out to be your beloved leader." Nik raised his eyebrows but didn't say anything. "Devin is no one's leader," I went on, "I can promise you that much. Devin is a pain in the fucking arse who needs moving out of the area for the sake of my fucking sanity, if nothing else. And," I scowled at them both in turn, "before you say it, I'm not being selfish. I'm being *sensible*. You can stop that right now." This was to Nik, who was audibly snorting. "He is going to get us into trouble if we don't do something soon. I caught him parkouring over the top of Paddy's sodding Wigwam last night, for fuck's sake." The Metropolitan Cathedral of Christ the King might be one of the most spectacularly modern places of Catholic worship in existence, but its space-age shape earned its affectionately informal nickname almost as soon as it opened back in the late sixties and it's not hard to see why. Although if you want to know what impressive looks like, hunt out the designs for what *would* have been there had the original architect got his way. The Anglican cathedral down the road would have rapidly lost its spot as eighth biggest cathedral in the world, put it that way. And no, I don't know why all these random facts take up real estate inside my head, but at least I'm never short of topics of conversation with tourists. Anyway, Paddy's is huge and spiky, and I'd caught Devin swinging from its spires the previous evening, after going awol from the flat. I'd had to bring out The Voice in order to make him listen and even then he was reluctant. And despite doing my best to keep the shouting to a minimum, I'd definitely heard the crack of breaking glass in the windows of the cathedral's tower.

"Is that why the glaziers were up on the cathedral roof earlier today?" asked Nik, as if reading my mind. "I wondered if you might have been involved."

"Don't start," I snapped. "You try dealing with a thirty-something newborn revenant with zero boundaries. See how you like it."

"We already did that," he said. "With you. Remember?"

"Anyway," I decided to ignore Nik entirely and turned to Eadric, "something needs to be done. Didn't you say you had contacts in Scotland?"

"We do," said Eadric. "And I'm sure Alba will be happy to help their new queen." I rolled my eyes. "If she asks them herself."

"Oh no," I said. "No, no, no. I am not dealing with even more territories when I still don't entirely know how to manage this one. *And* I've got Chester to sort out. You do it and I will, I don't know," I smiled in what I hoped was a winning fashion, "love you forever? Will that do?"

"How can anyone resist you?" said Eadric, shaking his head in resignation. "You are *utterly* ridiculous, Lilith. And yet you are all ours. Aren't we the lucky ones?"

"Yes," I said. "Yes, you are. People should appreciate me a bit more, if you don't mind me saying. It makes me happy. And happy queens are nice queens."

"Don't push your luck," said Eadric, but he was smiling. "I'm still doing most of the paperwork for you—it wouldn't take too much organising to get it all transferred into your name. If you want *real* appreciation, that is."

"I'm sure we're all just fine as we are," I said hurriedly. "So, you'll sort Devin out?"

"I will sort Devin out," said Eadric. "And in return, you will do something about Chester. Do we have a deal?"

"Deal," I said, far too confidently. "I'll bring Devin over tonight, and head down to Chester tomorrow. After all, how difficult can one little city be?"

I loped across Aigburth Drive and headed past the obelisk dedicated to Samuel Smith—the liberal politician with distinctly puritanical views—into the darkness of Sefton Park. Made up of over two hundred acres of land bought from the Earl of Sefton in the late eighteen-hundreds, the park is an impressively natural landscape containing endless quiet corners and secret shadows, and is the perfect hiding place for shape-shifters who'd rather not be spotted by the local dog warden. It was late enough for it to be fully dark, but I still spotted a couple of overenthusiastic joggers running ahead of me in the gloom. As I walked slowly in the direction of Sefton's famous Palm House, I wondered—not for the first time—just how many varieties of paranormal creature might actually be real, after all. I'd grown up with a love of creepy stories as a little kid, once spending several weeks wearing a green ribbon tied around my neck and answering only to 'Jenny'. With hindsight, it was no wonder I'd struggled to maintain friendships until Izzy came along.

And now here I was—undead and loving it, as the movie said. Although I'd love it more if the immortal lifestyle came with marginally less drama. The cats were actually one of the least weird things out there. Everyone's heard tales of big cats living in the British countryside, and anyone living in or near said countryside knows they're mostly true. "Finn!" I hissed at a shadowy bush. "You in there?"

"Why are you shouting at a shrubbery?" said a voice. I spun around to find Finn standing behind me. He was wearing jeans and a t-shirt, but his feet were bare.

"I was trying to find you," I said. "If that wasn't obvious."

"As it happens," he said, "no, it wasn't obvious. Because I only go into the bushes when I'm a cat. And when I'm a cat, I can't talk to you, can I?"

"I hadn't thought of that," I admitted. "What happens to your voice box?" Finn looked confused. "When you change," I went on. "What happens to your voice box when you change into your cat form?"

"How should I know?" he shrugged. "I'm just a cat."

"Anyway," I said, determined not to get sidetracked, "I've found you now."

"I found you, more like."

"Whatever," I sighed. "We're both here, and I need to ask you some questions."

"Wasn't me," said Finn.

"What wasn't you?"

"Whatever it is you're asking about."

"You don't even know what it is yet," I said, "so how can you be sure it wasn't you?"

"Doesn't matter," he said. "Still wasn't me."

"Will you shut up and just bloody listen to me?" I said. "This isn't about anything you might have done. Or didn't do," I went on, "before you say it. I just wanted to ask you about what happened on the night Katja was killed."

"That *definitely* wasn't me."

"I know it wasn't! Fucking hell Finn, will you at least let me speak?"

"I ain't stopping you," he said. He was grinning now, and I could see why Finn was popular with his customers. He had an easy grace about him, and an air of happy carelessness that made him incredibly likeable. Even when he was being super annoying.

"What did you see that night?" I asked. "By which I mean I only want to know what happened to Katja, not anything else you might have been up to."

"You're getting very suspicious these days, Lil," said Finn. "Don't want to be getting cynical in your old age."

"What did you—"

"Okay, okay," Finn interrupted, "take a pew and I'll tell you." He gestured to a nearby park bench. I dutifully sat down and he sat next to me, although he somehow curled himself up on the bench with his legs underneath him, rather than sitting upright like humans generally do. "So," he started, "you know how I like to hang out down here when I've got nothing else on?"

"Yes, but that's not—"

"It's relevant," he said. "So I was down here doing cat things, like." I decided not to ask what 'cat things' might be. There's some knowledge I can live without and the intricacies of feline interaction definitely fall under that heading. "Just chilling, hanging out, that sort of thing. Chased a really fat squirrel," he grinned, "and fuck me if I didn't nearly catch it! Okay," he saw my expression, "I'm getting to the interesting bit. So I'm chasing and running and all that stuff, when something prickles the back of my neck, you know?" I shrugged, not wanting to get bogged down in one of Finn's all-too-regular conversational rabbit holes. "Like when people say someone must have walked on their grave. I stopped and asked the others, but no one else had noticed. But they're mostly idiots, to be fair, so I didn't really expect anything else. Anyway, the feeling went away, but I couldn't concentrate. It was as if a mouse was lurking just out of sight. But it was a metaphorical mouse, y'know?" This was obviously rhetorical, because he immediately carried on. "So I raced round looking for the mouse, but I think it was in my head." He frowned. "A white mouse. Dunno how I knew it was white, but it was. And then something told me I had to get over to Harrington Street."

"What," I asked, "like a premonition or something?"

"No," said Finn, "an actual voice. Speaking in my head as if someone was standing right there in front of me. But it wasn't any of the other cats, and there wasn't anyone else there." I resisted the urge to ask him how cats spoke to each other. "Posh, it was."

"A posh voice in your head told you to go to Harrington Street?"

"Yup," said Finn, blessing me with a radiant smile. "Exactly that. And I've never had voices in my head before, on account of how I'm not mad." I raised an eyebrow, but managed not to say anything. "So I figured it was probably important and that I should do what it said."

"And you ran all the way back into town?" I didn't go down to Sefton Park very often, but by my reckoning it was a good three or four miles from Harrington Street.

"I'm fast," he said, "and I go the straight route, innit. As the crow flies, like." He grinned. "That's if the crow doesn't get eaten first, of course."

"Of course," I said. "So you ran back to Harrington Street. What happened then?"

"I could see someone up on the roof," he said, "as I ran across the top of Coopers." He meant Coopers Building, a massive old-fashioned department store on Church Street. "Thought it was weird then, on account of how Katja always tucked herself further down, closer to your place. I come that way a lot and she liked to jump out at me and I'd pretend to be scared." His smile faded. "I miss Katja."

"We all do," I said. "Which is why I'm trying to find out what happened to her."

"Maybe when you find out who did it, I can chase them round for a bit," he said, perking up. "You know, play with them 'til their blood's properly pumping, sort of thing. Makes stuff tasty, that does. Then Rachel can have 'em as a snack." He looked pleased by the thought. It was certainly tempting.

"We'll decide what to do with them when I've figured out who it is," I said. "So Katja was up on the very top of the roof?" That was presumably when she spotted a potential intruder. I couldn't imagine any human going to those lengths to break into my flat. Most burglaries are opportunistic—even if someone had spotted my open kitchen window, I was pretty sure they wouldn't have come prepared with a wooden stake.

"No," said Finn, "I'm pretty sure it was a bloke. At least, someone human-shaped. Anyway, I sneaked, right?" I nodded encouragingly. "Got myself across the road and up onto the roof of the fried chicken place on Lord Street. I like 'em in there. They give me extra bits for my cat when I go in."

"You don't have a cat," I said.

"They don't know that. Anyway," he went on, "I'm higher there, right? Roof of your place is lower, so I wriggled myself across so's I could see the door to your flat. Blokey on the roof is still there, mind—had to be really careful he didn't see me. Lucky I'm not bright ginger, innit." Finn was certainly pale enough that it had always confused me how his feline persona was entirely black, but I had to agree that black cats were definitely lucky, under the circumstances. "Saw Katja then, didn't I? She was arguing with someone lower down the roof. This other person was shorter and looked like they weren't very good at climbing." He sniffed. Finn has very little tolerance for anyone who can't climb well. "But they'd got themselves up on there and honestly, I think they might have been stuck? They must have got onto Katja's bit via one of the other buildings though, cos you'd have heard if they'd been scrabbling round outside your kitchen door." I wasn't entirely convinced—we'd had the television on pretty loud that night. And anyway, I'd felt secure, what with having a vampire guard on the roof and being immortal. That sort of thing lulls you into a potentially false sense of security when it comes to personal safety.

"So this other person—the bad climber—it was them who killed Katja?"

"Nah," said Finn, "I reckon it was old blokey up there on the roof. At least, I think it must have been him. The other human didn't look like their heart was really in it, you know? They had a stake in their hand, though! A really obvious one, like something out of a movie. They were sort of waving it at her. Katja was laughing at them, I think." He trailed off.

"What happened next?" I knew from experience that I needed to get the entire story out of Finn in one go, because once he starts rambling, there's no stopping him. "Didn't you see who actually killed her?"

"No," he sighed. "I spotted the bloody mouse, didn't I. Right there on the stair."

"Did he have clogs on?" Finn looked bemused. "Never mind," I said. "So you spotted a mouse. What did you do?"

"What d'you think I did?" said Finn. "Chased the little bugger, din't I? Couldn't help meself. Shot over the roof and after the little snacky-snack. And there was a bloke standing there as well! Just remembered that." He frowned. "Weird looking, he was. I think the mouse ran to the man? They disappeared—into thin air, seemed like. Anyway, I crashed into the railings outside your kitchen door, then someone fell on me from the roof. I was just turning to give 'em a good nip," he bared his very human teeth in an approximation of a cat snarling, "but then Katja went and thumped onto the doorstep, like a dead weight. Literally, as it turned out. Anyway," he brightened up, "I thought I'd snag whoever it was who'd fallen on me, but then I saw someone running across the roof above me and that looked more fun. So I went after them." He shrugged. "Lost 'em towards Pilgrim Street."

"How did you injure yourself?" Finn looked confused. "When you got back here," I said, "you were limping. What happened?"

"Oh, that." He looked sheepish. "The bloke disappeared mid chase," he said, "and it took me by surprise. I tried to stop a bit too quickly, din't I? Ran straight off the roof of the Cracke and landed in the car park over the back. Took the wind right out of me, that did."

"And whoever it was you were chasing just literally disappeared?" The only paranormal weirdos I knew who could do that were ghosts, and I was pretty sure it wasn't a ghost who'd killed Katja. Apart from anything else, they wouldn't have any incentive to hurt her. Nor me, come to that. Ghosts tend to just...exist, regardless of what's going on around them. I'd seen it with Billy—who'd 'lived' on Harrington Street for a very long time without ever really interacting with anyone—and also with Kitty, who mostly just wafted around, looking happily bemused at the world.

"Yup," he said, "right into thin air. And I've got cat eyes, innit." He scrunched his eyes up to look suitably suspicious. "So I don't miss much."

"What I don't understand," I said, "apart from the whole ghosts and mice and random vampire killers and people disappearing into nowhere, is how I didn't hear any of it. You're sure this all happened on my front doorstep?"

"Yup," said Finn. "It was quick, mind. Reckon maybe a minute or so between me spotting the mouse and taking off after blokey there." So it probably all happened in the time it took me to realise the crown was getting agitated.

"Hang on," I said. "What happened to the other attacker?" Finn looked blank. "The one that fell on you," I went on. "You said there was another person on the roof, threatening Katja with a stake."

"Oh yeah," he said, "them. They ran off, I think. Staggered off, maybe. Looked a bit wobbly on their feet, they did."

"Which direction?" Finn gave me the blank look of someone who'd got bored with the conversation and was thinking about what they were going to do next. "Which direction did they stagger off in?" I said. "Up on the roof?"

"Nah," he said, "they went down the steps. Slowly though, like a boring old human." Brilliant. As if I didn't already have enough enemies, now the humans were getting involved. "Anyway," said Finn, "is there anything else you wanted? Cos I'm not one to be rude, like," I raised my eyebrows at that, and he completely ignored me, "but I've got cat stuff to do."

"Nope," I said, "that's all. Thanks Finn." But the only response was the sound of something feline and slinky swishing through the underground away from me. Sighing, I turned for home.

One For Sorrow

"Where did you find all this?" I asked Nik the next morning. We were in my kitchen, Nik having unexpectedly arrived carrying a blue plastic bag filled with photocopy paper before I'd even had my first coffee of the day. To give him due credit, Nik's really good at research. He says all those years of competing against his ridiculous literary friends made him 'appreciate the sanity of the factual word'. Presumably as opposed to the endless flowery language of the dead poet's society. Anyway, Nik has contacts up at Central Library and I like to make use of them. I'd fully expected him to be dating—or, at least, seducing—the head librarian by now, but he swore they just chatted about bookish stuff.

What I wasn't going to tell him was that I'd already found what I was looking for. Having been given a surname by Joe Williamson, Jonathan Hulls had been an easy man to find. He even had his own Wikipedia page, although it didn't go into any great detail. From what I could gather from the sparse information available, Jonathan had been blessed with a clever imagination and cursed with not having enough financial wherewithal to actually do much with his inventive ideas. He appeared to have got as far as trialling an idea for an early form of steam ship, only for his scaled down prototype to sink into the River Avon to the general mockery of his peers.

"Mick's interested in the history of engineering," he said. "I suppose it comes with the territory when you're the head librarian in a city built on industry."

"Mick?" I squinted at him. "The head librarian's called *Mick*?"

"Considering you made your first undead dalliance with someone known as 'the Bastard'," said Nik, "you're hardly in a position to mock. Anyway," he went on primly, "Mick's not my type."

"What *is* your type, then?" I asked. "Apart from 'anything with a pulse'? Cos let's face it, even that's optional these days."

"Some of us have standards," Nik had retorted. "I do at least try to ensure they're not secretly a power-hungry tyrant on the make."

"We all make mistakes," I snapped back. "It's not my fault the only person I've jumped since I died turned out to be William the sodding Conqueror, is it?" Nik snorted. "How was I supposed to know that a bloke I bumped into in the pub was a manipulative asshat? Anyway," I huffed, "I threw him out of a window soon as I found out. No one can accuse me of not dealing with issues in a prompt and decisive manner."

"True," said Nik. "Anyway, Mick said I could copy these for you." He pulled a large and clearly heavy envelope filled with photocopies out of the plastic bag, and held them out to me. I slid the paper stack out onto the table and discovered it was a pick'n'mix of anything and everything that might have something to do with Jonathan Hulls or engineering in general. There were a lot of old diagrams of what looked like machinery, handwritten minutes of long-forgotten council meetings, and even the odd planning application. There was an entire collection held together with a large bulldog clip that contained nothing but endless copies of applications for patents. "I just asked him to stick to things that perhaps weren't entirely normal," Nik said.

"That's us all over," I sighed. "Not entirely normal. Thank you," I said. "I really appreciate it."

"And you think you might find this Jonathan in Chester?"

"I know he's there," I said, "but what I don't know is where. Or why."

. . .

Nik headed off back down to the Liver Building, after promising that, should I need it, Mick had more paperwork where that lot came from. I laid the papers out in their separate piles on the kitchen table, before turning to finally switch on the coffee machine. Thanks to Mapp, I at least knew how to make it work now. Just as I pressed the start button, there was a tapping at the kitchen window. "For fuck's sake, Grimm," I said, turning to the window with a sigh, "can't you see it's open—oh!" An enormous magpie was sitting on the sill of the open window, its feathers shining petrol-black in the sunshine and beady little button eyes flashing with curiosity. It tilted its head this way and that, as though sizing me up. "Who's a pretty birdie, then?" I said, moving slowly closer so I could see it properly. "What a gorgeous little boy you are!" I had no idea of the bird's actual gender, or if it was even possible to gender a magpie from its plumage in the first place. But I figured a friendly voice was the important thing. It really was a glorious creature, and also dangerously brave. "If the cats come home," I told it, "they'll munch you up as a snack. Are you listening to me, mister magpie?" The bird tilted its head again as though considering my words. Then it let out a laughing, guttural squawk and did a small jig on the spot. "You're a cheeky little bugger," I said, and the magpie made a chuckling noise. Slowly, I inched my hand towards it. Maybe it was a tame one that had escaped from an aviary somewhere. Or maybe I just had yet another strange friend to add to the gang. "Are we going to be friends, mister magpie?" I asked, reaching my fingertips out towards it. The bird stayed absolutely still as I slowly stroked its wing, marvelling at the prisms of colour the light created on the black and white feathers. The bird tilted its head back but didn't move. "Are you enjoying that?" I asked, daring to run my fingers down its soft, downy throat. "Christ," I said quietly, "I'm turning into Snow bloody White." The magpie made a noise that sounded distinctly like a human chuckle. "Do you understand what I'm saying?" I asked. "Are you a messenger from someone?" I narrowed my eyes at it. "You'd better not be spying on me, Liam O'Sodding Connor," I said, "or I will make an entire collection of quills out of those beautiful feathers of yours." In response, the magpie bounced forward a tiny step and pressed its head against my hand. I heard the yowling noise just in time. It was coming from the car park, and getting closer. "You need to go," I hissed at the magpie. "Grimm's home, for god's sake." The magpie turned on the windowsill and cocked its head to peer down to where Grimm was stalking up the fire escape. His vast grey bulk was flattened against the metal of the stairs and his ears were tight back against his head as he slunk steadily upwards. "Go!" I said, giving in and just flapping at the bird. "There's no point wanting to be my friend if you get eaten on the first day, for heaven's sake. Go!" The magpie reluctantly turned away from me and bounced to the edge of the windowsill, but instead of taking off, it just stared at the approaching cat as though mesmerised. "Don't you dare, Grimm," I hissed, but I knew he wasn't listening. Nothing comes between Grimm and his prey, and his victims have to be bloody fast movers if they're to have any hope of surviving the encounter. Before I could do anything to stop him, the cat launched himself—and so did the magpie. They collided in mid air, and for a brief second there was a spinning cloud of feathers and fur. "Pack it in!" I yelled, and shot out of the kitchen door in the hope of saving the bird from becoming cat chow. Before I could reach them, the magpie shot upwards out of the fight, then immediately turned and flew back down again. To my utter astonishment, I watched as it smacked Grimm hard across the face with its wing, sending the cat sprawling. With a loud screech, the magpie spun upwards, twisting like a feathery tornado. Below it, Grimm sat on the top step looking dazed, as though he had no idea what had—literally—just hit him. As I stepped forward to check he was okay, I heard wings flapping close above my head. The magpie swooped down past me towards the scrubby rubble of the car park, before pulling upwards in an arc so steep I thought it was going to go backwards into a full loop. At the very last second, the bird veered to the right, flying round and over my head again, before disappearing off toward the river. "Well," I said to Grimm, who was currently puffed up into a ball of fluffy fury, "that told you, didn't it?" He made a dismissive growling noise under his breath and stalked past me into the flat.

∽

"Gonna work from the back room today," I said to Izzy as I wriggled carefully through the hatch in the counter in Flora's. My arms were filled with paperwork, which was in turn wedged against my ancient laptop. "Need the table space."

"Not that I don't love having you around," said Iz, "but what's wrong with the table in your own kitchen?"

"This *is* my own kitchen," I said. "Got two, haven't I? Upstairs and down."

"If you're after company, you only have to say." Izzy's looked sympathetic. "You know you're welcome down here whenever you like."

"That's very kind of you," I grinned, "letting me come sit in the building I actually own."

"All heart, me," said Izzy. "Anyway, you might own it, but I do the work. So yeah," she grinned back, "I'm *allowing* you to come sit down here, if you don't mind."

"Aye aye, guv'nor," I said. Then I made myself a double espresso and settled in for a bit of detective work. After all Nik's efforts with the librarians, it was one of Eadric's diaries that held the first useful mention of Jonathan Hulls. Even after narrowing the possible time range down from the information Joe had given me, it had still taken a couple of hours of squinting over tiny handwriting to come up with anything. I also had to force myself to avoid going down a very tempting rabbit hole when I spotted references to the strange animals that had taken up residence in the south Shropshire hills during the early eighteenth century. I'd been on enough family trips to Cardingmill Valley as a child to be curious about what really caused the giant paw prints that my dad always insisted were put there by pranksters, but it was going to have to wait.

It was the end of the nineteenth century before Jonathan turned up in Eadric's diaries, and even then, his surname wasn't mentioned. The diary merely noted, *'An interesting man, with some strange ideas'*, and that he seemed *'childlike, in some ways, which is at odds with his appearance as a gentleman and a scholar'*. He was apparently *'aggrieved by matters unexplained'*. Eadric had assumed Jonathan was bearing a grudge against someone—possibly his supposed patron—but clearly didn't think any of it was important enough to go into further detail. Jonathan Hulls peered out of the screen of the laptop that sat next to me on the table, as though checking I was doing my due diligence on his personal details. The etched portrait on his Wikipedia page showed him dressed in what looked very much like the clothes he'd wearing when I'd met him down in seventeenth-century Toxteth, although by that time it had been more the faded, shabby outfit of a formerly privileged gentleman who'd fallen on hard times. This was presumably the same portrait Joe Williamson remembered from centuries earlier. It was titled *'The Inventor of the Steam Boat'*, but reading the rest of Jonathan's entry made me wonder whether he'd requested the moniker himself, rather than it being an accepted fact. Born in Gloucester at the end of the seventeenth century, there was precious little to confirm his title other than a complicated-looking patent that was granted in 1736. Even to my eyes, it was clear Jonathan had invented *something* potentially interesting, but I wasn't entirely sure what. It appeared to be small, steam-powered tugboat. And fully half a century before Watt delivered the steam engine that would change the entire world. The Wiki page also mentioned Jonathan's patron, the owner of a nearby estate, who at some point appeared to have decided that his money was better spent on maintaining his enormous stately home than on indulging the local would-be da Vinci. Dead before he reached sixty years old, there was precious little other background information available. And there certainly didn't appear to be any wife or other family left to mourn him. Poor Jonathan—it was no wonder he felt stuck, having spent the last three centuries watching others succeed where he couldn't.

Or perhaps he just wasn't a very good inventor, said the city in my head.

Maybe, I said. *But he clearly said he was trapped, rather than still being here by his own choice. So, who would do the trapping?*

Wasn't the Bastard lurking in the south west before you met him? Gloucester's within that territory.

Fucking brilliant, I sighed. *Just what I needed—another run-in with the nobhead of Normandy.*

He speaks highly of you as well.

Huh, I said, refusing to take the bait. *I'm going to have to find Jonathan, aren't I? Chester's a big place and it clearly doesn't want me there, so I'm going to have to be subtle and sneaky about it.*

You? Subtle and sneaky? The city made a snorting noise. **Good luck with that.**

Don't start, I warned. *I'm not in the mood for silliness.*

We're inside your head, Lilith, it said. **You can hardly ignore us.**

YES I CAN.

Silence for a long minute. **There's no need to be like that**, it said eventually.

There is clearly every bloody need, I snapped, *if I'm going to get anything done around here.*

You need to think more laterally, said the city. **Whoever's keeping Jonathan captive, they can only do it somewhere they'd have been able to tempt him to in the first place.**

How do you mean? Surely ghosts just wander all over the place?

Why would they do that? it asked. **Ghosts usually have as much a sense of purpose as the living. Often more so. As we said, your bewigged friend will be somewhere he himself would have found interesting.**

Sighing, I pulled out the ordnance survey maps that Nik had helpfully added to the stash of library papers. There was one for Chester, one for Shrewsbury and several covering different areas of Liverpool. He hadn't bothered with the Wirral side of the Mersey, I noticed. He probably didn't consider it important enough. Which just showed that Nik Silverton might be a literary genius, but he's definitely lacking in the spooky history department to a worrying extent, for someone who'd been a literal walking example of the genre for centuries. Wirral had popped up endlessly in Eadric's diaries, with mentions of strange creatures vying for space on the pages with tales of Viking invaders who never really left. But that was a rabbit hole for another day. Right now, I needed to get close up and personal with the inner workings of Chester. I opened out the OS map and looked for the canal. Canals are almost always a good indicator of which bit of a town or city would have been the most important in centuries past. They brought in the goods and took out the waste, for one thing. Rivers are just fine and dandy—and are often a good part of the reason a settlement is founded in the first place—but they meander wherever they choose, and have a nasty habit of rising and flooding any random bits of conurbation that humans foolishly build in their way. Canals, on the other hand, mean business—literally. If there's a canal in or near your hometown, it will have been put there for a reason. And that reason is usually 'making money'. I knew the Shropshire Union Canal ran right through Chester city centre, but not exactly where. I'd assumed it would be close by the Roman ruins—maybe I'd subconsciously tied the important landmarks together—but after ten minutes of fruitless hunting, I gave in and opened Google maps instead. It's not that I'm a technophobe, it's just that I have a nasty habit of breaking electronic equipment so avoid touching any of it as much as possible. This wasn't a recent thing—I'd been just as good at accidentally destroying mobile phones and the like back when I was still alive. The most expensive mobile I'd ever bought was broken in the fall that dumped me unceremoniously into immortality, and I still bore a grudge. These days I carried a second-hand iPhone that I'd bought from the Lord Street branch of CEX and it was already so outdated that I didn't use it for much more than the occasional text. I'd never been overly bothered by social media, which was lucky because no one had even noticed when I closed down all my accounts shortly after I died. It wasn't as though I'd be snapping selfies with my new undead acquaintances. Most of them considered mobile phones to be a form of witchcraft, anyway. And I didn't want to risk comments about how I never seemed to age. Thirty-two had been a good time to die, I'd decided. Not that there's ever a great time to die, unless it's at the age of at least ninety, whilst lying in a comfortable bed with zero pain and a collection of loved ones to see you off. But being in your early thirties means you're already a fully grown adult (Izzy would probably argue against that sometimes) but haven't yet started noticeably ageing. With any luck, I'd be able to carry on for a long time yet before I had to worry about whether to fake some grey streaks. I'd already had the laptop for several years by the time I'd died, and it was second-hand to begin with, so it was a miracle it had survived this far. It was slow and heavy, and the fan kicked in loudly if I dared run it for more than fifteen minutes, and I'd had to switch back to paper accounting within six months of opening Flora's after it collapsed under the strain one morning and lost all my records for the previous three months. But it would still load up maps, and that was all I needed. I switched to the satellite view and waited for the little coloured wheel to stop spinning in the middle of the screen. Using the A5480 road as a rough western boundary on the principle that whatever I was looking for, it was likely to be somewhere central, I zoomed in at creakingly slow speed until I could read the place names. Following the canal along past small boatyards and vast blocks of student accommodation, I spotted Telford's Warehouse on the corner where the canal took a sharp left turn. Izzy and I had once had a very drunken night out there, long before either of us had moved to Liverpool. When you grow up in Shrewsbury, you learn to find the nearest accessible cities at a young age. You also learn how to hold your bladder all the way home because the single train toilet is usually blocked and stinking late at night and you have to clench until you can find a dark corner to wee in on your stagger home from the railway station. No more bladder-holding for me, though. Toilets were now merely an unused accessory in my life, along with tampons and razors. I'd shaved my legs and armpits not long before I'd died, and hadn't needed to do it since. Weirdly, I kind of missed the ability to grow body hair—I'd sometimes grown it out just for the hell of it and quite liked the feeling of having soft, downy legs. I gazed up and through into Flora's, where Izzy was busy serving customers. Todd had come in for the lunchtime shift and was filling the dishwasher and pouring coffee to Izzy's orders at the same time. Izzy was wearing a loose-fit dress that I knew as her 'bloating frock'. She only wore it on the days when PMT made her tiny flat stomach swell slightly. Yeah, I definitely didn't miss PMT. Sighing—although I wasn't sure whether it was wistfulness or sheer relief—I got back to peering at the map. I thought I was maybe onto something when I spotted King Charles Tower on the corner of the city walls. Sadly, a brief google informed me it had been occupied by the guilds of painters and barbers, and I didn't think either of those would have been relevant. It wasn't until I was following the line of the canal from the street view angle and just heading underneath the City Road that I saw it. Suddenly, I knew exactly where to find Jonathan Hulls.

. . .

It was bloody obvious, in hindsight. I packed my papers up and wedged them, along with the laptop, into the drawer next to the sink. Then I opened the drawer again and pulled out the map of Chester. It might be useful, even if only to stop me from getting completely lost. Then I grabbed Basil's keys from the hook behind the door, and pulled down the note we keep stuck to the wall because it has the access code for the Harrington Street traffic bollards scribbled on it. The council only drops them for a brief period each morning to allow deliveries through, and it had been an absolute pain in the backside for a very long time. Eadric had only recently given me the secret code to freedom and I still wasn't happy with him for making me wait that long. On the other hand, I now had to have a very good reason for borrowing his Alfa instead of using Basil. Mind you, this has the advantage of him not knowing what I'm up to all the time. I wasn't entirely convinced that today's trip wouldn't be another dead loss, and I could do without him looking annoyingly sympathetic when I told him. So, a secret Beetle road trip it was. "I'm nipping over to Chester," I said to Izzy, as I walked through into the cafe. "Should be back before you close up."

"You don't need to race back on my behalf." Izzy was refilling the small wooden rack that sits at the end of the counter in Flora's. It holds sachets of sugar, salt, pepper and the like. We originally had proper sugar bowls with cubes. I far preferred them to the sachets, but we'd discovered all too quickly just how dirty and sticky a sugar bowl gets when it's left on a cafe table for any length of time. Ditto sauces for the small range of fresh sausage rolls and cheese and onions pasties we sell. In a fit of enthusiasm when I first signed the lease, I'd bought a wholesale box of tomato-shaped squeezy bottles of the type you see in fifties-themed diners. Within a week, they were all clogged with plugs of dried-up ketchup. Izzy had spent half an hour running boiling water into their spouts in an attempt to unblock them, before declaring life was 'too bloody short for this fuckery' and throwing the lot in the bin. These days we just get boxes of sachets from the cash-and-carry and agree not to think about the environmental impact. Once she'd finished neatly packing the different compartments, she picked the box up and put it back on the counter. Then she realised she hadn't wiped the counter down first, so put the box back by the sink and wiped the counter down. When she'd finally arranged things to her satisfaction, she wiped her hands on her black apron and looked at me. "You're a grown up," she said with a grin. "You can do what you like."

"I know," I sighed. "But I still feel guilty about not being around more."

Izzy frowned. "Why? Oh, thank you!" This was to a pair of students who'd made the effort to bring their empty cups back to the counter as they left. "If only everyone was as polite as you!" The students—a pair of young girls who didn't look old enough to be out without their parents, let alone living unsupervised away from home—smiled shyly and nodded their thanks. "I'll still have to go clean their table, mind," she said as the door closed behind them. "Messy little buggers." I glanced across to where the vacated table was decorated with rings of spilled tea and what looked like sugar that had been poured out in order for the girls to draw diagrams in it with their fingers. "Chemistry students," said Izzy. "Guarantee it. They're always the worst. Anyway," she twirled a tea towel and slapped it down hard enough to make a bloke on the nearest table jump in surprise, "why the guilt?" She tilted her head to gaze at me. "Look," she said, before I could reply, "I know we were going to run this place together. And it would have been fun. Of course it would. But we weren't expecting you to end up—" her voice dropped "—*dead*, were we? Reckon we've done okay, under the circs. And it's not like you don't have other stuff to do." She shrugged. "If it comes down to a choice between serving coffee and cake to mucky students or taking charge of an entire undead society, I don't think it needs a genius to realise which one's going to take up the most time. What?" She narrowed her eyes at me.

"I just can't get over how well you've dealt with all this," I said. "Most people would have run a mile the minute they found out."

"Well, I'm not most people, am I?" Izzy huffed. "And I'm not saying it hasn't been a steep learning curve. But, well," she shrugged. "You're my mate, aren't you? Doesn't make much difference to me if you're dead, so long as you're still here. And I've got Todd and Missy helping these days, so I'm not exactly run off my feet. I'd have been on my own this afternoon anyway, it's a quiet day. You go sort Chester, and I'll supervise the manky students. 'Kay?"

"'Kay," I said, heading for the door. "Oh, and Iz?" I turned as I stepped out onto the pavement.

"Yeah?" She was standing next to the counter in her flowery dress and apron, the tea towel now slung over her shoulder.

"Love you," I said, blowing her a kiss. I thought she was going to say something sarcastic in return, but she blew a kiss back.

"Love you too, dead girl," she said. A nearby customer looked up at that, but decided it must just be a strange form of affection and went back to staring at their phone. "Now go kick Chester's arse."

Right, Said Fred

As I pulled Basil slowly out onto Harrington Street, someone shouted my name. Looking up towards Button Street, I saw Sean waving as he headed towards me with a friendly grin on his face. "Hey," he said when he got close enough, "off anywhere nice?" He was dressed in his usual corduroy jeans and flannel shirt, the shirt hanging loose and open at the neck in deference to the warm weather, and his hair was as floppy as ever. Sean is basically the human equivalent of those puppies you used to see on toilet roll adverts, all cute and fluffy and just begging for a kindly pat on the head.

"Chester," I said, omitting the bit about it hopefully turning into a meeting with a bloke who'd been dead for nearly three centuries. "Boring stuff."

"Nothing boring about Chester," said Sean. "Can I come with you?"

"What?" I looked at him blankly. "You want to come to Chester with me?"

"That's what I said," he grinned, unperturbed by my response. "I like it there. And I haven't been for ages."

"Honestly," I scrambled around for an excuse, "I'm going to a really dull meeting. Just sorting something out for the Silvertons. And it'll take me ages. You'll get bored waiting."

"That's okay," said Sean, "I can go for a wander while you're busy being a boring businesswoman. And we're friends, aren't we? That's what you said," he shrugged. "And friends go places together. So?" He raised his eyebrows in query. "Can I come with?" I absolutely could not take Sean Hannerty to Chester. For one thing, it's the sort of place that attracts the kind of would-be intellectual tourists who'd probably recognise him. I generally tried to avoid attention as much as I could, which was why my hair was currently twisted up into a bun. It's easier to go unnoticed when you're not wandering around like a sentient Belisha beacon. And how would I explain that I needed to go walk along the canal on my own before potentially breaking into a listed building, without Sean insisting on coming with me? Nope, absolutely no way.

"Get in," I sighed. It would be nice to have company. Hopefully, it wouldn't take me long to check things out. Maybe we could have coffee afterwards. Sean walked round to the passenger side and got in, dumping his satchel in the footwell by his feet. As he went to fasten his seatbelt the strap jammed, and I leaned over to help.

"It needs coaxing," I said, letting the strap roll backwards into its housing before starting again. "Slowly, see?" Warmth breath on my face made me turn to see Sean smiling at me from approximately four inches away.

"Is that right?" he said, his eyes crinkling in amusement. For a second I nearly moved to kiss him—he was so close and eager, and I knew from experience that he tasted amazing.

"No," I said, more sharply than I'd intended. I fastened his seat belt without looking at him, then sat back in my seat. "Sorry."

"It's fine," said Sean. "We're just friends, too dangerous for anything else, blah blah. I kind of feel sorry for you," he went on. "I know it must be difficult to resist my manly charms." I did turn to look at him then. He sat grinning at me, looking absolutely unbothered. "Look," he said, "I get it. It's difficult. The whole 'dead and dangerous' thing, I mean. I promise I'll behave."

"I'm glad to hear it," I said, smiling despite myself. I pulled out into the traffic and started driving towards the Birkenhead tunnel. It's actually quicker to go up to the Kingsway tunnel and head straight down to Chester on the motorway, but I like the slower, more scenic route. Not that Birkenhead's known for its scenery. But Basil's less likely to get an articulated truck up his shiny chrome backside on the New Chester Road, and that's always a good thing. I'd thought it might be awkward having Sean in the car, but he turned out to be very easy company. He'd started telling me all about a plot hole in the latest book he was writing and how it was driving him mad.

"That's why I was coming over to Flora's when I spotted you," he said, as we drove through the light-spotted gloom of the tunnel. "I thought maybe a change of scenery would help."

"How do you think up the complicated plot lines?" I asked.

"You've read my stuff, then?" I could see his pleased expression out of the corner of my eye. "I've never liked to ask. And I thought they might not be your thing, anyway."

"I'd read one of them before I knew who you were," I said. It was only a half-lie. Izzy and I had actually both downloaded the first in one of Sean's early series just after we'd discovered our quiet but pleasant regular's real identity. We'd been impressed by his knowledge of devious murder methods—and even more impressed by his ability to conjure a very sexy sex scene out of seemingly nowhere.

"The plots are easy," he said. "It's the romance I struggle with." I forced myself to keep my eyes on the road. *Please gods tell me he can't read my mind*, I thought to myself. I was getting sick and bloody tired of not being able to keep anything to myself. Especially when thinking about things of an intimate nature. And even more so whilst sitting right next to the subject of those thoughts.

"Aah, they seemed fine to me," I managed. "Not that I'm an expert or anything."

"On writing, or romance?"

"I meant writing," I said. "But, well. Yeah," I went on, "it applies to both, I reckon." I turned slightly and grinned at him.

"I reckon I could help with that," said Sean. "If you'd let me."

"Writing or romance?" I pulled onto the slip-road to the motorway —you can't avoid it entirely, just put it off for a while—and floored the accelerator as a gap appeared in the traffic.

"Christ," said Sean, "this car's got more oomph than I expected."

"Basil's a good boy," I said, patting the steering wheel fondly. "And Eadric's mechanic did a lot of work on him." That was an understatement. Basil had been all but rebuilt from the chassis upwards. Long gone were the days of plodding at sixty miles-per-hour with everything crossed that nothing fell off en route. These days I can get to seventy for a good few minutes before everything starts shaking. And as any Beetle owner will tell you, that's a miracle in itself.

"Course," said Sean. "I'd forgotten about the tunnel collapsing. Bit mad how that just happened to occur right by Flora's, don't you think? After it had been stable for so many years."

"Abercrombie Square was affected as well, don't forget." I could feel his eyes on me and concentrated on keeping my expression as bland as possible. "Wasn't just me."

"But that's over the line of the tunnels as well, isn't it?"

I flashed Sean a sharp look. "I've no idea what you mean," I said, looking back at the road and quickly pulling round a milk tanker that was suddenly right in front of me. "No one really knows where those tunnels are."

"Not even Joseph Williamson?"

"What are you talking about, Sean?" My voice was sharp.

"Lil," he said, putting his hand on my thigh in what he clearly thought was a reassuring manner, "I write fiction. Which means I'm good at picking up on potential ideas, and even better at researching them. I stood there and witnessed a weird alien sitting on top of your television, for christ's sake! Did you think I'd forget something like that?" Well yes, I thought, I actually did. I really thought I'd wiped your mind enough for you to forget it. But I kept my mouth shut and my foot on the pedal and said nothing for another mile or so.

"Daisy isn't an alien," I said eventually. "She's an Asrai. It's a kind of mermaid," I glanced across to where Sean sat calmly listening, "but different. And she's my friend."

"She didn't look very friendly," said Sean.

"She was looking for safety and came to me to me for help," I said, thinking back to the day Sean and I had walked into my flat after a very nice date, only to find a feral water creature eating stinking fish in my living room. "It wasn't her fault."

"Uh huh," said Sean. "Are we going the usual way? Only you're about to miss the exit."

"Shit!" I swung Basil across two lanes of traffic and only belatedly remembered to put the indicator on as we came off the motorway onto the slip road for the A51. I waited until I was safely heading down Vicars Cross Road before speaking again. "You remember Daisy, then?"

"Who couldn't?" said Sean. "Although I've only thought about it fairly recently, which is weird. You'd think the first thing I'd have done was to come straight back to Flora's once you'd sorted things out, and ask you what the fuck had just happened. But I don't think I did. What I think," he squeezed my leg, and I raised an eyebrow at him, "what I think," he went on, not moving his hand, "is that you had something to do with me not remembering it."

"That's ridiculous," I said, as we pulled up to a set of traffic lights. I carefully didn't look across at him. "What on earth could I do to affect your memory?" The lights changed to green, and I turned off onto Christleton Road. Another right turn and I was on Spital Walk, as the ordnance survey map had informed me I would. I pulled Basil into a space alongside the canal and cut the engine. Then I turned to look at Sean. "Kiss me?" he said.

"What the fuck?" I spluttered. "What makes you think I'm going to kiss you? And you can get your hand off my bloody leg." Sean withdrew his hand, but he was smiling.

"I wasn't asking you to kiss me now," he said. "I meant that I think that's how you affected my memory. By kissing me."

"Well, that would be one hell of a power to have," I said, covering my floundering by making a point of undoing my seat belt and opening the car door. "It all sounds very far-fetched to me."

"Is it though?" said Sean, clearly not giving up easily. "I know you kissed me that day, Lil. I can't remember it, which is weird in itself. But I can feel it. Somehow. And then something messed with my head, and I forgot about it all until just recently."

"If that had happened," I said, "if it had happened. Which it didn't," Sean raised an eyebrow, but didn't say anything, "why on earth would you suddenly remember it months later? I can't be very good at wiping memories, if they come back eventually anyway."

Telling on yourself there, girl.

"And you can fuck right off!" I snapped. "Popping up like an eavesdropping lurker!" I belatedly realised Sean was staring at me with a concerned expression on his face. "Not you," I sighed. "I was talking to someone else." Sean looked up and down the empty road we were standing on, then back at me.

"Right," he said eventually. "Someone else. Someone I can't see. Is that someone in your head, by any chance?"

"I'm not hearing voices," I said, "before you ask. Well, okay, I am hearing voices. A voice. But it's the voice of lots of people. And it's real, before you call the men in white coats."

You're not supposed to tell him about us, said the city. **No good can come of it**.

"Well Izzy knows about you and she hasn't lost her marbles just yet, so you can just shut the fuck up. Sorry," this was to Sean, "it's a pain in the fucking arse some days. Are you listening to me?"

"Yes," said Sean hurriedly, "of course I'm listening!" He walked around the car to stand next to me and tried to catch hold of my hand. I snatched it away.

"That wasn't to you," I said. "Not the last bit. It really is a pain in the arse, though."

"It certainly sounds like it," said Sean. To my amazement, he looked...amused? Tolerant, at least. And he wasn't running very quickly in the opposite direction, which is what I'd have done had I been human and facing this sort of behaviour from a friend who was strange at the best of times. "Dare I ask who it is that's being so annoying?"

"Best not," I said. "It'll only make me sound absolutely unhinged."

Like anyone would notice a difference.

"If you're not going to be of any practical use," I muttered, "then you can shut the fuck up entirely."

"Not to me?" Sean definitely looked amused now.

"Not to you," I agreed. "Right, I need to go sort some things out. You okay wandering on your own for a bit?"

"I'll be fine," said Sean. "Going to head over to the amphitheatre, I think. Thought I'd check out the atmosphere." He winked. "Maybe I could set a book there. All about a strange woman who talks to the voices in her head."

"If you do that," I said, "I will expect higher royalties. And possibly a witness protection programme." I locked the car and squinted down the canal. "I really don't know how long I'm going to be. Shall I just call you when I'm done?" If I was wrong and Jonathan wasn't there, I might be at the amphitheatre myself before Sean even got there. Jonathan had told me he was trapped, but not how or by whom. My money was on Liam—it seemed like just the sort of manipulative crap he'd pull on someone. But why would he need Jonathan? His determination to win me over, I could understand—he needed me to keep control of the netherworld in order to feel secure, even in his own territory. Mostly because Ivo Laithlind was definitely going to try to destroy him at some point. Ivo would have spent eternity peacefully and properly dead if it hadn't been for Liam disturbing his burial mound all those centuries ago. The legends had come true, and Ivo had risen from the grave in order to defend his country from the invaders. That Ivo was himself originally an invader seemed to be lost on all of them. Even Eadric—the only one who could claim British lineage as far back as anyone could find—was descended from noblemen who veered between loyalty to the crown and the marauding Danes, depending on who seemed the more powerful at the time. My theory was that both Eadric and Ivo's antagonism towards Liam was mostly based simply on him having been the last of the three to arrive on British shores. It was basically like a village that considers 'incomers' to be anyone who hasn't lived there for at least thirty years, just on an epic scale.

"You do whatever you need to do," said Sean. "I'm in no rush."

"Okay," I said, but I didn't sound as confident as I'd have liked. "Could you put the car keys in your bag?" I'd had enough experience of this sort of thing to know I might well drop everything at some point and, whist I could live without a phone, I'd long lost Basil's spare keys.

"Course," said Sean, holding his hand out. I lobbed them towards him, and he caught them neatly before tucking them into the satchel he always carries. "At least now I know you have to come back for me," he said.

"I won't abandon you in the wilds of Chester," I promised. "And I definitely won't get on any fairground rides." Our last attempt at spending time together had ended with me falling off a carousel horse and into a time slip, because that is the sort of shit that happens in my world. "But I really might be quite a while."

"I'll wait as long as it takes. See you later!" He grinned and gave me a wave, then turned and headed off towards the city centre. Why had it taken my literal death for men to start declaring their eternal loyalty? Both Liam and Ivo had already firmly signalled their determination to wait forever for me to choose them, and now Sean was at it. *I could have had a much more interesting love life when I was alive*, I grumbled to myself.

You probably weren't as interesting then, said the city. **Or as useful**.

Cheers, I said, setting off down the towpath. *And there was me thinking it was my innate charm and sparkling personality.*

That as well, of course. Famed for your charm.

Are you going to be useful, I said, *or just lurk there winding me up?*

You already know where you are heading.

"Be nice to have some confirmation whether it's the right thing to do," I muttered, half to myself.

There is no use in second-guessing yourself, Lilith. A pause. **You are the only one who has to live with your conscience, therefore also the only one who can make your decisions.**

But what if I make things worse? Eadric and the others have left Chester alone for centuries, I went on, *what if I stir something up that shouldn't be bloody stirred?*

Then you will no doubt deal with the consequences in your usual inimitable way.

It was only a short walk to where I thought I might find Jonathan Hulls. I'd spent some time going through lists of Chester's notable buildings before leaving Liverpool. I thought wherever it was would probably be connected to industry, because of what Joe Williamson had said about Jonathan being an engineer. It also had to be isolated enough for the general public not to notice potentially weird behaviour in and around it. We get away with a certain level of strangeness in Liverpool because most of us look enough like average humans to go relatively unnoticed. Plus—well, it's Liverpool. That city is so used to oddities and outsiders that aliens could land in Clayton Square and the worst that would happen is they'd maybe get their spaceship clamped. Its occupants would have been dragged off to the pub for a good chat and some photies within five minutes of them stepping a single grey-skinned foot on Scouse soil. I thought the people of Chester might not be quite so blasé. So, somewhere tucked out of sight. Old, and connected to engineering or industry. There was only one place that fit that very specific bill, and I was standing right outside it.

The Steam Mill towers over the Shropshire Union Canal, where it runs alongside the imaginatively titled Canal Side. The version that still stands today dates back to around 1819, but the mill's first incarnation was built in 1785. And the earlier mill contained something that would have been the height of engineering grandeur at the time—a 'Boulton and Watt' steam engine. The building went on to house one of the country's first ever automated flour mills. So yeah, I could see Jonathan liking it here. I had a slight problem, though. The mill was in the process of being refurbished and turned into the sort of office spaces that have on-site gyms and open meeting spaces and tiny partitioned cubicles that make the occupants want to throw themselves through the nearest historically accurate uPVC window. I was pretty sure it wouldn't affect any ghostly occupants—although I'd pay good money to be a fly on the wall that Jonathan walked through into a room filled with reluctant blue-sky thinkers—but it was definitely going to affect my chances of getting in without drawing attention to myself. There was scaffolding surrounding most of the lower half of the main mill building, and a gaggle of workmen stood drinking coffee from Costa takeout cups while a man in a suit stood next to them, staring forlornly at a clipboard. I leaned casually against the wall and held my phone to my ear as though I was taking a call. Where would I be if I were based in an old industrial building? I held the phone in front of me and turned the camera on, switching it to selfie mode so it gave me a very unflattering view up my own nose. Doing my best to ignore the fact that I really probably should at least put some mascara on occasionally to avoid the piggy-eyed look I was currently sporting, I angled the view upwards in order to see above my head. The steam mill tower was huge and forbidding, and mostly built out of perfectly flat bricks that—from this angle, at least—appeared to be unhelpfully lacking in foot or handholds. Then I switched the phone off, put it in my pocket, and walked briskly off. Three strides took me round the side of the building and yup—there were the scaffolding ladders, zig-zagging up the mill's main tower. There wasn't anyone else in sight, and I wasn't going to get a better chance. Before I could bottle it, I hopped the laughably low portable fencing that was apparently supposed to stop people trespassing. I'd have more chance of not being spotted if I raced up at full speed, but that risked me knocking the entire scaffolding rig down as I did so. Being as careful as possible, I loped up the chain of ladders until I got to where the scaffolding ended just underneath the top floor. There was a window just above my head, and one section was pushed open to allow fresh air into the sterile interior of the newly refurbished mill. I jumped up and caught the windowsill with one hand, then swung like a monkey until I'd built up enough impetus to swing my legs up. Unfortunately, just as I was about to launch myself upwards, the works foreman came round the corner at street level and looked up.

"Oi!" he yelled. "What the hell are you doing?" Shit. I gave one last swing with my legs and threw myself bodily up at the window. Unfortunately, I was overenthusiastic in my panic and went straight through one of the closed sections of the window. As I scrabbled to my feet inside the building in a puddle of glass shards, I could hear shouting increasing below me and looked around for a possible escape route.

"In here!" called a familiar voice from the end of the corridor. I swung around to find Jonathan Hulls peering around a solid cast iron door of the type more usually found on old steam ships. The Premier Inn down on Albert Dock back in Liverpool has several sets of doors just like it, from when the building was still a functioning dock warehouse. No one's allowed to change the internal layout because it's a listed building, so the hotel chain has settled for building what is, in essence, a collection of modular rooms that have simply been wedged inside the available space. And there's no point putting money into new doors and stairwells when you're already well supplied with an entire industrial revolution's-worth of the blessed things, all made to last many centuries. Jonathan pushed the door a fraction further open. "Come on," he urged, "before they see us!" I ran through the doorway, the shouts of angry construction workers getting louder behind me. Jonathan pulled the door closed behind us with a heavy thud. He then pressed his hand against a small square of metal within the door itself, and I heard what sounded like the noise of several deadbolts sliding themselves across within the frame. The sound of my pursuers faded away to nothing. "We're safe now," said Jonathan, turning around to face me with a smile. "Welcome to my humble abode, Lilith." His wig was even more unkempt than the last time I'd seen him, the random tufts sticking out making me suspect a family of mice had possibly set up home on his head. Even as I thought it, a pair of tiny black button eyes popped up above Jonathan's left ear and gazed beadily at me.

"That's, erm..." I gestured to where the mouse was now sitting up and washing itself, "I mean, there's..."

"Oh, don't mind Horace," said Jonathan brightly, patting his hair. "We've been friends a good while now. I don't disturb him and in return, he keeps on top of the follicular side of things."

"Quite literally," I said faintly. That certainly explained Finn spotting a rodent on my fire escape on the night Katja was killed.

"Well of course," beamed Jonathan. "I do like things to be straightforward. Black and white, as it were. Anyway," he swung himself around with enthusiastic speed, forcing Horace to cling tightly to Jonathan's ear with his tiny paws, "what do you think?" He gazed around the enormous room as though he himself was seeing it for the first time and was completely in awe. "Isn't it marvellous?" It was certainly something, although I wasn't entirely sure what. The top floor of the Steam Mill was one gigantic open space, with a high vaulted ceiling that was almost entirely glass. Cold, grey light illuminated a shabby collection of sofas and armchairs, all of which appeared to have been placed entirely at random. The most well-used chair sat facing outwards in front of an enormous window, presumably to give its occupant the best view of suburban city life going on below. "I sit there to watch the boats," said

Jonathan, following my gaze. "I like to think about where they've come from and where they might be going."

"Do you go out much?" I asked. "Apart from when you've visited me in Liverpool, I mean."

"Oh no," said Jonathan hurriedly. "No, no, no. He doesn't know I can do that. I'm not supposed to leave the mill, you see. It's not safe."

"What isn't safe?" I asked. "And who's this 'he' you keep talking about?"

"Come and say hello to Fred," he said, ignoring the question. "She'll be so pleased to meet you. We haven't had company in a long while." Jonathan took my arm and led me to where a corner had been closed off with a tall room divider. It comprised three wooden panels, each decorated with ornately carved birds. Even to my untrained eye, it looked like it was probably worth more than the entire contents of my flat. "Fred!" he called, "we've got a visitor! Isn't that nice?" He gestured me forward.

"You can go first," I said.

Jonathan frowned. "There's nothing to fear," he said. "Fred's been a friend of mine for a long time. Haven't you, Fred?" There was a muffled response from behind the panels that sounded very much like someone was telling Jonathan to fuck off, but couldn't be bothered to open their mouth properly.

"Yeah, but you would say that, wouldn't you?" I pointed out. "There could be someone waiting to chop my head off round that corner, for all I know." Jonathan looked affronted, but just as he opened his mouth to speak, a woman appeared from behind the divider and stood with her hands belligerently wedged on her hips.

"I'm not sure I'd describe you as a friend," said Fred, "when one considers the circumstances." She appeared to be in her late thirties and was healthy and well-scrubbed, as though she spent a lot of time outdoors. "How do you do?" she said, reaching a hand out towards me. I took it and she gave mine a reassuring squeeze. "I'm no danger to you, Lilith," she said. "What these men haven't fully considered is the danger we might pose to them."

"It's not my fault you're here," said Jonathan, "as well you know. You might as well shout at the moon for help, as ask it of me."

"I do shout at the moon," said Fred, "and you tell me to be quiet."

"It scares Horace," said Jonathan defensively. "He doesn't like loud noises."

Fred rolled her eyes at him. This was clearly an old argument. "Come sit down," she said to me, "and tell me the news from Lerpul."

"They call it Liverpool now," said Jonathan. "Changed a long time ago, actually."

"I wouldn't know," said Fred sharply, "would I? On account of how I've been stuck here all these endless centuries. It's about time someone filled me in on what I've missed." She gestured at me to join her behind the room divider. When I stepped tentatively around, I discovered a compact but cosy living area laid out in front of one of the bigger of the side windows. Shelves were lined up along the end wall, each of them stacked with ancient-looking books. The divider formed the opposite boundary and in-between sat a large, well-upholstered chaise longue beside a massive armchair with cushions that were so squashed from overuse that they appeared to be slowly melting off the chair frame. A large embroidery frame was set up next to it, with a needle trailing yarn stabbed viciously into the middle of the canvas. "Keeps me busy," said Fred, nodding towards the frame. "And I get a lot of satisfaction out of designing my own patterns." I stepped forward in order to look more closely. It looked very much like a panel taken from the Bayeux Tapestry, but there was something slightly wrong in the way it was laid out. "I've used a bit of poetic license," said Fred. At first glance, it appeared to be a reproduction of the scene in which William the Conqueror is sitting under an awning with his half-brothers Odo and Robert, ahead of the Battle of Hastings. But when I looked more closely, I could see that rather than openly holding a sword as he did in the original, Robert had it concealed behind his back. And instead of the blankly amiable gaze portrayed in the Bayeux tapestry, Robert's eyes were narrow with concentration and focused on William. For his part, Odo's position was much as I remembered—sitting with an open and unthreatening posture and appearing to gesture to William in some form of explanation. A small object behind Odo turned out to be the stitched representation of a poison bottle. I could feel Fred's gaze on me as I peered carefully at her handiwork. She'd designed it as a single scene and rather than the usual scrolling text and imagery above and below the main panels, it was framed with images of what I assumed were Williams' soldiers. Every last one of them had been killed in one of many different ways. Some had knives sticking out of their throats, others were shown with arrows poking out of various soft bits of their anatomy. One poor unfortunate lay on the floor with an arrow in his neck, a sword in his stomach and another man standing over him with an enormous boulder, apparently about to drop it on his face. "I was quite angry that week," said Fred. I looked up, and she shrugged. "Got to take it out on something. Anyway, if you don't mind, I've got an evisceration I'd like to get finished today." With that, she dropped back down into the chair, pulled the tapestry frame in front of her and went back to stabbing the fabric with efficient fury.

∽

"You need to tell me who it is who's got you trapped here, Jonathan." I was sitting cross-legged on the floor, my back against the bare brick wall. The sun had come out fractionally too late to warm the place up, but it lit our surroundings brightly enough to show the cracks in the roof glass and every tiny cobweb in the corners of the bare room. Jonathan was perching on a rickety chair at his drawing table. Horace occasionally popped up and looked around, as if checking whether I was still there. Fred was doing a very good impression of being asleep in her chair. "I can't help if I don't know who I'm dealing with."

"I can't let you take that risk, Lilith." Jonathan spoke quietly. "If I don't tell you who it is, you can't go after him. And if you don't go after him, you might be safe. For a while, at least. He takes my thoughts and ideas, and he twists them up and uses them against me. He's a thief, Lilith. A thief of the worst kind. He steals my dreams and turns them into weapons. Not guns, or bombs," he looked up at me, "but just as dangerous. More so, in fact."

"How?" I asked. "And, probably more importantly, why?"

Jonathan gave me a sad smile. "The 'why' is easy enough, don't you think? Some men desire nothing more than power. Over other men, over women, over entire countries. It's all he's ever wanted, from the moment he stepped upon these shores so many centuries past. So very many centuries." His voice was wistful. "It must make life easier, I think," he went on, "being focused on one thing above all others. Power is all he wants, and he doesn't care how long it takes to acquire it. Nor does it matter who gets in his way." I sighed. Liam O'Twatting-Connor had a lot to answer for. Why did it have to be him I bumped into by accident in the Duck & Swagger that night? Why couldn't it have been some other random immortal I'd indulged in a well-overdue fling with? If it had been someone else, I might have been in a perfectly happy 'friends with benefits' situation by now. Instead, I was being given a list of all the reasons I'd made a really bad decision to even get involved with Liam in the first place.

"He was away for a long time," I pointed out. "He can't be that bothered about power if he was happy to leave it to others all that time."

"He wasn't away," said Jonathan with a rueful smile. "He's never been away, Lilith. He lurks. Like a sewer rat. Always in the shadows, always just a small step away from everything that's happening. It was him who told me about your own arrival in our world."

"Hang on," I frowned, "I thought it was my...arrival that woke things up? Like a sleeping dragon, or something like that."

"He was never unaware of what was going on. He just had to bide his time."

"For what?" I asked, although I already knew the answer. When I got hold of Liam, I was going to kick him into the middle of the next week. Whilst wearing the pointiest boots I could find.

"For you," said Jonathan. He looked thoughtful. "It isn't as romantic as it sounds, though, I don't think."

"None of it's romantic," I said. "It's all bloody stupid and confusing and has been since the day I woke up dead."

"What I mean," said Jonathan, "is that it didn't have to be you in particular. And it doesn't matter who wears the crown, come to that. Not so long as someone does."

"I'm never wearing that crown again," I said firmly, "so the whole thing's moot. It's got ideas above its station, that thing."

"The wearing is metaphorical," smiled Jonathan. "The crown is yours, and always will be."

"Unless someone steals it," I said, remembering Katja's sticky end on the fire escape.

"I wouldn't like to be the person who dared try to take the crown from you," said Jonathan. "It wouldn't take that sort of thing kindly, I don't think." I was about to point out to Jonathan that the crown wasn't sentient and therefore couldn't make its own decisions, but then I remembered the feeling it gave me when I touched it and kept my mouth shut. "But people forget the role that chance plays in all our lives," he went on. "In the destiny of kingdoms and slums, rich and poor. It didn't have to be you, Lilith." Jonathan gazed at me with a lopsided smile on his face. "It just had to be the right person at the right time."

"Well, that's just marvellous," I said. "Not only am I lumbered with the eternal guardianship of potentially the entire country, you're now telling me the stories about it being my destiny are actually bollocks? That it was entirely accidental and, I dunno," I sighed, "it might have been Izzy instead? She could have fallen off the manky steps outside her flat and cracked her head. It's happened before." Izzy really had come an absolute cropper a year or two before I died, when the pair of us had a rare night out and stumbled drunkenly back to her flat in the early hours. She'd tripped over the handbag she put down whilst fumbling her keys into the lock and split her head open on the pavement. But that had led to nothing more dramatic than a sudden sobering up (me) and a long wait in A&E for stitches (her).

"Yes," agreed Jonathan, "that might have happened. But it didn't. It was you who fell, Lilith. It doesn't matter whether it really was an accident, because those involved had no idea of the weight of history they were about to unleash. That was a secret for the land and its many rulers, not for bit actors in your own play. Shakespeare would have liked you, I think."

"Please tell me he's still around?" I squinted up at Jonathan. "Cos I want to give him a bloody good kicking. All those stupid sentences that are complicated enough for English teachers to still be lecturing them centuries later." Strangely, for someone who ended up doing a history degree, I'd never got on with English Lit at school. It all seemed too much like academics turning fun stories into instruments of mental torture.

"I don't think so," said Jonathan uncertainly, "although I'm not sure I would know, even if he was. We were a century or more apart and it wasn't until a long time after his supposed death that he began developing his current reputation. I've read some of his work over the many years since, of course."

"Do you remember being alive?"

"I don't think so," said Jonathan. He frowned. "Some little things, possibly. Eating cheese that turned out to have maggots in it. That's a clear memory. And the death of my dog, who got himself caught in a poacher's trap and had to be put out of his misery by my father. I miss my dog." I wasn't enjoying Jonathan's reminiscences as much as I'd thought I might, but he was on a roll now. "Sometimes I think I remember a place," he said, "but it's all so fleeting! I'm afraid, Lilith, that I am no longer sure what's real and what isn't."

"Can you remember what you did for a living?" I asked. It felt like one of those tests the paramedics do to check you're in control of your faculties. Although I very much doubted Jonathan could identify the current Prime Minister. Come to think of it, I wasn't sure I'd know the answer myself. Leaders come and go, and even newborn immortals rapidly realise that human politics is far too irrelevant a subject to waste much energy on.

"Oh yes," said Jonathan enthusiastically, "I made things!" Still self-aware, then. "So many ideas, all written neatly and stored away for the day I could find a proper patron." He glanced towards the shelf where Horace appeared to be having a dust bath in the shredded paper. "So many ideas," he said quietly. "I was too far ahead of my time, I think."

"Perhaps you could get them going again," I said. "People like inventors more, these days."

"Oh no," he smiled. "Bless you, though. My ideas would be rather outdated now, I think. The ones he stole from me were a very long time ago and all he did was to use them against me." I'd noticed Jonathan was careful not to say Liam's name out loud, as though it might tempt him to appear. Beetlejuice, Beetlejuice, Beetlejuice, I thought. All I needed right now was a red lace wedding dress, and we'd be sorted. "I was very proud of an engine I designed, mind. It was as precious to me as any child could ever have been. I had the idea it would transform shipping, you see. But now," he waved an arm towards the windows overlooking the canal and the streets beyond, "well. Everyone seems to have their own personal engine these days."

"Do you have any children? I mean, did you?"

"Gosh no," he said, "I didn't really see the point of them. Too busy inventing things. Children would have impeded my work. I lived with my parents, I think? For a very long time." He got up and brushed himself down, as if he didn't already look like Worzel Gummidge. "Anyway, we're all here now," he said brightly, "and that's all the family anyone needs. Don't you agree, Fred?" I'd almost forgotten Fred was even in the room, she was so quiet. I looked over to where she lay on the chaise, still as a statue. Eventually one eye blinked open, and she gave a heavy sigh.

"I could do with you inventing a way to get some of that newfangled electricity up here," she said. "That would be more entertaining than any kind of family, I should imagine."

"There's no power up here?" I looked around the cavernous room and noticed for the first time that it was missing anything that looked remotely like an electrical switch or socket. "What do you do for heat and light?"

"We've no real need of either," said Fred, pulling herself upright, "so it isn't an issue. I would like to see how it works, though."

"What do you do with your time?" I asked. Fred pulled a face.

"A whole heap of nothing," she said, "apart from the needlework. And obviously I can only do that when there's enough light. Bored, bored, bored. Although," she brightened up, "I did spend some of the nineteen-twenties learning how people speak in the modern world. I'm from a time before modern language," she said, seeing my expression. "What I would call English isn't very much like the version you use."

"The great vowel shift," I said. "Same words, different pronunciation."

"Well," said Fred, "that and the fact I spoke in what you'd know as Old English. Not this newfangled version with its skiffle and rocket ships."

"Ummm," I said, "I think your information might be a bit out of date. If you don't mind me saying."

"Huh," said Fred, "I thought as much. When's the last time you brought any newspapers in, Jonathan?"

"Not for a good few decades," he admitted. "I tend to forget."

"How often do you go outside?" I asked him. "Couldn't you go to the shops occasionally?"

"How would this," Jonathan waved a hand up and down himself, "work in a modern setting?" I gazed at Jonathan's ancient, flea-bitten outfit and had to admit he had a point. Horace peeked out from his nest in the wig, as if for emphasis. Something else occurred to me.

"Are you a ghost?" I asked Jonathan, "or a revenant? Or something else."

"He's annoying, is what he is," offered Fred, but I ignored her.

"I'm both, I think?" said Jonathan. "Or perhaps neither. Who knows?" he shrugged. "I haven't met many others of our kind, so I'm sure I don't know what's normal and what isn't."

"I'm not sure normal exists as a concept in our world," said Fred. "What is normal, anyway?"

"You'd been to Liverpool before the day I met you," I said to Jonathan, changing the subject before it all got way too deep. "You said as much."

"I'm sure I don't know what you're talking about," he said apologetically.

"Yes, you do," I insisted. "You told me the city was protective over its people, and you knew it from personal experience. So," I raised my eyebrows at him, "what happened?"

"Yes, Jonathan," said Fred, "what did happen?" She folded her arms and gazed at him. "I remember you disappearing for almost an entire moon cycle, many years ago. I thought you'd gone forever, and I'd been abandoned to go slowly mad, up here in this stupid tower," she banged her heel down on the floor for emphasis, "but then you suddenly reappeared one night."

"Did I?" said Jonathan faintly. "I'm sure I don't remember."

"Well I'm sure I do remember," said Fred. "I also remember you had the fear of almighty God upon you when you got back here. You never have told me what really happened."

Jonathan shuffled his feet, pink spots of embarrassment flushing his cheeks. "If you must know," he said finally, "I thought I might seek help from the wild man up in the tower. But the birds spotted me and oh!" he put a hand up to his face as if it still frightened him all this time later, "what vicious little beasts they are!"

"What wild man?" I asked. "And what tower?"

"The two towers," said Jonathan, "you know them, of course. They hold the birds."

"The Liver Building?" Jonathan nodded. "You went to see Eadric?" Another nod. I knew enough of Eadric's fairytale history to understand the reference. There are still people to this day who are daft enough to think Eadric Silverton will go galloping across the Shropshire hills if ever the country is in serious danger. As if that man would ever leave Liverpool for long enough to go hacking in the shire. "How do you do it?"

Jonathan kept shuffling. The sole was loose on one of his shoes and it made a really annoying flapping noise each time. "I don't know," he said eventually, "and that's the truth. I used to write everything down in the ledgers but, well," he shrugged, "Horace likes to sleep in them and I haven't the heart to tell him no." I glanced across at the shelves laden with paperwork and Horace popped his head up right on cue. By the flurry of confetti that accompanied his appearance, I assumed Jonathan's records had been turned into mouse bedding long ago.

"How long has Horace been with you?"

Jonathan squinted over at the mouse and then back at me. "A few seasons," he said, "I think? I don't follow the years too well these days, I'm afraid. But Horace here has definitely seen me through a couple of winters."

"So, you only lost the paperwork recently?"

Jonathan looked briefly confused, but then his face cleared into a beaming smile. "Oh no," he said brightly, "they've been gone centuries. Many Horaces back."

"So Horace isn't always the same mouse?"

"Oh my lord no," laughed Jonathan, "how could that even be?

Everyone knows mice only live for a brief time, Lilith. Did you not have an education?" His face fell. "I was rather hoping that had changed," he said. "I never understood why it's only the boys deserving of the learning."

"Girls get educated," I said, "don't worry. And I know mice don't live long. But some of my closest friends are several hundred years old, so immortal mice wouldn't be the strangest thing I've dealt with."

"How are the cats?" Jonathan asked suddenly. "I've forgotten to ask you about them! I do like the cats."

"You knew about the cats?" Jonathan nodded. "The big cats?" Another nod.

"The cats were an accepted thing, when I was a boy," he said. "We all grew up being warned not to go too far into the woods alone. Mama said it was because there was a witch who lived in a hut on legs deep in the woods, and if she caught me, she'd boil me up for broth. But I knew it was really because she was worried about the cats. I honestly don't know why she had such concerns. They were lovely beasts."

"You met them?"

"Oh, yes!" said Jonathan. "I even had favourites—always the black ones. My friend David said the spotted ones were the better looking—he thought they were perhaps related to real wild cats from the jungle, you see. I told him they were very different, but he was never swayed. Said they must have swum over from Africa. I ask you!" He chuckled to himself.

"I've got one of the black ones living with me at the moment," I said. "Perhaps you could visit him sometime."

"I saw him!" Jonathan brightened up. "Oh," his face fell, "I was going to keep that secret!"

"The fact you were on my doorstep the night Katja died?" I raised my eyebrows at him. "Can I ask why you were there, or is it going to be more quantum bollocks that I really don't want to think about?"

"I was going to tell you," said Jonathan quietly. "About what's been going on here. I was going to tell you everything and hang the consequences."

"You can tell me now," I said. "Get it off your chest, spill the beans, all that jazz. It'll make a change for me to actually have some idea of what's really going on."

Jonathan shook his head. "Too dangerous here," he said. "Far too dangerous."

"You can come to Liverpool whenever you want," I said. "Talk to me there."

"As if he'd dare," snorted Fred, before Jonathan could answer. "As if he ever does anything other than sit around daydreaming over his stupid drawings."

"That's not very nice," I started, but Fred was up and out of her chair and stalking over to us.

"I have been stuck in this building for centuries, Lilith," she said. "Centuries of watching humanity growing across my land like the parasites we all truly are. Centuries of being locked up and ignored because apparently men are still terrified of powerful women. You need to watch yourself," she fixed me with a steely glare, "or you'll be locked away the same as me."

"We're not in the Dark Ages now," I said. "Women are allowed to be powerful in their own right."

"Are you sure about that?" said Fred. "Because from where I'm standing, it looks very much as though you're being taken for an absolute fool."

"By who?" I got to my feet, indignant now. "I'm well aware of who my enemies are, thank you very much."

"I said the same." Fred's voice was bitter. "Back when I took over from my father and thought I could change the world. But I had a brother, didn't I? So he took the credit whilst I did the work. Mercia considered me their Queen back then, you know. But the Saxons thought me nothing more than my brother's sister, and theirs is the history people remember." She tilted her head as she gazed at me. "It doesn't matter which history gets remembered, Lilith," she said. "But you have to ensure you are never trodden down by it." A little tinkling bell of recognition was ringing in the back of my head as my mind sifted through what I could remember of mediaeval history.

"I know who you are," I said slowly, as the jigsaw pieces finally slotted into place. Fred, I ask you. "You're Alfred's daughter."

Fred grinned. "Finally, she gets it! Aethelflaed, Lady of the

Mercians," she dropped into a mock curtsey, "at your service." She looked up at me and winked. "Ma'am."

Our Lady, Who Art In Mercia

Our Lady, Who Art In Mercia

Aethelflaed started out in life a mere princess, in a time when being a princess was a reasonably common vocation. And not a bad one, considering the other options would have been servant or peasant. Daughter of Alfred the supposedly Great, she had nothing much planned for her life other than wafting around draughty castles in a dramatically mediaeval line of fancy frocks. But Alfred had an approach to child rearing that was unusual for the time, and insisted on his daughter having the same education as her brothers. She would achieve more than all her other siblings combined, yet was all but written out of history. I vaguely remembered Kitty watching a television series in which Aethelflaed was portrayed as submissive to her younger brother, Edward of Wessex, presumably because too many people still consider a strong-minded and successful woman only acceptable in the role of backbone to a man's achievements. Changing history for the sake of drama has always been a pet peeve of mine. Like it's not already dramatic enough as it is? I'm just waiting for someone to write my biography and I'll be haunting their asses until they take the dramatic fakery out.

Not that anyone's ever going to want to write a book about me, I sighed to myself. *It's not as though anyone would believe it.*

Don't bet on that, murmured the city. I ignored it and gazed across at Fred, who had apparently decided to give me time to let this new information settle in my head, then sat back down. She met my gaze with a crooked smile.

"Not what you expected to find in Chester, I'd imagine," she said.

I blew out my cheeks. "You could say that," I said. "Although given what else has been going on this last couple of years, I'm not sure why it's come as such a surprise."

"How well do you know your history?" Fred asked.

"Erm," I was almost too embarrassed to admit it. "I have a degree in it. Not that it's proved much use so far."

"I bet you studied the Romans at school," she said. "Then the Tudors, then nothing until the Industrial Revolution and the Victorians. Aah," she sighed, "the Victorians. I do so wish I'd been able to see some of that for myself."

"You mean you didn't?" I was surprised. Fred had, by my calculations, been in Chester for more than a thousand years. And the Victorians definitely made themselves known in Chester. "Why not?"

"I've been a prisoner all this time," she said, her face impassive. "First in a section of the old walls—which were built on my orders, by the way, me not realising they would become my own prison—and then up in here."

"Haven't you tried to escape?"

"Once." She shook her head. "Got as far as the door and felt myself sort of..." she trailed off. "Thinning out? I don't really know how else to describe it. There was nothing to stop me from leaving—there never has been. But if I take so much as a single step over the boundary, it's as though I'm breaking apart. Not emotionally," she smiled. "You learn to be very much in control of your emotions when you've lived the sort of life I have. Physically, I mean. It's as though I truly am a ghost, and the molecules of whatever make me, well, *me*," she shrugged, "start spinning away from each other. As though I might be blown away in the breeze."

I gazed at her stupidly, the whole story so fantastical that I was beginning to wonder if I was dreaming. Me, the woman who never sleeps and lives in a fantasy world as it is. "So, I stay here," she shrugged. "Where I can, at least, watch over my city."

"How does it work?" I asked. "Surely between us we could find some way of reversing it?" This was my territory, for fuck's sake. How *dare* Liam keep people prisoner right under my nose? "This isn't wizardry," I said, "and revenants can't do magic. So whatever trick has been used to keep you trapped here, it's got to be something I can do as well. And if I can do it, I can undo it."

～

"Is it anything I can help with?" said a voice from behind me. I was up and out of my chair as fast as I've ever moved, spinning round to find Ivo Laithlind standing less than two feet away. I could have reached out to touch him without even stretching. "Afternoon, Red," he said, as though we did this sort of thing all the time. "Need a hand?"

"Not unless you know how to undo ancient curses," I said. I was so relieved to see him I didn't even bother with my usual bitching. If anyone was going to help me out of a tight spot, it was Ivo. I could live with being made to feel grateful for once, if it meant getting Fred out of the tower and me out of Chester, hopefully for good. For his part, Jonathan had run into the furthest corner of the room, where he was hunching himself up as tightly as possible, presumably hoping no one would notice a large man in a wig sitting on the floor with a mouse on his head.

"Oh, but that would be Mr Hulls's department," said Ivo, turning to Jonathan. "Wouldn't it?"

"I can't remember," whispered Jonathan. "I can't remember how I did it!"

"This was *your* doing?" I stepped towards Jonathan, and he cowered. On top of his head, I was sure Horace was waving a tiny mousey fist at me. "It was you who trapped Fred?"

"I was forced to do it," said Jonathan. "I didn't want to!"

"Hang on," I said, "you died in the seventeen-hundreds?" Jonathan nodded. "And Fred here was trapped long before that."

"I most certainly was," said Fred. "And I never knew who did it, nor why. But it can't have been Jonathan," she went on, "because he didn't arrive until much later."

"But you can travel through the time-slips," I said to Jonathan, "can't you?"

"He made me!" wailed Jonathan. "He made me go back and I was scared, and I lost my Horace. I don't know why he did it," he looked up at me with pleading eyes, "but I promise you, it wasn't my choice."

"What would be the point of trapping someone in a city for so long?" I asked Ivo. "And apart from that, do you have any idea how to fix it? Because if you've got any more secret talents I don't yet know about, now's the time to show them to the class." Just then, a shadow passed over the roof. I was just wondering what my chances were of being picked off by a vulture—which wouldn't have been the weirdest thing to have happened since I'd died—when something exploded through the glass and hit the floor in front of me. The surprise visitor dusted himself down before standing up and grinning.

"I thought you might appreciate some company," said Liam O'Connor.

Everyone stood frozen for a split second—and then all hell broke loose. Jonathan was shrieking in panic, Horace clinging on for dear life on top of his wig. Liam didn't bother with niceties—he picked up Jonathan's drawing table and threw it straight at Ivo, who ducked. The heavy wooden table sailed right through one of the enormous windows and the noise of it crashing to the ground was rapidly followed by screaming from the street outside. Fred ran to the broken window to look out and then dropped to the floor, presumably to avoid being blamed for any collateral injuries. Liam stalked around the edge of the room whilst Ivo circled on the spot, watching him carefully. "What the *fuck* are you doing here?" I yelled at Liam. "You're not James sodding Bond, for fuck's sake!"

"I am *trying* to help," said Liam, not taking his eyes off Ivo. Revenants might be supernatural, but we don't have superpowers. No flying, or throwing lightning bolts out of our fingertips. At least, not without hitting the ground with a bloody great splat shortly afterwards.

We're strong though, and I wouldn't have liked to bet on who'd win in a straight fight between Liam and Ivo. Although I was apparently about to find out.

"By keeping Fred prisoner?" Liam flashed me a sharp look, but was too distracted by having to keep an eye on Ivo to answer. "Is this what you get off on, Liam O'Connor?" I yelled. "Trapping women and forcing people to do what you want?" Before he could respond, Ivo launched at him and both men went crashing into the wall. Remnants of old plaster and brick dust showered down, and I heard Horace making a squeaky sneezing noise. When I looked, Jonathan was still hunched in the corner behind me with his hands over his face like a scared little kid. Fred just looked shellshocked, alternating her panicked gaze between me and the pair of brawling idiots at the other end of the room. I needed backup, but clearly wasn't going to get it from my present company. Then my brain suddenly made one of those random connections that seem bloody obvious with hindsight but have somehow eluded you until you're right up against it. I had the stone with me—the one the little girl had given me over at the amphitheatre, and which was also presumably responsible for Flora's poltergeist infestation. I'd put it in my pocket with the vague idea of taking it back while I was in Chester, and maybe finding out who the girl really was. But now I needed to break up a fight without getting in the middle of it, and the stone would make a handy weapon. It was warm as I pulled it out of my pocket, and I had a weird sensation that it was somehow fizzing. *Come on, girl,* I thought to myself, *show me what you're made of.* I felt the power building beneath my fingertips as I considered my next move. Just then, Ivo swung Liam around by his leg and threw him into the wall with such force that I felt the entire building shudder. "You are going to bring this whole place down if you don't pack it the fuck in!" I yelled, but neither of them were listening. Okay, so I had major issues with both men, but I really didn't want to be responsible for either of them offing the other. Apart from anything else, the paperwork involved in transferring all their belongings would be enormous. And like I said, I'm not fond of admin. I threw the stone as hard as I could, aiming for the middle of the ongoing fight. I'd hoped to break an ankle or two, just enough to stop the carnage without causing major harm. Unfortunately for Liam, he launched himself towards Ivo at just the wrong moment and the stone hit him full in the temple. I heard a sickening crack as the small, innocuous pebble embedded itself in Liam O'Connor's head, and then he pitched forward onto the floor.

"Quickly," said Ivo, "come with me." He grabbed my arm and dragged me towards the door. "Before he gets back up!" I stared at where Liam lay, Fred and Jonathan both standing over him with horror-stricken expressions on their faces. Behind Fred, a glowing apparition was forming. I recognised her face even before she became fully clear, and suddenly I knew who she was.

"Fred," I said, "look behind you." I had just enough time to see Fred turning to the ghost with a look of pure shock on her face before Ivo pulled me out of the room. The door slammed behind us with a heavy thud, and we were alone.

It was a different room than the one I'd run through to find Jonathan. Ivo must have taken us through another exit that I somehow hadn't noticed. It was weirdly quiet—even more so than in Jonathan's room. I could hear muffled sounds I assumed were Jonathan and Fred dealing with whatever was going on the other side of the door, but it felt as though I was listening from a distance. "Where are we?" I asked Ivo. This room had no windows at all, but its old brick walls were topped with a full skylight that lit it from above. The sun was high in the sky now. "Shit," I said, "Sean will be wondering where I am."

"He'll wait," said Ivo. He was sitting on the floor, with his back against the wall. "We can't go out until I'm sure it's safe."

"Safe for whom?" I asked. "What about Fred and Jonathan?"

"They'll be fine," said Ivo. "They've been here for centuries. A while longer won't hurt them."

"How do you know?"

He shrugged. "When you've been around as long as I have," he said, "you learn to keep an ear to the grapevine."

"Well, I'm not waiting," I said. "I need to rescue the others."

"Who from?"

I turned and looked at him as though he'd lost his mind. "From

Liam, of course," I snapped. "They're stuck in there with him! God knows what he'll do when he comes around."

"With any luck," said Ivo mildly, "you'll have killed him permanently. And he can spend the rest of eternity burning in hell."

"You don't honestly think I might have actually killed him?" The possibility hadn't even occurred to me. "Well, that's it," I said. "I'm going back in." Ivo frowned, but didn't say anything. "Stay here then," I snapped, "I'll sort it out myself." I turned back to the door and wrenched the handle, but nothing happened. I could hear the lock mechanics clicking into place, but the door itself refused to budge. I turned to Ivo for help, but he had his eyes closed with his head resting back against the wall. Fuck him. I'd sort it out on my own. Taking a step backwards, I eyed the door to work out my aim, then launched myself at it, feet first. The heavy wood creaked, and I heard something splinter, but it stayed intact. I bounced straight back off it onto the hard concrete floor. Getting to my feet, I turned to see if Ivo had decided to make himself useful yet, but he was still determinedly ignoring me. "Aaaaargghhhh!" I yelled, using the force of my anger to propel myself forward with as much strength as I had in me. This time it worked. The centre point of the door itself splintered outwards, disappearing into the darkness. I bounced around in excitement for a few seconds, unashamedly thrilled by my own abilities. Girl power, indeed. And then it occurred to me that there should have been something on the other side of the door.

When Ivo had rescued me from Liam, we'd come through a doorway from Jonathan's room, straight into this one. But now there was nothing but darkness outside. Considering I'd knocked out most of the door, Jonathan and the others should have been right there in front of me. Even if they'd all somehow escaped, I should have been able to see the room we'd been in. I leaned forward carefully, trying to see around without making myself a target. As I put my face to the doorway, I felt a prickling down the back of my neck. Something was very wrong, but I didn't know what.

Any ideas? I asked the city. No response. *Oh, come on,* I said, *you can't leave me in the lurch right at the moment I need you!* Still nothing. I stepped back into the safety of the room, where Ivo still sat with his eyes closed.

You're back! said the city, making me jump. **We were about to panic.**

I frowned in confusion. *What do you mean?* I asked it. *I've been here all the time.*

You were here, it said, **but then you weren't. We were with you when you broke the door, but then you disappeared into thin air.**

A horrible feeling was making itself known in the pit of my stomach. I stepped forward towards the broken door and tried to look through it again. The cold was bitter against my skin and I realised I was struggling to focus. I pulled back sharply and stared in mesmerised horror at the door.

You did it again! said the city accusingly. **How are you doing that? It isn't safe to shut us out, Lilith. Who knows what might happen to us if we lost you.** A pause, then a hurried, **We were worried about you as well, of course.**

Glad to hear it, I said absentmindedly. *Let me know if I disappear again.* I went back to the door, and this time I stuck my head right through it. Or I would have, if my mind hadn't broken apart.

It was exactly as Fred had described it. My thoughts fragmented and I lost control of what I was doing, as though I was literally coming apart at a molecular level. Luckily, I fell backwards with the shock, rather than forward through the door.

Yes, said the city in what sounded suspiciously like a panicked tone, **you disappeared. We need you to stop doing that.**

I don't want to do it, I said, *something's making me. Something's keeping me—us—prisoner behind this door.*

Surely Laithlind will help you.

I have a sneaking suspicion Ivo is enjoying the entertainment. Now, tell me again. I stepped forward and, gritting my teeth, thrust my arm into the hole. Nothing happened—at least, nothing happened inside my head. My hand, however, had disappeared. I pulled it back out and stared down at it in confusion.

Tell you what?

Nothing. I put my hand back into the hole—and something grabbed it. I screamed like a hysterical banshee, and it finally spurred Ivo into action. Leaping to his feet, he grabbed me from behind and pulled hard. We both went tumbling backwards onto the floor, but I rolled and was back on my feet before he could take advantage of the situation. I'd been in a very literal tight spot with Ivo Laithlind on previous occasions and let me tell you, he is not averse to making the most of enforced proximity. He grinned as I bounced backwards away from him, and I couldn't help but smile back.

"What the fuck just happened?" I asked him.

Ivo sighed. "I'm pretty sure we're trapped," he said. "Did you feel as though you were losing your mind when you tried to get through?" I nodded. "It's the same thing that was done to Aethelflaed," he said, "all those years ago."

"Well, I'm not staying in this stupid bloody room for centuries," I snapped, "so you'd better think of a way to get us out of here."

"I don't know how to do it," he said. "Anyway, why are you suddenly so interested in Chester?" He tilted his head and looked at me curiously. "I don't recall you bothering to visit before now."

"Chester's within my territory," I pointed out. "I can come here whenever I please."

"But you don't, do you?" said Ivo. "None of you have been here for centuries. You stay up there in your fancy new city, forgetting your roots. No one likes people who forget their roots, Red."

"Oh, cut the crap," I said. Ivo's face twitched, but he didn't say anything. "You're full of hot air and prime bollocks, as per bloody usual. You don't get to stand in *my* territory and criticise how I do things, Ivo Laithlind. How is Fred being held here? More to the point, how are *we* being held here?"

He shrugged. "Time doesn't have the same meaning when you live as long as we do. You'll realise that yourself, eventually."

"Oh, I think time has exactly the same meaning," I said. "No matter how long you've been around. I think most people start losing their tiny little minds after a while. Even the brightest, sharpest minds that ever existed get fuzzy around the edges after a while. All those memories jostling for attention. It gets confusing in there eventually, don't you think?" Ivo's eyes narrowed, but he didn't say anything. I sighed and slumped to the floor. "When I find out who's done this," I said, "I am going to kick their stupid arse into the middle of next fucking week."

"That's more like it, Red," said Ivo. "That's my girl."

Prisoner Cell Block WTF

"You know," said Ivo, "this is a bit like one of those romance novels." He'd gone back to leaning his head against the wall with his eyes closed. By my reckoning, we'd been trapped for at least two hours. Two sodding hours, and I already felt as though I was losing what was left of my marbles. How on earth did someone like Fred cope with being stuck like this for centuries?

"In what way is this," I waved my arm round the room, "romantic? In any shape or form?" Ivo smiled and opened his eyes to look at me.

"A...friend of mine liked to read them," he said. "The sort of book literary types consider trashy, but are usually far more enjoyable to read than the more worthy stuff. People getting stuck in lifts together and having to make the best of it. That sort of thing."

"If you think romance is even remotely on my mind right now, then you are even more insane than I thought."

"What else is there to do?" He opened his eyes a fraction to look at me, a lazy smile on his face. Gods, but that man was as annoying as he was hot. And Ivo Laithlind was *hot* stuff, if you know what I'm saying.

"I thought we might try to escape," I said. "That would be the obvious course of action, no?"

"I don't think we can," said Ivo. He got to his feet and started pacing. "I've seen this done before. Only once or twice—it's a rare thing."

"What happened to the ones you know about?"

"As far as I know," he said, "they're still stuck."

"Did you know about Fred?"

"Yes," said Ivo, turning to look me in the eye, "I did."

"And you just left her here to rot."

"I'd forgotten about her until recently, which is different. A lot has happened over the intervening centuries, Red."

I stared at Ivo in disgust. "You knew the Queen of Mercia was trapped, and you just...*forgot* about her?"

"Fred isn't my problem," he said. "It was a fight for power and she was unlucky enough to get in the way. Collateral damage, you might say."

"Because she isn't worth anything more?" I demanded. "That's how you work, isn't it? Everything has to have worth, whether it's through money or power. And if you meet someone with neither, then they're irrelevant."

"That's harsh," said Ivo. "I'm nice to Izzy and your other friends, aren't I? I could have taken them out of the picture a long time ago, but I chose not to." Not getting a response, Ivo turned to look at where I stood shaking with fury. "Oh, come *on*, Red," he said, seeing my face. "They do say all's fair in love and war, after all."

"You don't know the meaning of love," I spat, anger fixing me to the spot. "And you certainly don't know how friendship works. How dare you threaten Izzy? How *dare* you?" Ivo gazed impassively at me. "I don't care how powerful you are," I said, "nor how old. Or how many acres of stupid bloody land you own, or the grudge you've been holding against Liam for all these centuries. No," he opened his mouth to speak, "you shut the *fuck* up and listen to me for once. You think the entire bloody world owes you, and that you're just taking what's yours. None of it's yours, Ivo," I struggled not to stamp my foot like a toddler, fury bubbling up like a geyser about to blow its top, "not one tiny bit. You don't get things just because you've decided you deserve them. This isn't the twelfth bloody century, or the eighth, or the dawn of fucking time, for that matter. This is here and now, and you, Ivo Laithlind, are a fucking *brat*." I finally ran out of things to say and just stood staring at him. Daring him to make something of it. Ivo gazed back at me thoughtfully, and for a moment I thought I might have taken it a step too far. Fuck it. All or nothing, that had always been my approach to life. Mind you, it had historically been more often directed at cream cakes rather than powerful undead Vikings.

"Do you really think I'm a brat?" he asked finally. The ghost of a smile twitched at the corners of his mouth.

"Yes," I said firmly, "I do. You act like a kid who's had his sweeties taken away by one of the bigger boys and is going to make everyone's lives hell because of it. Even the ones who have nothing to do with any of it."

"Maybe I'm just older and wiser," he shrugged. "You don't survive as long as I have without a decent amount of both."

"Eadric's almost the same age as you," I pointed out, "and he's managed not to turn into a complete pillock."

"We're very different people, Eadric and I," said Ivo. "We may have ended up in similar situations, but we came to it in very different ways."

"How do you work that out?" I said. "Cos from where I'm standing, you were both over-privileged man-babies in a patriarchal world that gifted you an overly strong sense of entitlement. The only difference between the two of you is how you've used that power over the years."

"So. Eadric's good and I'm bad?" asked Ivo. "That's how you see it? It's a rather simplistic theory, don't you think?"

"Eadric wouldn't have left Fred stuck in this bloody tower like an undead Rapunzel," I said. "If he'd known she was there, he'd have done something about it."

"You sure about that?" Ivo raised an eyebrow. "Because from where I'm standing, Red, no one comes out of any of this very well. Not even you."

"What are you talking about?" I said. "What have I done that's anything like the sort of things the rest of you get up to?"

"You lost Billy in the past, for a start."

"I wouldn't have had to *go* back into the sodding past if you hadn't been messing round with it," I snapped. "That was *your* fault."

"Regardless," said Ivo smoothly, "you chose to take Billy with you and put him at risk. In the same way, you risk Isobel's safety every single day of her human life." I stared at him, completely speechless. How could anyone think I'd ever put Izzy at risk?

She's at risk purely by knowing you, said the city. *It would have been better for everyone if you'd taken the offer of a quiet flit to Scotland at the start.*

Don't you fucking dare, I hissed silently. *You're supposed to be on my side!*

And we are, it said. *Which is why we speak the truth. Were you not a friend, we'd lie for the sake of an easier life. But we are entwined with you deeply enough to feel you deserve the truth.*

I'm currently thinking I'd rather be lied to.

Of course. But it wouldn't help.

"The city agrees with me, doesn't it?" Ivo gave me a strange look that was a mix of satisfaction and sympathy. "And I think you know it yourself, Red. At least, you do when you let yourself really think about things, rather than just bouncing through life like an over excited baby elephant."

"A baby elephant?" I snorted. "Cheers, mate. Best compliment I've had all week, that is."

"Quiet week, then?" grinned Ivo. "Look," he held his hands out in supplication, "I'm not here to cause trouble. I've been straight about my motives from the start."

"Fuck off," I said, "you absolutely have not. You pretended to be my friend at the start of all this, but you were in cahoots with Maria bloody Silverton all the time. You were shagging Eadric's *wife*, Ivo! You fathered her child when she was still human, for fuck's sake. Then you set Eadric up and pretended you didn't know his new wife. You know," I scowled at him, "the wife who never really loved him. The one who tried to kill me, then Billy." I'd never forget the expression of howling agony on Billy's face as Maria had tried to exorcise him, pulling his spirit up out of his body and high into the air over Harrington Street. And people wonder why I chopped her horrible little head off. "There *has* to be a way out," I said, forcing myself back to the immediate problem. "I can't just disappear! Izzy and Kitty would be beside themselves! We have to do *something*."

"Like what?" Ivo didn't look nearly worried enough for my liking.

"Like, I don't know…" I trailed off. "Ring Eadric," I rallied. "We'll ring Eadric. He'll think of something."

"Do you have your phone?" Fuck's sake. How had I forgotten the eighth wonder of the modern world?

"Yes, of course—oh *shit*." I'd put the phone down on Jonathan's drawing table when I first went in. Even if it wasn't broken, I couldn't get to it anyway. "Surely you have a phone?" Ivo travelled all over the place and stayed at fancy hotels—I couldn't imagine him not being contactable, even if it was just so he could meet up with his silly little human girlfriends.

Why are they silly? asked the city.

Don't start, I muttered silently. *Can't you make yourselves useful and find me a way out?*

We can't rescue you, Lilith.

Why the fuck not? What's the point of having an entire city in my head if it can't help when I'm having a crisis?

Lilith, it said in an annoyingly calm tone, **your entire afterlife has been a series of crises so far. We'd never get any peace if we helped every time. Anyway, we can't. Help, we mean. We don't know how this is done. Or who did it.**

Liam did it, I said. *Obviously. And I'm going to rip his stupid bloody head off when I get hold of him.*

It wasn't William.

Then who? I frowned. Then I opened my mouth to speak, but immediately shut it again.

We don't know, it said, **but it wasn't William. He doesn't have as much power as he likes people to think. That's why he needs you. If we could help, we would. It might not seem like it**, I was sure I heard the city give an embarrassed cough, **but we're rather fond of you, Lilith. We'd like to keep you around.**

I didn't reply. But I clearly hadn't hidden my response well enough, because Ivo was watching me with a curious expression. "You're cute when you smile," he said. "Has anyone ever told you that?"

"Nope," I shrugged. "Sucks to be me."

"You should smile more," he said. "It suits you." He stepped forward, so he was just a couple of feet away from me. Close enough to touch. My hand twitched involuntarily, and I had to make a conscious decision not to reach out. Izzy would have been shrieking had she been there, practically cheerleading in the background and encouraging me to make the best of a bad situation. And there really were many worse situations I could have been in than stuck in a room with an ancient Viking who wanted nothing more than to claim me as his own. An ancient Viking who was, by any standards, hot as the surface of the sun. Yup, there were definitely *way* worse things I could be doing right now. I half-closed my eyes and stepped forward. Ivo didn't need any encouragement. His hand reached out to cup my chin and I opened my eyes just in time to see his closing as he moved in to kiss me—and then, with every ounce of my undead strength, I punched him right in his perfectly chiselled jaw.

The blow sent him reeling backwards onto the floor. Before he could think about getting to his feet, I kicked him harder than I'd ever kicked anything in my life. If I'd done that to a human they'd have been a goner, but whilst revenants don't have magical powers, we're definitely made of sterner stuff. Ivo curled into a protective ball and rolled over onto his knees, shielding himself from my punches. I didn't let up, even as he got to his feet. A lifetime's worth of pent-up fury was coming out, and Ivo Laithlind was bearing the brunt of it. "You bastard!" I yelled as I caught him across the other side of his face. "You lying, deceitful, evil *bastard*!" Suddenly developing moves I didn't even know I had, I swung round on one leg and hoofed him straight in the ribs. The cracking sound echoed in the empty room, and I'd have felt sick if I'd had time to think about it. But I didn't—Ivo was still coming at me. I wasn't fast enough this time and he grabbed me from behind, pinning my arms to my sides.

"You really need to stop trying to fight me, Red." I could hear the pain in his voice. Good. "I don't want to hurt you," he went on, his voice soft against my ear, "I just want you to see sense." Remembering something Damon had taught me and Izzy when we'd been talking about how to fend off an attacker, I stamped my foot backwards, hard against the inside of Ivo's right ankle. He fell to the floor with a yell, clutching at his leg. "You broke my fucking ankle, you idiot!" he yelled. Without taking his eyes off me, he reached down and twisted his foot back into the right position with a horrible crunching noise. I backed off to give myself some space to move. Ivo was already pulling himself upright, and I couldn't help but wonder at his healing abilities. Did it get faster as you got older, or was Ivo Laithlind just a freak of undead nature? Whatever the science behind it, he was on his feet and walking —carefully, but with weight on both feet—towards me. I could hear sounds from outside now. Indistinct, but definitely there. Whatever was holding me in this room was weakening.

"It was you, wasn't it?" I said flatly. Of course it was him. Ivo Laithlind had been fucking me over from the start, and I'd been endlessly giving him the benefit of the doubt. What an absolute fucking muppet I was. And now I was trapped in a room with the oldest and strongest immortal I'd ever met, and I'd managed to royally piss him off. "You win," I said. "Gold star for Ivo, blah blah. But you don't win my territory. And you *definitely* don't win me."

"Are you sure, Red?" he asked. "We could still do this together, you know. Me and you, against the world. Think of it!" He was smiling now. Okay, so it was a pretty evil-looking smile, but he'd stopped moving. Maybe if I played for time, Jonathan might—well, I had no idea what Jonathan might do. Probably nothing useful, unless he suddenly came up with a plan for a battering ram made of bits of old table that was capable of breaking through metaphorical doorways, like a steampunk psychologist. The obvious answer in any other hostage situation would have been to throw things out of the windows until someone called the police, but the last thing I needed right now was the authorities turning up en masse. And I wasn't even sure there *was* an outside.

"Why are you trying to force things?" I said. "Look, there's no denying you're the hottest man I know. I actually fancied you a bit when we first met. God knows why."

He raised an eyebrow. "You certainly hid it well." I remembered the first time we spoke, not long after I died. He'd tried to use some kind of mind trick on me, and I'd nearly leaned in to kiss him.

"I've never been attracted to people who try to trick or bully me into it," I said. "And I'm not going to start now."

"I'm not a bully, Red," he said. "That's where you're getting things very wrong."

"What are you then?" I snapped. "Because from where I'm standing —in a locked room with you looking extremely predatory, if you don't mind me saying, and with two other people also trapped in the room next to us—you're definitely coming across as being a bit fucking mean, if you ask me. Not that anyone's asking me, obviously," I was feeling behind me for something solid to lean against, but there was nothing. "You forget that I *know* myself, Ivo. If this last year has taught me anything, it's that I never truly appreciated life until it was taken from me. But somehow I got given a second chance, and I'm not going to waste it." Still no sound from the other room. What the hell could they be doing in there that was keeping them so quiet? There was only so long I could waffle vague platitudes before I started boring myself, let alone Ivo. "Yeah," I ploughed on, "I've got friends. Even if you think they're pointless humans, they're still my friends. Do you even know what friends are, Ivo?"

"Forging connections makes you weak," he said. "Look what happened with the Bastard. He thought he'd just swan back in here and take over, probably with you as his queen. I wouldn't have given you the crown, Red." He smiled thinly. "William thought he was being clever. That flattery would push you over to his side and he could just wait for your arrival, like the arrogant bastard he's always been. And now he's gone for good, because he let himself be ruled by his heart instead of his head. I don't have a heart, Red." His eyes narrowed. "And I'm not in the habit of leaving dangerous people free for long enough to become a threat. Whether that's to me, or to my territories."

"You said I was dangerous, once."

"I did indeed," said Ivo. "And I still think you're dangerous. Which means you cannot be allowed to continue." I needed to edge further back towards the door. I might not be able to get out, but someone else might be able to get in. And then Ivo Laithlind was going to be sorry, oh yes. *Three ounces of pure rabid mouse to the face, see how you like* that, *you ridiculous son of Odin!* Okay, maybe I needed more than a mouse. Acting on pure animal instinct, I ran straight at Ivo and barrelled him to the floor. He rolled with the blow and pinned me down, kneeling astride me and grinning devilishly as he gripped my wrists. The grin disappeared as I brought my leg up and kneed him hard in the bollocks. He gasped and loosened his grip just enough for me to throw him off and punch him in the face again. This time I connected with his nose, and he went down, his face looking suddenly lopsided.

STOP THIS NOW, I said, the voice in full effect. ENOUGH.

"For christ's sake," he garbled, a hand up to his face, "don't you ever give up? That doesn't work on me, Red." He pushed at the bent and broken cartilage until his nose was back where it should be, and scowled up at me. That's the trouble with fighting revenants—you never get to see the fruits of your labours. I punched him again, just for the hell of it. His arm came up even as his head rolled back and he grabbed my wrist with such force that it should have broken. But my dad had been a coach at a local martial arts club when I was a kid, and I sometimes sat in on classes if I had nothing better to do. Twisting my body to follow Ivo's movements, I flipped myself over his head. My weight pulled him off balance and the back of his head hit the floor so hard that it creaked under the strain. But you don't get to be a Viking warrior without learning how to fight, and being immortal just makes you less likely to die from your injuries. "Red," he said, clambering upright again, "why can't you just accept your destiny and save us both this endless ridiculous bickering?"

"What if I enjoy bickering?" I danced from side to side as adrenalin raced round my undead circulation. "And just whose destiny are we talking about here, Ivo? Cos from where I'm standing it looks more like you decided on your own destiny a long time ago and have spent all this time just forcing people into it against their will." He stood watching me, but didn't make a move. His nose still didn't look quite right—hopefully I'd done enough damage to leave him permanently scarred.

That would be a suitable reminder not to meddle in the affairs of women who were sick of his bullshit. "Jonathan was right," I said. "You really are a thief. A thief of dreams. You steal other people's dreams and ideas, Ivo Laithlind. They have something you want and you take it, even if it ruins them. And do you know why?" I bounced around a bit more, just for the show of it. I was surprised to find I was actually enjoying this. When you're a revenant living in the human world, you get little chance to make the most of your newfound abilities. People notice that shit. But here in a magically locked room with only a love-interest-turned-nemesis for an audience, I suddenly felt like the hero of a ridiculously cheesy movie. The sort where the protagonists fight like cat and dog whilst the world burns around them, only to decide they fancy each other after all and probably get down and dirty amid the carnage. But I didn't fancy Ivo Laithlind anymore. Not one part of me was tempted by the bruised and angry man standing in front of me. "I'll tell you why," I said. "You're a coward, Ivo. A fucking *coward*. You're not strong nor clever enough to succeed on your own, so you take what you need from others. And you don't care what it does to them."

"Why should I care?" Ivo took a deep breath. "I can smell you. Did you know that?" I did not know that, but I was careful to keep my expression blank. "You smell of lust and excitement and deep, dark fear. You're *scared*, Red. Scared of immortality, scared of things going wrong, scared of *everything*. Including me."

"Yup," I said, still bouncing. "I'm scared. Because I've still got some humanity and it would be stupid *not* to be afraid of what might happen. But you got one thing wrong, Ivo." Shitting hell, why wasn't anyone coming to rescue me? Had they assumed Ivo had finished me off already and decided to just get the fuck out of Dodge? Or worse—maybe they thought I'd side with him after all, and they were just getting out of the way in case we both came after them. Fuck it—I'd just have to do the best I could. "I'm not scared of you." I ran at him so fast even he—mister 'great Viking warrior, don't mess with me puny humans'—didn't see it coming. Before he knew what was happening, I grabbed hold of his head and bit straight through his ear. As he yelled, I kicked out hard enough to send him sprawling and bounced back as far away from him as possible. Ignoring a sudden overwhelming urge to vomit, I chewed good and hard on the piece of gristle in my mouth before spitting it out onto the floor between us. "I might not be able to take you down," I said, wiping my mouth onto my t-shirt, "but I can make sure you don't look quite so dashing." Ivo was still clutching his head, but I didn't think he was going to bleed to death. Sure enough, he dropped his hand and I saw the wound on his ear was already healing. The only consolation was that he was now permanently disfigured.

"Satisfied?" he asked.

"Nope."

"You're not getting out of here," he said calmly. "At least, not without my help. So we can carry on bitching and taking chunks out of each other, or you can give in to the inevitable and discuss how we move this situation forward." Jesus bloody Christ, he sounded like an office manager at a team meeting. He'd be asking me to indulge in some blue-sky-thinking next.

"Had enough, big fella?" I crowed. Clearly even Odin had his limits. "Want to strike a peace deal? Cos unless it involves you fucking right off out of my life for ever and a fucking day, it ain't gonna happen. So we're *stuck*, Ivo Laithlind. Stuck with this stupid situation where I'm never going to give in and you're never going to give up. But you're not going to win *me*, I keep telling you that."

"But I don't need to win you, Red," said Ivo. "I just need to conquer you." He launched himself across the room so fast I didn't see it coming. Before I realised what was happening, he had me pinned up against the wall with his hand around my neck. I started choking, before I remembered I didn't have to breathe. I settled for kicking him instead. Silently, mind, because it turns out that having your windpipe gripped by a large and angry Viking stops your larynx functioning, even if the rest of you is fully conscious. Ivo had me pinned like a butterfly, holding himself just out of range and ignoring the blows that did manage to hit their target as I flapped stupidly at him. "We can stay here forever," he said, "if needs be. I've got all the time in the world." I shook my head and pointed to my mouth, indicating I needed to speak. Amazingly, he loosened his grip just enough for me to get the words out.

"I don't think you have, actually," I choked out.

"Red," he said calmly, as though trying to pacify a mardy child, "from now on, we're doing things my way."

I grinned manically, then spat in his face—a pretty neat move for someone who was way down on her coffee quota for the day and who was also currently being throttled. "It's behind you," I said hoarsely. Ivo turned just in time to see what was plummeting towards him through the glass roof. And then Bella hit him.

This wasn't the Bella I knew and loved. Nothing about the vengeful whirlwind whipping round in front of me bore any resemblance to the huge metal bird that creaked happily to herself on top of the Liver Building. This Bella was made entirely from fire and fury, and she was about to make it Ivo's problem. She swiped at him with one of her gigantic wings and he staggered backwards, dropping me heavily to the floor. I'd automatically shielded my face when she appeared, but I was realising now that there was no heat. This was the spirit of Bella, rather than her physical form—the version I sometimes watched dancing in the sky over Liverpool, a vision of pure joy above the city lights. There was nothing joyous about her now. She ripped through the room like a fiery tornado, the force of her flaming wings pulling the very fabric of the building away from its framework and sending floor tiles and plaster spinning through the air. Ivo was scrabbling across the floor in an attempt to reach the door. A screaming noise built from the depths of Bella's fire, making my ears ring and my head throb. The bird filled the entire room as her vicious beak grabbed Ivo by the arm and flung him into the wall. Glass splintered from what was left of the roof, and outside, a car alarm wailed into life. Bella stalked slowly towards Ivo, a red-gold raptor cornering her prey. Fear rippled across his face, as clear as the gleaming hatred in the Liver bird's eyes.

There was a hammering sound on the other side of the door. "Lilith!" shouted Fred, "the building's going to collapse!" Oh, thank fuck, the mediaeval cavalry had finally arrived. But even as Fred was shouting, an ominous crack rippled through the bare bricks where the plaster had come down, wide enough for me to see daylight through it. I thought I could hear screaming from outside, but it might have just been inside my head. Sirens were approaching—Bella might not have been made of actual fire, but anyone witnessing it from outside would assume the entire building was going up in flames.

"Bella!" I screamed her name as loud as my lungs could manage, hoping to distract her. The bird ignored me in favour of grabbing Ivo's leg and throwing him across the room like a rag doll. *BELLA.* And suddenly the words were inside my head, the voice slotting into place like the missing piece of a jigsaw puzzle. By the way Ivo was staring across at me in horrified awe, I assumed he could hear it too. *LEAVE HIM.* She heard me that time. The flames were still swirling around us, but she stopped moving forward towards Ivo and twitched her head slightly. *LISTEN TO ME*, I said to her. *YOU HAVE TO LEAVE. NOW.* She shook her refusal, her entire phantom body juddering. By the crashing noises and screams from outside, the roof tiles had clearly begun sliding off. *I CAN DO THIS*, I said. The shaking lessened just a fraction. *TRUST ME, BELLA. LIKE I TRUST YOU.* There was shouting outside now, and engines. My money was on a fire engine, complete with extending ladder. Fire brigades are fast—by my reckoning I had a minute at the very most in which to somehow salvage the situation. Shit, shit, *shit.* "Let me out of here, Ivo," I shouted.

"Fuck you," he yelled back, all pretence of being a gentleman long gone. "Fuck you and fuck that ridiculous fucking bird you rode in on," he spat, clambering to his feet. "I hope they have to dig the remains of your pathetic shattered body out of the wreckage, you traitorous little bitch. How *dare* you ignore everything I've offered you!" But I wasn't listening anymore. Ivo himself had told me the way out. I ran at Bella, and she ducked down to make it easier for me. I tried not to think too much about the fact I was now sitting on the back of a mythical creature made of nothing but metaphysical fire, and settled for wrapping my arms tightly around her neck.

"Come on, girl," I whispered into the bird's ear, "let's go home." I glanced back as we ripped upward out of the building and into the sky. The last thing I saw was the furious face of Ivo Laithlind falling towards the ground in a tsunami of rubble.

THE DREAM THIEF

We hit the headlines, of course. Or at least, the Steam Mill did. Amazingly, there had been no injuries to anyone on the ground, other than a small girl with a grazed knee who'd fallen out of her pushchair when her mother had panicked and tried to run. The mill had fallen helpfully sideways, most of it landing in the canal. The local waterways commission was frantically clearing it out, but other than a few pissed off narrowboat owners, the destruction of one of Chester's most well-known buildings had caused surprisingly little upheaval. The contractors were already back at work and making plans for a full rebuild. There'd even been a mention in a news article of them having found a white mouse in the rubble and semi-adopted it, which pleased me. According to the many newspaper reports, no one had been inside the building at the time, despite the contractors insisting they'd chased a woman up onto the top floor just before it happened. It wasn't entirely surprising they weren't believed, because they'd freely admitted that whoever the woman was, she'd disappeared in front of their eyes. I'd found plans of the mill online and discovered that the door Jonathan had ushered me through at the start didn't even exist—in reality it had been a brick wall with nothing on the other side except, well, the outside. The working assumption was that Jonathan's section of the mill had been yet another glitch in the stupid sodding matrix, existing outside of time and space. Like I hadn't had enough of that bullshit already. A specialist firm of architects had been brought in to supervise the salvage operation, and the only thing they'd found that didn't belong in there was a battered and very broken phone that was thankfully unsalvageable and which they decided was too old to be relevant, anyway. I was currently using Izzy's old iPhone 7 and perfectly happy with its limited abilities. Having heard the commotion and realising I probably had something to do with it, a worried Sean had eventually remembered he had my car keys and drove Basil back to Liverpool. Bella and I had been back a long time by then, giving Eadric plenty of time to lecture both of us at great length about our 'ridiculous behaviour' and how 'people must have noticed a bloody great big fire bird flying across the sky'. We'd both sat patiently while he ranted, me smiling helpfully and Bella creaking in what I think she considered a supportive manner. Then Nik had ushered Sean up onto the tower and he and Eadric took it in turns to shout at us until Nik reappeared and informed us that tourists on Pier Head were trying to figure out where the noise was coming from and did we really want to end up on the front page of the *Echo*? So everyone agreed to never discuss any of it ever again, and we all went home.

Nobody Expects The Nan-ish Inquisition

"Know what occurred to me the other day?" Sean was leaning against the living room doorframe, watching as I wrangled coffee out of the machine. I still wasn't sure what I was doing with it, despite Mapp's instruction.

"Nope," I said, realising the steam pipe was switched on and rapidly delaminating my worktops. I wrapped it in a tea towel before twisting it to the 'off' position with enough force that it would probably never work again. "What occurred to you the other day?"

"All you need to do is press the buttons for strength and size," said Sean, trying not to sigh as he leaned across me to tap buttons on the coffee machine's display. "How do you work the one in Flora's?"

"That one's practically antique," I said. "None of this ridiculous computer nonsense. You just grind the beans and wedge the dispenser thing onto it."

"The filter," said Sean. "It's called a filter. The bit you twist onto the machine with the ground coffee in it."

"No one likes a smart arse," I said. "Anyway, you still haven't told me what occurred to you the other day."

"You don't know where I live," said Sean.

"Eh?" I looked up from the coffee machine in confusion. "Am I supposed to?"

"I just thought it was weird, is all." He shrugged. "That you've never asked."

"Sean," I said, turning to face him properly, "I generally consider myself lucky to get through each day relatively unscathed and without either me or my friends and family being threatened with some new and unusual form of horrible death. It doesn't matter to me where you live, so long as you're safe."

"Awww," he said, "you do care, after all."

"Of course I bloody care," I said, trying to hide my embarrassment. "You're my friend."

"Just your friend?" he asked. He stepped closer and raised a hand to push my hair back from my face. "Do you think maybe—"

"Fuck*sake*!" I moved so quickly that Sean lost his balance and nearly fell flat on his face. But I was already out of the door and grabbing the intruder I'd spotted through the kitchen window. They were shorter than me and dressed entirely in black, complete with a full-face balaclava. I wrenched their arms behind their back and twisted. "Drop it," I hissed, roughly where I thought their ear would be.

"Shan't," came the belligerent answer. I twisted their wrist again. The burglar made a strangled noise and dropped the weapon.

"Sean!" I shouted, but he was already out of the door and gaping in astonishment. "Grab this *fucking* idiot, would you?" Before he could say anything, I threw my would-be assailant at him and jumped from the top of the fire escape. The second intruder was slower than the first and hadn't even made it out of Harrington Street before I rugby-tackled them to the floor. "You," I snapped, as I dragged them to their feet, "had better have a bloody good explanation for this." They might not have been very good at running, but they fought like a demon and made it as difficult as possible for me to keep hold of them. In the end I resorted to flinging them over my shoulder like a sack of potatoes, gripping them by the ankles and ignoring their attempts to pummel my back into submission. It actually felt quite nice, a bit like the overpowered massage chairs they always sit you in when you're having a pedicure in one of those backstreet nail salons. When I got back up to the top of the fire escape with the would-be burglar hanging down my back, I found Sean still hanging onto the first intruder. They were putting up a good fight too, mind. Sean's hair had flopped over his eyes, and he looked a bit like Velma holding back Scrappy Doo, his serious face confused above the flailing figure he was gripping onto for dear life. "Shouldn't we call someone?" he asked worriedly, as I headed up towards him.

"I *am* someone," I said. "This doesn't need anyone else. Take that idiot inside, would you?" I followed him into the flat and turned to lock the door behind me, swinging my prisoner round so their head knocked against the kitchen wall. "Oh, I'm sorry," I said, "did I hurt you?" I dropped them heavily down onto the floor and they scrabbled backwards towards the living room. A noise from the room beyond them made them look up—right into Finn's aggressively slanted eyes. "Oh, hi Finn," I said casually, "I didn't realise you were here. Could you keep hold of that one for me, please?" A heavy paw thudded down onto the burglar's shoulder, the claws stretching out and then not quite retracting, so that Finn's prisoner could clearly see the razor-sharp tips out of the corner of their eye. "As for you," I stalked towards where Sean had wedged himself into the corner of the kitchen, still gripping the original intruder with their arms behind their back, "how bloody dare you! And after we'd given you free cake, as well." I ripped the balaclava off and the woman underneath it glared balefully at me.

"You're an abomination, that's what you are," said Judith. Gone was the friendly woman I'd seen in Flora's, just happy to have a free scone. "You all need staking! Just like that other one."

"So, it was you who killed Katja?" I asked, leaning in close. Judith's angry eyes glittered with fury. "She was my *friend*, you murderous little bitch."

"I don't know anything about any killing!" Delphine wriggled frantically on the kitchen floor, but it made no difference. Finn's bloody heavy when he's in cat form. And no, I don't know how the physics of that works, any more than you do. "She kept telling me there was something wrong with you," Delphine went on, "but I told her she was just being silly. 'There's nothing weird about Flora's', I said. Apart from the poltergeist, of course."

Nobody Expects The Nan-ish Inquisition

"Apart from the poltergeist," I agreed. "The poltergeist is the least of your worries right now, I can promise you that much. What a nasty, spiteful pair of old witches you are. And that's an insult to witches. What had Katja ever done to you?"

"My Georgie came home with bite marks on his neck," snapped Judith. "He's always been such a good boy. Then he met this ridiculous gothic girl and suddenly I barely ever see him! He's out all hours of the day and night and even when he is around, he's either asleep or away with the fairies and not even listening to me."

"Georgie's her grandson," said Delphine helpfully. "His parents live down Oxford way, so he's staying with his nan while he's at university. It's ever so expensive to rent somewhere these days, you know. He's a nice lad, but a bit—"

SHUT UP. Delphine shut up, her eyes wide with terrified confusion. "Sorry." This was to Sean, who clearly wasn't as used to the voice as he thought he was. "So you," I turned to Judith, "got upset about your grandson living a normal student lifestyle. And you decided to get it out of your system by staking my friend?"

"People always used to say there was something weird about this town," muttered Judith. "Something not quite right. Something making it different from everywhere else. I used to think they were all jealous, that we should feel sorry for them because they didn't have the clothes and the music we had. They didn't have the *spirit*. But then," she made a spitting noise, "then I realised what was causing it. It was *you*," she stabbed ineffectually at me with a shaky, crooked finger. "All you weirdos who aren't quite human and don't know how to behave properly. It's disgusting, is what it is."

"I thought you were losing your marbles, Judith," said Delphine, from floor level. Finn had decided the easiest way to prevent her from escaping was to sprawl entirely across her, like the world's heaviest fur throw. Delphine was currently lying flat, her head just visible behind Finn's enormous furry backside. *Oh dear*, I thought, *he's had prawns today*. "I was just humouring you, because I thought it might do you good to get out a bit more. I didn't know you were going to attack this lady!"

"She's no lady," snapped Judith.

"So, you weren't with her when she killed Katja?" I asked Delphine. The woman shook her head—or at least, she shook it as much as she could without sticking her nose up a cat's unmentionables.

"I didn't even know anyone *was* dead until you mentioned it just now," she said.

"I didn't kill her," said Judith. "I wanted to, but that other bloke beat me to it. Figured he'd saved me a job, so what with her landing on the doorstep and that bloody cat turning up out of nowhere," she nodded towards Finn, "I just toddled off back home."

"You toddled off," I said. "Toddled off. Who the hell says 'toddled off' after they've just had a dead vampire dropped at their feet?"

"Those who think all vampires should be got rid of," snapped Judith. "Not kept like horrible little pets, all bite-y and smelling of the sewers." I opened my mouth to defend vampires from accusations of poor hygiene, then shut it again. There's no denying that vampires really do have a very distinct smell, and it isn't a pleasant one. "Anyway," Judith went on, "no. No, I didn't kill it."

"But you were going to kill me," I said. "Right on my own doorstep. And in the middle of the day, as well."

"And I didn't know she was planning to attack you!" Delphine's voice was muffled by the cat draped across her face. She wriggled until her head popped out enough for her to look at me.

"You'll have to excuse my confusion here," I said slowly, "but what the fuck did you *think* she was going to do? You're gussied up like a pair of ninjas, for chrissakes! What is this, a reboot of Golden Girls, the Marvel edition?"

"She told me she was dropping off a card," said Delphine indignantly. "You know, to thank you for the other day. And we're on our way to the Women's Institute." She looked sheepish. "It's fancy dress week."

"Are you on fucking *glue*?" I squinted at Delphine. "Who on earth sends a thank you note to a cafe after witnessing a poltergeist attack?"

"I've never witnessed a poltergeist attack before," said Delphine with calm logic. "I'm sure I wouldn't know what the usual etiquette might be."

"Oh, will you just stop bloody talking before you make everyone think you're simple in the head?" said Judith. Both me and Delphine swung round to look at her. Even Finn tilted his head sideways and eyeballed her with curiosity. "She's telling the truth." This was to me. "She had nothing to do with it. And yes," Judith rolled her eyes, "I told her I was dropping a card round. Not my fault she's a bit daft now, is it?"

"Ohhh, you cheeky—" Finn rolled over onto his back and splayed his back legs out either side of Delphine's head. She leaned away as far as possible, the back of her head pressed against the tiles. She didn't finish the sentence, presumably because she was too scared to open her mouth. Let's just say Finn has definitely not been neutered.

"So, you," I prodded Judith in her bony chest, "decided to kill my friend—"

"Your friend was sitting on the roof in the middle of the night, like the freak she—"

"You tried to kill my friend," I went on through gritted teeth, "and then came back for me."

"We can't have vampires in Liverpool," snapped Judith. "It's just not right."

"I'm not a fucking vampire, Judith!" I was getting very close to the end of my tether with the pair of them. To Sean's credit, he was still holding Judith's arms behind her back, but now he was doing it with a grin creeping across his face.

"Well, what are you then?" Judith frowned at me. "Because you're certainly not normal, that's for sure."

"Who are you to say what's normal?" I asked her. She held my gaze, glaring at me with her little piggy eyes. She had some brass neck, I had to give her that much. "But you're right, Judith." I leaned right in and felt her panicked breath against my cheek. "I'm *not* normal. I'm about as far from being normal as your tiny little mind could ever imagine. But I'm not a vampire. And I've got nothing to do with whatever your grandson is getting up to in his own free time." I did, however, make a mental note to check with Aiden, in case one of his proteges needed a refresher course in How To Care For Your Human. "What I *am*, Judith," I pressed up against her, so that my eyeball was millimetres from her own, "is your worst fucking nightmare." I doubted she'd be able to focus well enough that close up to notice the silver ring around my iris that gives me away as being dead, but she got the idea just the same.

"What are you going to do with us?" asked Delphine, her voice quavery. "You're not going to eat us, are you?" I looked down to where she still lay pinned to the floor. Finn appeared to have gone to sleep, but he was twitching and his claws occasionally extended, as if he was dreaming about hunting something small and squeaky.

"I'm not going to do *anything* with you," I sighed. "I just want you to promise to stay away from me. And my friends," I added, turning to Judith. "No turning up on my doorstep like an episode of Old Age Ninjas. And definitely no killing vampires. Do you hear me?"

"No," said Judith. "No, I don't hear you, actually." She glared at me through pinched eyes. "I'm going to tell anyone who'll listen exactly what's going on in this godforsaken hell hole. Just you try to stop me, you nasty little witch."

"Okay," I said. Judith, Delphine and Sean all looked at me with confused expressions on their faces. "You tell everyone, Judith. Tell them everything you know about me and my friends, and what you think goes on inside Flora's."

"Bad things is what goes on," spat Judith. "*Evil* things."

"Cool," I shrugged. "I look forward to reading the Echo's piece on it all. Actually, maybe get in touch with the Post as well. They like to do a deep dive into strange goings on. I'm sure they'll be just fascinated by your stories."

"Lil—" started Sean.

"Nope," I said to him, "don't tell me I need to keep it secret. Judith here knows what she has to do, so we will let her do it." Judith herself just gaped at me, the wind taken completely out of her sails. A strange noise near my feet made me look down. It took me a good few seconds to realise that Delphine, still squashed underneath Finn, was laughing. The noise woke the cat up and he rolled off her, but she stayed where she was. Tears were running down her face and I thought maybe she'd turned hysterical, and I was going to have to slap her. It would have certainly been satisfying. But before I could do anything, Delphine pushed herself upwards and grinned at Judith.

"You silly old woman," she said, struggling to get her breathing under control. "You silly, *silly* woman. Who's going to believe you?" Judith frowned, but I could see realisation slowly dawning on her face. "I'd like to see you tell everyone about how Flora's is run by zombies who have vampires for friends," Delphine snorted. "It'll be a week at most before that daughter of yours is taking you off to the doctor for a friendly checkup. Why don't you tell them about the giant bloody cats whilst you're at it?" She actually patted Finn as she said it, and he purred in response. That creature was a grade-A tart, and no mistake. "It'll be the Sunshine Care Home For Mad Old Bats before you know it. Ha! Come on," she got to her feet and steadied herself against the kitchen table, "let's go home. Leave these nice people alone, aye. They've done nothing to hurt you."

"But my Geor—" started Judith. Finn gave a low growl, and she shut up.

"Your Georgie is an absolute trollop," said Delphine. "And enjoying every minute of it, from what I've heard. Now do come *on*, Judith. We're leaving." Ignoring the poisonous look her friend was giving her, Delphine caught hold of Judith's arm and steered her towards the door. I opened it for them and stepped back with a flourish to let them out. "I'm very sorry about this, Lilith," said Delphine as she pulled Judith past me and onto the fire escape. "I hope this little contretemps won't affect me coming into Flora's? I do so love your scones."

"You are both more than welcome," I said brightly. "Just remember that stakes are off the menu." To her credit, Delphine pretended to laugh.

"You're weird," said Sean. We'd finally managed to make coffee and were sitting at the kitchen table. Finn had gone to sleep in the corner of the living room, and Kitty had reappeared just in time to see Delphine and Judith leaving. She was currently curled up on the sofa with Grimm, watching old episodes of *Doctors*.

"Tell me something I don't already know." I raised an eyebrow at him. "Any particular reason for saying it right now? Or is it just my general demeanour?"

"Those women wanted to kill Katja," he said. "But you let them go with barely a telling off."

"Judith tried to kill Katja," I said, "on her own. But it was Ivo who did it. It all makes sense now. The crown kicking off when the trouble started, Finn chasing a strange man on the roof, all of it. I think Ivo probably assumed he'd be able to talk his way into the house." And probably into my bed, although I kept that bit to myself. "Awful as it all is, if Judith hadn't turned up and confused everything, maybe Ivo *would* have got in that night. And then things would have been a whole lot worse."

"What about the mouse?" I looked at Sean, confused by the question. "The mouse," he went on, "where did that come from?"

"Oh," I said, "that was Horace." I smiled. "He's living his best life up in Chester."

"Right," said Sean. "A mouse called Horace. Gotcha. Anyway," he went on, having clearly decided the mouse story was a diversion too far, "do you think Ivo would have tried to steal the crown? If he'd got into the flat, I mean."

I stirred my coffee thoughtfully. "Yes," I said, "I think so. He'd have tried to connive his way into me letting him get close to it and then possibly just tried to do a runner."

"Would he have been able to steal it, though?" said Sean. "I thought it had a mind of its own."

"It does," I said. "But it's still just a fragile piece of metal. It doesn't have legs to run away, or superpowers to destroy its enemies."

"What would have happened if he'd taken it, do you think?"

"Not much," I shrugged. "He'd claim it was symbolic of something or other and everyone would have ignored him, and it would have all just simmered down eventually."

"Seriously?" Sean looked incredulous. "All this drama and you're telling me he could have just taken the crown and been done with?"

"You're forgetting something," I said. "It's *my* crown, Sean. Not Ivo's, not Liam's, not the country's. Mine. It would have found its way back to me. And with any luck," I grinned, "it would have turned Ivo Laithlind completely mad in the meantime. But it's still my crown. Regardless of whether it's actually with me or not. What?"

"Nothing," said Sean quickly. "It's just...well." He sighed. "Your eyes kind of, well," he faltered. "Changed. Flashed. I don't know," he shrugged, "something like that, anyway. As though there was someone else hidden in there. Just behind your eyes."

He can see us, said the city. ***That is...unexpected***.

"Nope," I said brightly, "just me. Sorry about that."

"Aah," said Sean, "you're more than enough for me, Lil. More coffee?"

Service Station Subversion

The definition of 'unexpectedly out of place' has to be the sight of one of the most famous muses of the nineteenth century sitting at a plastic table in a motorway service station cafe just off the M40. Elizabeth of London was wearing a long green smock dress over flat sandals, the narrow straps snaking over and around her tiny feet. Her long red hair was braided into a rope that hung heavily over one shoulder, and her slender hands were folded neatly in her lap. She sat calmly with her legs crossed and smiled as she saw me approaching through the queue for Starbucks. I glanced around the atrium, but couldn't see her loyal companion anywhere. Not that the absence meant anything. Jude was almost certainly hovering in the background, ever-ready to protect their lady from annoyances caused by the northern branch of Undead Anonymous. "A'right?" I said, dropping into the seat opposite Elizabeth. The chair made a squeaking noise at the sudden weight, something it would never have dared to do under the presence of Elizabeth's bony behind.

"I'm very well, thank you," said Elizabeth politely. "It's nice to see you again, Lilith. It's been a while."

"You know what it's like," I said. "Busy, busy."

"I can imagine," said Elizabeth with a smile. "Aah, there you are,

Jude." Knew it. Wherever the metropolitan leader went, her tall and lithe companion went too. Jude was dressed in a loose-fitting jacket and trousers in dove-grey cotton, with black pumps on their feet. *All the better to swing you over their head and out of a window if you annoy their beloved master*, I thought to myself. I'd never met Elizabeth without Jude in tow, although I had met Jude alone. Only the once, mind. They'd arrived like an avenging angel sent from God—in reality, sent from London—the previous year, to assist my escape from the Anfield catacombs. But I'd then let the bad guy—aka Ivo sodding Laithlind, yes I've learned my lesson now, thank you for asking—escape, and Jude had never forgiven me. I wasn't entirely sure Elizabeth had forgiven me, either. She might be many centuries younger than Ivo, but Elizabeth held more power, and she knew it. London's a weighty place, both physically *and* metaphorically. She also holds land that has a boundary running along the edge of what we call the 'wild territory'—an unclaimed area that runs above Middlesex from the Midlands across to the East Anglian coast. The problem is, we all do. The section Eadric and I are in charge of has a narrow border with it to the east, and Ivo joins it to the north. But Elizabeth's lands have the longest of all the joint borders, so historically she's been left in charge. And she doesn't seem to want to do anything at all with it, which drives Ivo mad. His centuries-old beef with Liam means he doesn't see why any land should lie unclaimed, because then there's a risk that HRH Liam the First might step in and claim it. Ivo already has a border with Liam to the north and, given Liam's the reason Ivo's been wandering the country for a millennium anyway, he's never been keen on having him as a neighbour on one side, let alone two. "I was saying," Elizabeth interrupted my rambling train of thought with an amused smile, "that it will be nice to have another woman taking charge." I blinked at her. "Of her own territory, of course," Elizabeth went on. "First amongst equals, as they say."

"Absolutely," I replied, smiling brightly and ignoring Jude's low-level scowling in the background. "We're all in it together, as far as I'm concerned."

"So, you won't object to me taking on the wild territory, then," said Elizabeth. She was still smiling, but now there was a sharp glint in her eye. "Just to keep it safe, you understand."

"I understand nothing," I said. "Why does it suddenly need to be kept safe? You haven't bothered with it for a century or more. Why now?"

"You know exactly why, Lilith." Elizabeth shrugged. "Chester proved that by harbouring Laithlind's spy for centuries without anyone thinking to check it out until you went there. Yes, yes," she'd clearly seen my face, "I understand that Mr Hulls was not a willing accomplice to any of it. Nevertheless, he allowed himself to be forced into servitude by Ivo Laithlind. He also allowed Laithlind to take advantage of his ability to move through time, in order to imprison Aethelflaed. And to what purpose?" I stared at her blankly for a while before realising it wasn't a rhetorical question.

"We're not sure," I admitted. "The current hypothesis is that Ivo saw Chester as the grit in Liverpool's oyster shell." That had been Mapp's suggestion, and I could see from Elizabeth's expression that she agreed with me it was a pretty rubbish one. "Trying to irritate it from the inside," I ploughed on. "Personally, I think he had been readying himself for the day Maria Silverton deposed her husband and he could walk in like the conquering hero and take over."

"And then you turned up unexpectedly and changed everything."

"That's what they say," I shrugged.

"And became the city's living pearl." She smiled wryly. "Anyway," she went on, "Eadric himself is yet more proof that the north-west territory is unstable. He's never once left Liverpool in all time I've known him, but now he's happy to step back and let a newcomer take over?" She saw my expression. "I'm sorry, Lilith, but that's the truth of it. Things are changing, and you are part of that change. Maybe even the cause of it. And changes are always unsettling, especially to those whose egos rely on their power. No one can deny that both William and Ivo Laithlind are pushing their luck further than they have ever previously dared. And so far, you don't seem to have been making much of an attempt to stop them. If you don't mind me saying. None of us can feel truly safe in our own territories until the boundaries are set once and for all."

"Neither of them will accept you taking over the wild territory," I said. *And nor will Eadric*, I thought, whatever Elizabeth seemed to think. Although Eadric's response would be as measured as always, of course. He'd probably send a polite letter or two, maybe even arrange a cosy dinner for us all to chat about it. Whereas Liam would almost certainly lose his undead shit and make it everyone's problem. As for Ivo, no one had heard from or of him since the Steam Mill collapsed. I was certain—reasonably certain, at least—that he'd survived the unexpected demolition. Not that the lack of a body proved anything. Revenants have a horrible tendency to disintegrate into sticky dust when they meet their ultimate death, in the same way as vampires. But I didn't *feel* as though Ivo was gone. It wasn't anything I could have explained, and I didn't really understand it myself. But there was some kind of connection between me, Ivo and Liam, as though an invisible thread connected us all. I suspected Eadric was also entwined in it somewhere, but he was so close to me anyway that I wouldn't have noticed any extra entanglement. What I did know is that I wasn't prepared to do without Eadric. Not yet, at least. And that depended on keeping the territories separate.

"I'm not sure they'd have much say in it," Elizabeth was saying. "At least, not if you and I agree it first."

"You want *me* to agree to you taking over the wild territory?"

Elizabeth gave a small, elegant shrug. "Why not?" she said. "It's within your power to make such an agreement, and the others would have no option but to accept it. William was prepared to defend you in Chester, so I believe he would support any decision you might make." Jude arched an eyebrow at that, but didn't say anything. Jude never says anything. "Laithlind won't go up against you again," Elizabeth went on. "We both know that."

"I know nothing of the sort," I said. "You're talking about someone who was prepared to risk trapping me with him in Chester, Elizabeth. Possibly permanently. You're mad if you think I can tell him what to do." Jude bristled behind Elizabeth, and I gazed up at them. "Turn of phrase," I said to the glowering face, "innit?"

Elizabeth reached a hand back and touched Jude's arm with gentle reassurance. "Then I would be very interested in any alternative plans you might have, Lilith. After all," she said, "it's nice when us women work together, don't you think?" *Not when one of those women is a devious immortal who's already killed luckless opponents*, I thought.

"I'm all for girl power," I said brightly, "but not to the detriment of my own interests. I'm sure we can all work towards mutually agreeable arrangements, whatever our gender. Or lack thereof."

Elizabeth gazed at me for a moment, the cogs clearly ticking in her immaculate mind. Then she smiled. "Of course," she said politely. "I sometimes forget you're so much younger than the rest of us." *Oh do fuck off, you patronising cow*, is what I didn't say. Instead, I smiled back and stayed silent. Two can play the waiting game. "But you agree the wild territory should be allocated?" Elizabeth asked eventually. "For safety's sake, if nothing else. Let's call it a guardianship."

"No one needs to take over that territory," I said. "It's been just fine on its own for centuries. And assuming no one plays silly buggers with it," I looked from Elizabeth to Jude, and back again, "it should stay that way. Don't you think?"

Elizabeth couldn't hide the flash of irritation in her eyes. "You can't really think Laithlind will just leave it alone when it's unoccupied?"

"You're telling me there's nothing guarding your own boundary line?" Her expression answered the question. "Exactly," I said. "Everyone keeps an eye on their line, same as they've always done. It's a tiny piece of land, Elizabeth. Why's it so important now?"

"Wars have begun over smaller territories than this," said the Queen of London, straightening up to look me directly in the eye. "And they will be fought again."

"That rather depends on someone deciding to start a war in the first place," I said. "Doesn't it?"

"You are, I assume, aware of London's interest in the current situation." I knew she didn't mean her own version of the capital. "They're watching us, Lilith. More than they ever have. Watching and waiting, and just looking for a reason to tear us apart."

"And how are they going to do that?" I said. "I can't imagine the Home Office giving a public statement about how yes the supernatural is real and living in your neighbourhood and we've known for centuries but didn't think to mention it, oops. Also," I thought back to the officials who'd visited the Liver Building a few months earlier, "their staff are pretty shit, if you ask me. Stomping in like they're more important and can tell us what to do? Fuck that sideways," I said. "If you don't mind me saying."

"You've met the delightful Donna, then?" Elizabeth smiled despite herself. "Quite the character, don't you think?" Huh. If Donna Karnstein had thought I'd be unnerved by her position of authority, she must have been sorely disappointed when I'd all but threatened to dislocate her arm if she didn't get her stupid pinched face out of my town asap.

"She's certainly something," I said, noting that Elizabeth hadn't mentioned Eve, who'd accompanied Donna on her visit to the Liver Building. "Look, Elizabeth," I leaned forward and Jude's eyes flashed a warning, "I don't *want* to take over this country, whatever Fate and all its stupid spooky cronies might think." She raised an elegant eyebrow at me but stayed silent. "Liverpool's had enough of being told what to do by London. And I don't suppose you've allowed anyone to tell you what to do since the day you woke up dead."

"I woke up in a sealed coffin with only my ex-husband's repulsive family for company," Elizabeth said calmly. "I discovered the true extent of both my mental and physical strength as I extricated myself. I can promise you that much."

"I just bet you can." I grinned, despite myself. Elizabeth was inherently likeable, even when she was clearly also fully prepared to kill me on a very permanent level. "So, my solution is this. We both know I'm fated to take over everything eventually," she opened her mouth to speak, and I put a hand up to stop her, "but I don't want to. It's as simple as that. So, if you will pledge to stick with Middlesex alone, I will pledge to leave you alone."

"You expect me to, how do you people put it—stay in my lane?" I nodded. "Whilst you run riot across the rest of the countryside?"

"Nope," I said. "Just those bits that need looking after. I'm not planning to interfere with either Alba or Ireland, and neither do I think much of Wales needs my input."

"Your territory cuts across Wales," Elizabeth pointed out. "You may have little choice."

"Only the north," I said, "and that's a different country entirely." She didn't look convinced.

"What about Hereford?" she asked. "Will you allow William to take that as well? They are clearly in his pockets, for him to have hidden out there before making his move."

"Liam wasn't in Hereford," I said. "Or if he was, it was a brief visit in order to fit the storyline he gave me when he first appeared in Liverpool." I'd been through a *lot* of old paperwork since I'd last spoken to Elizabeth, and none of it implied that Liam had been anywhere but tucked away in his own territory all the time. It certainly explained why the north had been so quiet for so long—their leader had just been biding his time. I suspected that, if I hadn't arrived on the scene when I did, Liam would have taken advantage of any weakness caused by Ivo's inevitable eventual move against Eadric and simply taken over the lot. Probably with my crown wedged firmly on top of his pretty little head.

"So," I sat back in my plastic chair, "that's my offer. I stay out of your way, if you stay out of mine. Take it or leave it." Elizabeth took her time considering her answer. I wished she'd bottle some of whatever made her so self-assured, and let me have a spritz occasionally. I'd often felt obliged to make fast decisions in order to appear confident, often making mistakes as a result. Elizabeth of London took all the time she needed, her thoughts and considerations written all over her face as she did so.

"I'll take it," she said finally. "At least you have a mind of your own, Lilith. It's a refreshing change."

※

"Well handled," said Eve. The senior officer from the Department of Miscellaneous Affairs—aka 'the British government's monitoring unit for spooky shit'—stepped out from behind a tree as I headed back to my car. "Obviously, we'd prefer you to assert your authority over *all* of your undead acquaintances, Elizabeth included. But I thought it went reasonably well under the circumstances."

"What went reasonably well?" I asked. "And what the fuck are you even doing here?" Eve hadn't popped up for months, and I'd started to risk thinking London had finally decided to leave well alone. But now she was back and telling me they actually wanted me in charge of everything. Which, knowing the government, was purely to make it easier for them to keep an eye on things.

"You have to understand things from our perspective, Lilith," she said, putting a hand on my arm. "We can't risk being left in the dark when it comes to matters of, aah," she smiled. "An esoteric nature, shall we say? Come on," she gave my arm a squeeze, "I'll walk you to your car. We can talk there."

"I don't think I want to talk to anyone who's prepared to keep me under surveillance," I said, shaking my arm loose. "I thought you were on my side, Eve! Fucksake," I shook my head, "are any of you actually trustworthy?"

"No," said Eve, "I'm rather afraid we're not. And I'm sorry if you think I'm letting you down in some way, Lilith. I can assure you that's not my intention. But," she went on, "you're right to say I'm not on your side. I'm not on *anyone*'s side. And neither should you be."

"So you listened in on my conversation with Elizabeth?" Eve nodded. "Then you already know my plans. I've no interest in taking over London."

"Nor anywhere else," said Eve. "A brave move, indeed."

"In what way?" I asked.

"This country is weak, Lilith," she said. "Both the living and the dead are too busy bickering amongst themselves to keep an eye on what happens outside their immediate worldview."

"That's because we're not interested in what's happening outside our world," I snapped. "It's none of our business what others are doing."

"Your inexperience is showing." said Eve. "This naïve belief that things will always turn out for the best if people are left to their own devices, well." She pulled a face. "You'll see," she said. "Eventually."

"You think people need to be told what to do in order to survive?"

"Most of them do," she shrugged, "yes. It's the unavoidable truth, I'm afraid. Humanity is no more than a flock of over-educated meat-puppets, running determinedly towards disaster like lemmings falling off a cliff, if no one's around to divert them. That bit's not true, by the way."

"What isn't?"

"The thing about lemmings. Did you know the myth was started by filmmakers in the nineteen-fifties?" I shook my head. "Some idiots from a studio big enough to know better decided their new nature documentary needed a bit more drama. So, they pushed a load of lemmings off a cliff and filmed it as though the animals were jumping."

"Nice."

"Humanity needs all the help it can get, Lilith. There's always someone willing to push others off the cliff. Our job," she went on, "is to make sure that never happens."

"So you want me to join the undead police now? That can fuck right off, if you don't mind me saying."

"You can say whatever you like, when you're with me," said Eve. "I like the way your brain works." She smiled. "I always know where I am with you."

"Whereas I don't know where I am with any of you," I said, feeling for the Alfa's key fob in my pocket. I pressed the button and the doors unlocked with an expensive *thunk*. I glared at Eve over the car's glossy roof. "There's nothing more to discuss," I said. "Let me know if you ever decide to take a break from being a government shill." Eve's face crinkled in amusement at that, but she didn't say anything. "I'm going home."

∾

I couldn't go straight home though, because I'd promised to call in on Chester. None of the others had been affected by the building's collapse, because—as I'd suspected—they'd been in a parallel reality all the time. And it was a reality that still existed—through a door that no one else could see, on the side of an old brick storage unit behind the ruins of the mill. I'd persuaded Eadric to requisition it through his endless commercial connections. The room that Ivo had trapped me in had been genuine enough, though. Plans of the original mill showed a small, square room to the side of the office conversions that had been intended for conversion into a communal kitchen. But that was before the mill had collapsed under the weight of a furious liver bird.

At least the city itself had finally settled down. In fact, things were currently so calm that Nik declared it 'unsettling' and took himself off to his room to read John Fowles by candlelight in order to soothe his nerves. There was still no word on Liam, but I knew he'd surface again eventually. The crown would have let me know if he'd gone forever, I was sure of it. The crown itself was in a drab beige tote bag that I'd wedged under the passenger seat of the Alfa while I talked to Elizabeth back at the service station. It pleased me to think of both versions of London telling me what they thought I should do, whilst the one true crown was right under their stupid southern noses all the time. I handed it over to Fred, who jiggled the bag as though getting a feel for it. "It's lighter than I expected," she said, peering inside. She looked back up at me. "But heavy to carry, I shouldn't wonder."

"Very," I said. "You think you can do something with it?"

Fred grinned. "It will be my absolute pleasure, Ma'am," she said with a mock curtsey. "You can pick it up tomorrow."

"That soon?" I'd expected it to take her much longer, considering what I was asking. I'd spotted Fred's tools when she'd first shown me her embroidery, and an idea had been growing in my head ever since. I'd had to provide her with some new and very expensive equipment along with several bottles of propane gas, mind. But I was confident the investment would be worth it.

"It'll not appreciate being away from you for long," she said. "Best you come back for it as soon as possible, I think. Oh wonderful," she glanced over my shoulder, and I turned to see a glowing shape appear in the middle of the room, "Elf's back." The cake-smashing poltergeist from Flora's appeared out of the weirdly artificial light. Aelfwynn was the only child of Aethelflaed and her husband, Aethelred, Lord of the Mercians. After her mother's disappearance, Aelfwynn did her best to retain control of Mercia, but was soon deposed by her uncle, Fred's brother Edward. Or 'that pathetic churl', as Fred liked to call him. I'd resorted to googling some of Fred's choicer language and had discovered that a churl was a word for 'peasant'. It certainly wasn't the worst thing I'd heard her call him. Aelfwynn had been sent to a convent, from where she eventually escaped by throwing herself to her death from one of the towers. She'd been haunting Chester ever since—the tie to her mother pulling her there, but Fred's existence on another plane of reality preventing Elf from finding her—until I went stomping in with my argumentative nature and Elf's little stone in my pocket.

"Ooh," said Elf, "what are you going to do with this?"

"Just you wait and see, child," said her mother. "Just you wait and see. We'll do our Lilith proud, don't fret about that. Now come see what our helpful queen has arranged for us."

"All you need to do," I said, "is open the flap and take out whatever's inside it." I lifted the cover on the mailbox to demonstrate. I'd had it installed on the outside wall of the building, which luckily still had a postal address. 'Side House, Canal Side, Steam Mill, Chester', if you can believe it. They really didn't believe in putting a great deal of effort into naming things back in the day.

Fred grinned at me. "And the mail will be here?" she asked. I nodded. "Truly," she said, "you are the queen of dark magic." She bent down to peer into the black metal box that I'd had fixed to the back of a brand new letterbox on the back door of the steam mill. "Magic," she repeated, her voice muffled in the depths of the post box.

"It's known as online ordering," I said to the back of her head. "Anyone can do it. There'll just be a daily newspaper for now. I'll set up some magazine subscriptions when you've thought of things you might like to read about." I'd actually tried to get Fred onto the internet, but she'd decided it was a step too far. Also, the iPad I'd persuaded her to try didn't always recognise the touch of her fingers. And the internet connection in the steam mill was basic, to put it mildly. My long-term plan was to install proper broadband and give Fred a crash course in interacting on social media without coming across as a complete madwoman. But for now, newspapers would do. I'd arranged the delivery through a corner shop in Chester city centre and made sure the bill went straight to the Liver Building. No point being an immortal queen if you don't make the most of your expense account.

Fred straightened up and grinned at me. "Actual paper!" she exclaimed. "Can I have the Manchester Guardian? I used to like that one. When my resident da Vinci remembered to actually go out and get it." She narrowed her eyes at Jonathan, who was standing slightly apart from us and gazing at the letterbox with an expression of sheer wonderment on his face.

"Don't be too hard on him," I said. "He's been doing his best for a long time now. It's a wonder he hasn't lost even more of his marbles over the centuries."

"He's gone back to inventing," said Fred. "Yup," she clearly seen my expression, "I was surprised as well. I honestly thought he wouldn't bother after losing his rich patron. I was half expecting him to just, well…" she trailed off. "Fade away, I guess." She shrugged. "But the day after you dumped that Viking asshole in the rubble, I stuck my head round to see what he was up to and found him frantically tidying his drawing table. No idea what it is he's actually inventing, mark you. I suspect it involves mice." Right on cue, Horace popped his head out of the top of Jonathan's wig and gave us both a beady-eyed once-over. I didn't bother asking where the new Horace had come from. Some things are best left undiscovered.

"It's the Guardian I've ordered," I said, turning back to Fred. "It'll be different to how you remember it, though."

"I don't mind," she said happily, straightening back up. "I'll just be pleased to have some contact with the outside world. Now come back upstairs with me? I want to show you my embroidery." She grinned. "I've added a panel of you kicking Ivo Laithlind in the head," she said. "I think you're going to be impressed by my work."

Home Is Where The Heart Is

"What are you going to do about the OAP attack squad?" asked Eadric. It was the next day, and we were on top of Bella's dome, each of us sitting astride one of her gigantic feet. I looked across to where he sat with his chestnut hair blowing in the breeze. It was nice to see him outside. Eadric did check on the birds, but he'd been doing it much less recently. When I'd mentioned it to Nik, he'd said Eadric didn't worry about the birds anymore, because he knew I was around to look after them. I wasn't sure I wanted Eadric to be too comfortable leaving me in sole charge of anything just yet. I'd told him I'd only give him an update on things if he came outside with me. When he'd asked why, I'd said I liked to get Bella's input on things. It wasn't even a lie. I've got into the habit of talking most things through with Bella. Even though she can't speak, she still makes more sense than most of the humans I know. These days I recognise her different creaks and head-tilts and can figure out pretty quickly whether she approves of my various ideas. I know I've taken something too far when she shakes with laughter to the point I nearly fall off the building.

"Nothing," I said, turning my gaze back out over the water. I could see the ferry making its way across the Mersey, as it did all day, every day.

It looked like a small bobbing cork from this distance. A cruise liner was heading into port from the west, ready to spew its passengers out into the city for an allocated amount of sightseeing and carefully limited drinking time. To our left, teenagers milled around with skateboards on George Parade.

"You don't think they'll tell people about you?" he said.

"Oh, they'll tell plenty of people." I turned to look at him. "And all those people will assume it's the confused ramblings of a pair of old dears with overactive imaginations."

"What if they try to attack you again?"

"I don't think they'll take that risk," I said. "Not now they've met Finn."

"And if they report you to Environmental Health for the giant cat that's living in your building?"

"Then the council can come round and ask to see him for themselves, can't they?" I said. "They can walk into Flora's and come up to the counter and ask if it's true I keep an enormous were-cat on the premises. And can I please show them my teeth so they can check I don't have fangs." I grinned at him. "Do you honestly think anyone is going to take that sort of thing even remotely seriously?"

"Probably not," he admitted. "I'm still not sure about all this, though."

"All what?"

"We've hidden from public sight for centuries," he said. "Millenia, even. And now you're telling me it's fine for everyone to know all about us because they probably won't believe it's true anyway. It's the 'probably' I have concerns about, Lilith. It's not 'definitely'. And I'm not sure I'm entirely comfortable with our existence even being hinted at, let alone confirmed."

"No one's confirming anything," I said. "So you can stop being a baby about it." Eadric raised an eyebrow at me, but said nothing. "Honestly," I went on, "you need to move with the times, mate. Get with the programme, grandad. Etcetera."

"You think it will work?" he asked. "Hiding in plain sight?"

"Eadric," I said, "I am well aware that I don't know the first thing about how all this works. Any of it." I shrugged. "But, for whatever reason, I've been dropped into the hot seat. The only thing I can do now is just cling on for the ride."

"I'm not sure that works," said Eadric. "As a metaphor, I mean."

"You know what I mean," I said impatiently. "And I hung onto Bella well enough, didn't I?" I patted her leg fondly. "You're right, though—there's no guarantee people won't find out about us. But considering I've only been around for just over a year and we've already dealt with collapsing tunnels, vampire infestations *and* sodding bloody time-slips, I think it's highly likely people will start to wonder what's going on anyway. Better that we're all openly weird and everyone knows we're here. Because the alternative is to hide, Eadric. Hide away up here in your tower, or down in the tunnels with Joe and the vampires. Or tucked away in my flat, hoping no one will notice me and making myself thoroughly bloody miserable in the process. We didn't ask to be what we are," I was talking urgently now, only realising the truth myself even as I spoke the words, "and we're not hurting anyone else by existing. Okay," I paused, "maybe the vampires are sometimes hurting people. I need to have another word with Aiden about that. But most of us," I carried on, "are just trying to live our lives. You know? The fact our lives might go on for thousands of bloody years doesn't change who we are as people. It's fucking terrifying, like, but we're still...well. We're still us. What?" Eadric was staring at me with a weird expression on his face.

"Nothing." He smiled, and his entire face lit up. God, he was gorgeous. Shame he had a mythical wife to get back to. "It's just that sometimes, just sometimes..." he trailed off.

"Sometimes what?"

"Sometimes, Lilith," he said, "you surprise me with just how mature you can be."

"You cheeky fucker!" I glared at him. "I'm thirty-two, not bloody thirteen, for fuck's sake."

"And I'm around a thousand years old," said Eadric, "and still not always sure of the best course of action. What I meant was that you are turning out to be surprisingly adept at, well," he gestured around us, "all of this."

"Huh," I sniffed, "you needn't sound so bloody surprised. And you can stop sniggering," this was to Bella, who was starting to wobble ominously. "I am perfectly capable of being a responsible adult, thank you very much." The shaking increased until Eadric and I were both forced to cling onto her legs to avoid being thrown off the building.

"What on earth is going on up here?" Nik popped his head out of the tower door and craned his neck to look up at us. He started clambering up without waiting for an answer and came to sit between us on the top of the dome. "Honestly Lilith," he said as Bella slowly subsided, "you are a bad influence on these birds." There was a distinct muttering noise from the other side of the roof. "Not you, Bertie," Nik called across, "you're a good boy." A brief shuffling of metal wings and Bertie settled back down. "He'll insist on an extra chapter tonight," Nik said, keeping his voice low, "so thanks for that."

"Give over," I said, "you enjoy reading to him! I've heard you, doing the voices and everything."

"I can't resist," shrugged Nik. "They're just such brilliant characters. I like to think of myself as an immortal version of Granny Weatherwax."

"More like Magrat," said Eadric. We both turned to stare at him in astonishment. "What?" He grinned, and his ancient face looked practically boyish in the last rays of the fading sun. "No point living forever if you can't use some of it to catch up on the best literature."

"Can't argue with that," said Nik. A clanking noise behind us suggested Bertie agreed. "What about you, Bells?" Nik raised his face. "Never mind," he said, "that's not your best angle. Don't you dare!" Bella was shuffling in a manner that suggested she'd be laying something big, if only she had a digestive system. "God," said Nik, "you are nothing more than a bunch of heathens." He got to his feet and started scrabbling back down off the dome. "I'm going to see what Mapp's up to," he said as he went. "Can't be any worse than you lot."

"Then you don't know Mapp as well as you think," said Eadric.

"And you're just going to leave Fred where she is?" Eadric said when Nik had gone back inside and the birds had settled down.

"Yup," I said. "I don't really have much choice in the matter, given the circumstances."

"Because she's trapped by Laithlind?"

"Yup," I repeated.

"But you think she could free herself? If she really wanted to?"

I sighed. "She doesn't *know* she wants to. That's the problem. For now, anyway." The sun was setting behind the sea, laying out a golden carpet for the little ferry that was ploughing its endless way back and forth across the water. "I think her daughter might talk her round, eventually."

"You got out, though."

"Bella got me out," I said. "That's the difference. Plus, I was so fucking furious, it's a wonder I didn't explode."

"Yes," said Eadric politely, "I suspect the anger helped. And the satisfaction of punching Laithlind in the jaw, of course."

"Of course." We sat in companionable silence for a while, the traffic on the roads below our only soundtrack. Everything felt muffled up here, as though the building itself was cushioning us from the real world.

"It's Bella," said Eadric, unexpectedly. "She's very protective of you."

I swung round to look at him. "Are you reading my bloody mind now?" I demanded. "Because you can cut that crap out right this minute, Eadric Silverton."

"I can't read your mind," he said, "and nor would I want to. But I'm learning to read *you*, I think. I suspect the power's beginning to even out between us."

"Oh." I didn't know what else to say.

"I'm not going anywhere, Lilith," Eadric said. "Not yet, at least."

"I know," I said, "I have to reunite the territories before you get to disappear off to eternal rest, blah blah. Maybe I'll just take my own sweet time about it."

"It isn't going to be an easy or quick job anyway," he said, "however much time and effort you put into it." I thought he was probably trying to sound reassuring, but he actually came across as wistful. "The humans we know now will be long gone before it happens, I know that much."

"I'm not losing Izzy," I said vehemently, my voice cracking slightly. "That isn't happening. And I will not be discussing it further."

"You can't stop it happening, Lilith." Eadric's voice was gentle. "Humans are, well. They're human. Temporary. That's what makes them so beautiful."

"I'm not talking about it," I said. "End of. Anyway, she's got plans for Flora's."

"Really?" said Eadric. "Does it involve world domination?"

"This is me and Izzy we're talking about," I grinned. "Of course it does." I wriggled my leg from around Bella's giant claws and slid down the dome. "I need to go," I said, turning to look up at Eadric. "Got a parcel to collect from Chester."

∼

"Thank you for this," I said, when Fred showed me her handiwork. "It's beautiful. You still haven't explained where you learned goldsmithing, though."

"And neither will I," said Fred with a grin. Afternoon sunlight was streaming in through the windows of Side House, and I briefly wondered whether it was the same sun I'd see when I stepped back out into my own reality. "It pays to have many strings to one's bow when you're in a position of power, Lilith," she went on. "You never know when you might need to turn your hand to something. Oh, and don't forget this! Lord knows what might happen if you don't keep an eye on it." She handed me a small hessian bag. Inside it was what looked like a gold ingot. Probably because it was a gold ingot.

"Thank you," I said, wedging the bag into my pocket, where it pressed uncomfortably against my hip bone. "You've done an incredible job." In my palm lay a gold link necklace and a ring that looked like a wedding band. But it was much heavier than usual and had writing inscribed around the inside. I held it up to the light and read *'My Heart - My Soul - My City'* in beautiful script. I slid it onto my finger and it fitted perfectly, as I knew it would.

"Married to the city?" said Fred, seeing which finger it was on.

"Better than any man," I grinned. And I headed back home.

Cat Got Your Tongue?

ONE WEEK LATER
"I'm just running Devin's stuff over to the Liver Building."

"Eadric's found him a new home, then?" asked Izzy. She'd just closed Flora's for the day and was soaking mugs in the sink, carefully swirling bleach into the water. It doesn't matter how well you wash up or how efficient your dishwasher might be—if you put tea into white china, sooner or later you're going to have to deal with tannin stains. She turned to look at me, the gold chain around her neck flashing in the last of the evening sun.

"Yup," I said. "He's off to live with an old friend of Elizabeth's. Up in Glasgow." Eadric had been unsure about asking Elizabeth for a favour so soon after I'd forced her to rein in her takeover plans. I'd told him it was an excellent opportunity to show trust from our side. He hadn't looked convinced, but made the arrangements anyway. To be honest, I'd been more concerned that Dev would prove too much of a handful for his new caretakers. But then Elizabeth had called me directly to let me know who Devin's *in loco parentis* was going to be, and I'd stopped worrying. Anyway, I could always get the cats to send a scout up there, just to keep an eye on things.

"Isn't that a bit public?" asked Izzy. "I thought the whole point of moving him was to get him out of the way until he's calmed down a bit."

"Said friend lives in the Necropolis," I grinned. "One of the caretakers, I think." I didn't mention that the caretaker in question was very old, very dead, and suspected—by Eadric and Nik, at least—of being a golem. "There's plenty of space for Devin to run around. And if he does go rogue at any point, people will just think it's yet another local weirdo getting overexcited about the vampire legends."

"That's my girl," said Izzy. "Single-handedly repopulating Britain's spooky society." The mug she was holding slipped from her hand and I jumped forward, but it stopped in mid-air before I could catch it. "Aah, thanks, love," said Izzy, reaching out to take it from the invisible hand. "You're a gem." I stared in astonishment as she put the mug on the drainer and carried on as though nothing had happened.

"What the fuck?" I managed. To my astonishment, Elf materialised just enough for me to see her wink at me, before disappearing again.

Izzy turned round to grin at me. "She pops in occasionally, I think she's trying to prove to her mum that it's safe to leave the mill. And there's no point having a poltergeist if she doesn't make herself useful, now is there?"

∼

I went in through the front entrance of the Liver Building and headed over to Sylvie on the reception desk. "Are you not visiting us today?" she asked, as I dropped Devin's bag on the counter. "Mr Eadric said you might call in at some point." Although technically receptionist for the entire building, Sylvie definitely has favourites. She insists on calling the Silvertons 'Mr Eadric' and 'Mr Nikolaus' despite us all having asked her not to at some point. Her answer is always 'it's just me being polite, don't you mind now' and then she carries on exactly as before. It might be more understandable had Sylvie been an old-fashioned lady of a certain age, but she was actually a twenty-something trans woman (I only knew that last nugget of info because she'd insisted on telling me herself on her first day behind the desk, 'because I'm sick of people thinking they've got something on me'). She had a natty line in sharp trouser suits and an eyeliner game Amy Winehouse would have envied. I often thought she'd be better suited to donning a nineteen-forties dress uniform and role-playing for tourists over at Western Approaches. She certainly wouldn't have to practise the RP accent.

"Nah," I said, "gonna head straight home. It's been a long week."

"Oh dear," said Sylvie, sympathetically. "Then off to bed with you!" She flapped a handful of paperwork. "Catch up on that beauty sleep, my darling," she beamed. "Not that you need it. Now shoo!" I'd considered more than once that Sylvie quite possibly knew the truth about Silverton Properties and all who sailed in her. But if she did, I was pretty sure she wouldn't have mentioned it to anyone. Anyway, I was too weary to think about it.

"Will do," I said, giving a mock salute. "Night, Sylv."

"Night, lovey," said Sylvie, already up and heading towards the private lift that goes to Eadric's floor. "You take it easy."

I walked home slowly. The streets were all but empty, and I allowed myself to breathe. The air tasted of hot cars and sea salt, excitement and broken dreams. I could smell the diesel tang of the docks alongside the stale beer and tobacco of the bars and clubs. It smelled of Liverpool. I sighed and stopped for a moment, leaning against the wall of the Gin Distillery on Castle Street. The sounds of chatter floated out as I breathed in the scent of juniper and quinine, alongside rubber from the tyres of a lorry that was grumbling its way past me and around the bend towards James Street.

Despite my endless whining about not having chosen this lifestyle, I knew I wouldn't change it now, even if it were possible. This was my home, in a way Shropshire had never been. Shrewsbury might be written on my birth certificate, but Liverpool was written on my heart. I was—literally—a part of it, and always would be.

Forever is a very long time when you're immortal. As far as anyone had ever been able to figure out, revenants still have the same physical life span as normal humans. It's just that it runs out at a far slower pace. The popular theory—well, Mapp's theory, which amounts to the same thing—is that our bodies all have the same maximum usage. Revenant hearts will knock out as many beats as anyone else's, but because it's eked out over a longer time, we just... keep going. An average human heart runs at a rate of between sixty to one hundred beats per minute, whereas mine bumps along somewhere around once per hour. I can feel it, sometimes. It's an unexpected and subtle reminder from somewhere deep behind my ribs that I am, in fact, still human. If I meditate, I can get it down to once every ninety minutes or so. By my reckoning, if I kept it that slow I could live—'live' being a relative term, here—for over seven thousand years. Even accounting for the large margin of error needed for my terrible maths, that's a timescale big enough to give even immortals a cracking headache and a desire to do nothing except watch old episodes of *Jeremy Kyle* for a year or so, just to blank it all out for a while. Sometimes I wonder just how far I'd have to zone out for my heart to never beat again. Sighing, I pushed myself up off the wall and headed home.

There was no one else in when I got back to the flat. I managed to make a coffee without accidentally blowing anything up and was just wondering whether to run a bath when Grimm jumped in through the kitchen window. Izzy keeps telling me I'm a sitting target for opportunistic burglars, all 'Oh just leave a window open at the top of a handy staircase why don't you, might as well just dump all your valuables out in the carpark for them to take their pick and save everyone the bother.' But when you live with a ghost and a were-cat, these things are far less of a worry. "Christ," I said, as the ball of grey fur dropped past my ear, "give me some bloody warning next time!" I turned to look at Grimm, who sat in the middle of the floor, gazing up at me with his usual expression of feline indifference. "Yes, yes," I said, already reaching into the cupboard. "I bought the fancy salmon stuff. Hang on."

'I prefer the cod, in all honesty,' said a voice from behind me. I snapped upright so fast that my head went straight through the formica worktop with a loud crunch. I stood in the middle of a pile of smashed fibreboard and stared down at the cat.

"You always make a fuss for the salmon, though." I couldn't think of anything else to say.

'I like to make you feel useful,' he said.

"You're talking!"

'Finally, she gets it,' said Grimm. 'You took your time.'

"But..." I spluttered, "you're a *cat*! Cats can't speak!"

'I'm not speaking,' said the cat in question, 'am I? Yet you're still hearing me. Clever, no?' He raised a back leg and began methodically cleaning bits of him I'd rather not think about.

"Do you have to do that when I'm having an existential crisis?"

Grimm's big grey head lifted slowly, his leg staying upright like a chorus girl at the Moulin Rouge. A slow grin spread across his furry face —a real grin, all teeth and crinkly eyes. 'I'm just waiting for you to calm down enough to converse rationally,' he said. 'We have a lot to discuss, Lilith.'

"Where are you from?"

Grimm frowned. 'You found me in a rescue centre,' he said, 'if what Kitty tells me is correct.'

"You're telling me Kitty already *knows* you can talk? Actually no, don't answer that. This is weird enough as it is, without thinking about my aunt—my *dead* aunt—already knowing about this but choosing not to tell me. I mean, where are you from originally?"

'How should I know?' said the cat. 'And why are you even asking? Isn't a talking cat enough to stun you into silence?'

"I'm mostly wondering why the cat in question sounds like Christopher Lee."

'I have no idea who that might be, Lilith.'

I snorted with laughter, although it might have just been incipient hysteria. "Who the fuck has a talking cat?" I eventually managed.

'Well, you, for one,' said Grimm. 'Evidently. Look,' he went on before I could say anything, 'we need to talk. There are events occurring in the background of which you have no current knowledge, and this needs to be rectified. Immediately.'

"What are we supposed to be discussing?" I couldn't believe this was even happening. Okay, so I'd spent the last year or so getting used to being dead and most of my friends were paranormal oddballs, so you'd think I'd be practised at dealing with weird shit. Turns out talking cats are a step too far, even for me. And I loved *Sabrina* back in the day. "Are you suddenly my familiar or something?"

'Huh,' said Grimm, looking unimpressed, 'as if I'd be happy in such a lowly role. I ask you! No,' he tilted his head sideways as though examining me and finding me lacking, 'you and I are going to work together, Lilith. I suspect you're going to need my help.'

"Help with what?"

'It's not the crown they're after,' said Grimm. 'Or at least, it's not purely the crown. Where *is* the crown, by the way?' He tilted his head and gazed at me with very human curiosity. "It is noticeable by its sudden absence." I automatically shifted my foot to press my weight down onto a particular kitchen floorboard, which may or may not have recently been lifted in order to hide something from prying eyes. Luckily, I'd been so paranoid about being spotted that I'd checked the entire flat for lurking spooks before getting the crowbar out, so was pretty confident Grimm hadn't seen what I was doing. For a brief second, I thought I felt energy pulsing up from where the ingot lay, but then it was gone.

"I sent it away," I lied. "Things are dangerous enough as it is. Even with Ivo gone, it felt risky to have what is basically a magical beacon sitting on my dressing table." I caught movement in my peripheral vision and turned to see a magpie perching on the windowsill. Grimm followed my gaze and immediately went fully feline, arching up on all four feet with his hackles raised as high as they could go. I watched as the bird tipped its head and, with deliberate exaggeration, winked at me. I knew that look, and it didn't belong to Liam O'Connor. *If that's you, Ivo,* I thought, *I can promise you I won't be saving you from cats again. And I know some very big cats.* The bird cawed loudly, and I heard Ivo's laugh within the call. Just as Grimm was readying himself to leap, the magpie turned and flew off, familiar laughter echoing on the wind.

Grimm scowled—I mean, literally *scowled*—then settled himself back down. 'Your enemies are closer than you think, Lilith,' he said. He didn't know how right he was. Or maybe he did. 'They always will be. How will you protect yourself?'

"By *being* myself," I said. "That's all I can ever be. Myself."

'Yes,' said Grimm, dragging the word out into a slow drawl, 'that's what worries me.'

"I'm pretty sure Liam would help if needed," I said. "He tried to come to the rescue at the Steam Mill, don't forget." I hadn't heard from Liam since the incident at the mill, but I knew he was around somewhere. If anyone had asked me how I knew, I wouldn't have been able to tell them. But I was sure, all the same.

'And then you all but lobotomised him with a small stone, I hear. As for your earlier question,' he went on before I could say anything, 'no, Kitty is not aware that I can communicate. She talks to her ridiculous boyfriend without realising I understand what they're saying.' I tried not to think about all the things I must have told Grimm during my endless middle of the night ramblings. Lying on my bed and scritching his ears whilst confessing my deepest, darkest thoughts and fears. Everybody confesses to their pets, right? Cos pets never answer back, and they never judge. You could tell your dog you'd just offed your neighbour with his own garden shears in retaliation for him constantly playing Coldplay at full volume and the worst reaction you're likely to get is a sigh followed by a shuffling noise as they rearrange themselves in order for you to start on the next itchy bit.

I'd told Grimm *everything*. How excited I was when I first bought Flora's, how I loved that Izzy had chosen to come work with me, how much I still missed my baby brother even after all these years. All of it. A shudder went down my spine as I remembered lying on the duvet with him one sunny afternoon and telling him all about the night of physical fun I'd had with Liam and how I thought I'd maybe finally found someone who would suit me for literally eternity, only to discover within hours that he was a deceitful scrote who'd been working to his own agenda from the start. I'd whispered to the cat that I felt stupid for thinking someone just liked me for myself and not for what they could get, or how exciting it might be to date an immortal. Because however nice Sean was, there was always going to be a tiny part of him that was fascinated by my otherness. I just wanted to be *me*, for fuck's sake. And I'd said that to Grimm and he'd ignored me like cats do and it had all been fine because, well. Because he was just a cat. And now he was sitting on the kitchen table whilst I sat on a chair and listened to him.

Actually listened to him *talk*, like cats are absolutely never, no-how, absolutely *not* supposed to do. "Well," I spluttered, "who would even think their cat might talk back? Fucking hell." I thudded my head down onto the kitchen table and heard one of the legs splinter. "This is all entirely *insane*," I mumbled into the wood.

'Concentrate, Lilith,' said Grimm. 'There are more important things at stake than your sanity. They're after something, and you need to stop them.'

"What are they after?" I asked, not liking where this conversation was heading.

'You'd know it better by its common name,' he said.

"Which is?"

The cat smiled again, and this time it wasn't remotely comforting. 'The Holy Grail.'

~THE END~

Sign up to my newsletter to be the first to hear about upcoming releases and other interesting stuff - and get a FREE short story from Netherweird!
tinyurl.com/netherweirdstory

Next in Netherweird...

~DARK WATERS~

Netherweird Chronicles, Book Six

COMING OCTOBER 2024

Sign up to my newsletter to be the first to hear about upcoming releases and other interesting stuff - and get a FREE short story from Netherweird! tinyurl.com/netherweirdstory

Author's Notes

As with all Netherweird stories, many of the people, places and events mentioned in this book are inspired by real life. I have, however, taken enormous liberties with many of the finer details and no association with anything or anyone (whether dead or alive) is intended, nor should it be inferred. I just take the juiciest bits of history and mythology and twist them together into a tangle of fictional weirdness.

The vampire on Lil's roof obviously isn't the real Colin Robinson, but Izzy isn't wrong in noting the similarity. And if you don't know who Colin Robinson is, look him up. I promise you won't be disappointed.

Chester was one of the most important cities in Britain for a very long time. Whilst it's true that its decline as a port was, in part, due to the unstoppable rise of Liverpool just up the road, Lilith is correct in saying it wasn't entirely down to commercial rivalry—Liverpool's success in the shipping industry mostly rests on sheer geographical luck.

And Chester really is worth a visit if you've never been. The

Author's Notes

'Rows'—the balconied streets in the city centre where Lil looks for the city's spirit—are just as beautiful now as the day they were built (although the original residents probably didn't have to dodge quite so many weirdly dressed street performers).

The Steam Mill is a real building, and very impressive it is, too. You'll find it exactly where Lil does—just off Canal Side, on Steam Mill Street. She wasn't kidding about the literalness of local street names.

Aethelflaed (*sometimes* Eithilfleith), Lady of the Mercians, is described in the *Annals of Ulster* as *famosissima regina Saxonum*, or 'renowned Saxon queen'. Her daughter Aelfwynn inherited Mercia upon Aethelflaed's death in 918, but only held power for a few short months before being usurped by her uncle, Edward the Elder.

Jonathan Hulls was/is a very real person. He is also my own many-times-great uncle, which is how I knew about his beloved invention of an early form of steam engine. Considered by some to be the first person to make a serious attempt at developing a steam-powered vessel, the sad reality is that Jonathan's ideas never got past the theoretical stage. Such bright ideas might have changed his life (and the course of British industrial history) had his patron not cut funding. As it is, he was consigned to the footnotes of history and the glory he'd chased went to Boulton and Watt et al., long after his death.

Random interesting fact: according to my extensive family tree, Jonathan Hulls was a direct descendant of William the Conqueror. So yours truly is something like the Bastard's hundred-times-great-niece (exact amount of 'greats' may vary, and yes I am well aware that William's descendants number in the many thousands and I'm therefore unlikely to inherit the crown any time soon). If nothing else, I'm hoping the family connection will make them less inclined to haunt me for playing silly buggers with their legacies.

. . .

Whilst I was writing this book, it was announced in the media that researchers had finally confirmed the existence of DNA evidence suggesting big cats do indeed live wild in the British countryside. I could have told them that a long time ago.

∼

As always, this book would never have seen the light of day without the support of many, many people, including (but very much not restricted to):

Jayne Hadfield—beta reader, editor, general support system; Sal Geere—editor, proofreader, sworn enemy of my beloved commas; Toni Hibberd—beta reader, cheerleader, saviour of Wednesdays; Tracy Whitwell, writer and witch-sister; Tilly Melia, font of local knowledge and endlessly tolerant of stupid questions (hi Peter!); Pixie Purvis, who helped set up a Netherweird playlist (well worth checking out, there's a link on the website); Winston Gomez, who is somehow still putting up with my daftness; my boys, who are the light of my ridiculous life; Li Zakovics, loved and missed forever.

And Liverpool itself, without which none of this madness would even exist. Love youse.

Printed in Great Britain
by Amazon